THE TOWN THAT JACK BUILT

CONNER LEE

ISBN: 979-8-9882514-0-8

eBook ISBN: 979-8-9882514-1-5

Cover design and illustration by Isaac Holtorf

Library of Congress Control Number:

2023907568

For Lys

ONE

The morning sun shimmered off the surface of Vineyard Lake as I stepped onto the back porch of the cabin. I always thought it was a stupid name for a lake. I get that Jonesboro's a wine town and all, but Jesus, a little creativity wouldn't kill anyone. The cabin, owned by my former boss, Captain John Jameson—or Cap, as everyone referred to him—was nestled in a cozy little strip of homes with back patios twenty feet from the open water on the lake's north side. I stepped onto the sidewalk circling the lake and inhaled the dry air as I stretched to loosen my tight muscles. I had made some assumptions about Washington's climate based on Seattle's usual dreary atmosphere when I'd first come to town. While springtime still brought its occasional rainstorms, Washington's wine country was nearly as dry as what I was accustomed to back in California. Made my usual morning run less miserable, anyway. With a satisfying pop, I cracked my neck and eased into an easy jog counter-clockwise along the lake's three-mile perimeter.

If I'd known what that simple run was going to turn into, I would have packed up and left town.

I jogged past the empty vacation homes, many with an all too familiar "For Sale through Westcliffe Real Estate" sign staked into the grass. Some of them would fill up in the next few weekends, especially with Memorial Day just around the corner. But it was nothing like how the Fourth of July used to be on the Lakeside strip, with folks wandering from patio to patio, sharing bottles they'd purchased from the Jonesboro Winery, laughter carrying through the air only to be drowned out by the fireworks exploding over the lake. I only experienced it once before the "Independence Day Incident," as the locals came to call it.

The name's a bit overblown. Makes it sound like someone was murdered; nothing like that ever happens in Jonesboro. The local winery and vineyards are the town's main draw, particularly around the Fourth. Two years ago, Jonesboro was ready to celebrate the winery's 50th anniversary on Independence Day. Millions of dollars went into the preparations, branding, and advertising. Every hotel room and Airbnb in town was booked, and the event was billed with the biggest fireworks display ever. Then about mid-June, Liquor Enforcement randomly showed up and busted the winery's tasting room for serving underage locals. Whole operation got shut down, and all the tourists pulled out. Two years later, the town still hadn't recovered.

Lakeside Drive had been quiet those two years, so I didn't mind. Plus, the lack of tourism didn't slow down business at O'Callaghan's. Benefits of being the only bar in town. My regulars provided all the social interaction I needed, and all the info I could ask for. I only took the job in the first place to keep a pulse on the local goings-on. Old habits die hard, and I developed a lot of them in my time with the LAPD. My regulars in the bar always helped me get my fix, but none more than good old Jack Romero.

I looked out into the middle of the lake. Odd, I thought, Jack's not out this morning.

Every morning I'd go on my run and Jack would be out in his boat. Some days he had someone with him. I'd heard the excited shrieks of a child reeling in their first catch many times. All the locals had been out fishing with Jack at some point; it was a rite of passage. Hell, he had a fishing buddy out with him just the day before. And every morning on my run around Vineyard, Jack would wave at me from his boat, and I'd wave back.

But he wasn't out on the lake that day.

I rounded the northwestern corner of the lake, running along the drainage ditch between Vineyard Lake and the Jonesboro Golf Course's back nine.

He could have been sick, but I hadn't known that to stop Jack Romero. He spent every morning on the lake. After several hours fishing, Jack would tie his boat to his dock and proceed to saunter his squat little Italian body around town with an expensive cigar clamped between his teeth beneath his gray mustache, chatting with anyone he came across. He owned a tackle shop on Main Street, but you could rarely find him inside. Every now and then he'd be sitting behind the counter tying new flies, but more often than not, the front door of the shop would be propped open and he'd be walking up and down Main talking with people. He'd talk and talk until 7 pm, when the silver bell over O'Callaghan's door would jingle and the scent of expensive tobacco would waft in on the evening air. Jack would greet whichever regulars were there that night, awkwardly nestle his ass into his usual barstool and request that I make him a "Me and Coke," which I'd already made and was clearly sitting on the bar in front of him like every other night. Then he'd start talking and wouldn't stop until he wandered out the door around 11:00.

I didn't see him the night before, but that was normal. He always spent Tuesday evenings at a cigar shop ten miles out of town restocking for the week. But that Monday night, over the course of two drinks, Jack talked about the Fosters' new dog, Mayor Westcliffe's re-election, a huge fish he caught the other day, Chrissy Jenkins' crisis pregnancy, and The Masters Tournament, amongst other topics. I never asked for any of these details, but Jack always functioned as my primetime anchor for the local news each night, only pausing for a break when I stepped away to grab something for another one of the regulars. After his evening broadcast, he'd saunter back home and show up on the lake the next morning.

But he wasn't out on the lake that day.

As I continued along the path around the lake, the sun glinted off something abnormally shiny on the concrete ahead of me. I slowed my pace, eventually settling into a walk, taking deep breaths as I looked at the ground. It was a dark oil stain, sitting in the middle of the sidewalk. Seemed fresh. Weird. Hadn't seen anyone drive on the path around the lake before.

I stretched my back and prepared to set back off on my run when I noticed something at the bottom of the drainage ditch next to me.

My breath caught in my lungs.

The bells of Jonesboro Community Church chimed 11:00.

Jack Romero laid sprawled in the bottom of the ditch, eyes wide in shock, a bloody hole punched in the center of his forehead.

TWO

I've never been to confession. Dad pastored a church, but it wasn't Catholic, so confession was never part of my experience growing up. But I saw the practice represented in movies and TV shows, and books that I had to read in high school. I didn't understand how the priest could sit there in that booth and listen to people share their darkest secrets all day. As I stood next to the ditch with Sheriff Mike Wilson, I thought that surely priests had to tell someone the things they heard. No way they could carry all of that in silence, without anyone else to share the burden of knowing everyone else's shit. Especially *Catholics'* shit. Then I realized the sheriff was staring at me, awaiting a response to a question I hadn't heard.

"I'm sorry, what?" I asked.

"Do you think it's a suicide?" he repeated, tucking his thumbs through his belt loops.

I blinked. "What the hell are you talking about?"

"Jack." He gestured toward the body in the ditch as if that answered my question.

I blinked again. "Sheriff, what the *fuck* are you talking about?"

"Hey, simmer down there, CJ," Wilson said, putting up his hands in defense. "No need for the language. I was just asking if you think it's a suicide case."

I stared at him. "How could this possibly be a suicide, Sheriff? There's a bullet hole in the center of his goddamn forehead. There isn't a gun in sight. And why would he kill himself in the middle of a golf course drainage ditch?"

Wilson scratched his head, his hat tilting forward over his face. "I mean, I dunno, CJ. I just don't see what else it could be."

He hadn't been there ten minutes and Wilson already had me at a loss for words.

A siren chirped as a deputy's truck rumbled along the sidewalk, pulled over, and blocked the path. Deputy Jeremy Ralston, the only other officer in Jonesboro, hopped out of the driver's seat. "Good morning, CJ," Ralston said.

"I'd have to disagree," I said, looking back in the ditch.

"What's going on?" Ralston asked on his way toward us. "Sheriff told me to bring Catherine, but he didn't tell me—" Ralston looked down into the ditch and immediately spun back around to throw up.

"First crime scene, Deputy?" I asked him. Ralston heaved several times as a Jonesboro County Coroner's van pulled up behind him and Catherine Sinclair, Sheriff Wilson's assistant, stepped out with a camera around her neck. Catherine walked to the edge of the ditch and groaned in disgust when she saw the body.

"Where's Dr. Lancaster?" I asked.

"The Bahamas," she said, snapping a picture of Jack's corpse. "It's his 50th wedding anniversary."

"But why are *you* here?"

The sheriff said, "Catherine has a degree in forensics, so she's also been helping Dr. Lancaster out in the lab as an assistant coroner."

"Are you heading this case up, then?" I asked her.

"Guess so," she said. She looked at the camera screen and winced. "Still not used to this."

"Isn't this what you studied for?"

"Not this part," she said, raising the camera once again. "It's different when the bodies come to you on a cart. I've never had to see them like this."

I looked back down at Jack. To a certain degree, I understood what she meant. I'd seen dozens of crime scenes in my time in Los Angeles. On top of that, I'd looked over hundreds of photos and videos and been completely unfazed. But seeing Jack down there really got to me. Only the second time that had happened.

"Sorry," Ralston said. He wiped his mouth and walked over. "So what do we think happened here?"

"Suicide, I reckon," Wilson said, tugging on his belt loops again.

"Goddammit, Sheriff," I shouted. "It wasn't a suicide. There's literally nothing on this crime scene pointing to a suicide."

"What is it then?" Ralston asked.

I held Jack's undying gaze. "Murder," I said. "Jack was murdered."

"No way." Wilson shook his head. "We haven't had a murder here in Jonesboro in…" He trailed off, searching the skies for an answer. "Hell, I don't think there's ever been a murder in Jonesboro, honestly. The worst crime we've had in 20 years was when I busted those teens skinny-dipping a few years back. Never investigated a murder before." He rubbed his neck. "This couldn't have happened at a worse time, either."

"I don't think there's ever a good time for someone to be murdered, Sheriff," I said.

"No, I know that," he said. "But one of the winery's co-owners up and dying like this right before the winery's Independence Day Relaunch definitely won't look good."

The winery. Everything was always about the goddamn winery. The Independence Day Relaunch was meant to be Jonesboro's saving grace. The few businesses that had stayed open in the last two years were gearing up to do whatever they could to support the event, and everyone in town was buzzing about it even though it was still three months out. Most folks didn't know how much longer the town would make it if the relaunch didn't go well. I looked at the Jonesboro investigative team: Deputy Ralston still queasy, Catherine Sinclair grimacing in disgust with every picture she snapped, and Sheriff Wilson scratching his head.

"Suicide would at least go over better than murder would," Wilson muttered.

I couldn't take it anymore.

"I don't give a shit what would go over better, Sheriff," I said. I stepped right up next to him and leaned close. "Clearly you didn't get any formal training when your uncle let you onto the force 20 years ago, so here's a tip: you treat every death like a homicide until proven otherwise. Even if it looks like natural causes. And this?" I pointed at Jack's body. "This doesn't even look like natural causes. So give Jack the respect he deserves."

Wilson visibly swallowed. My face felt hot. I could tell the others were staring at me based on their silence. "Well then," I said and slapped Wilson on the shoulder. Probably harder than I should have. "You have my statement, so I'm going to leave now. Good luck with your investigation." I took one last look at Jack's body before storming off toward the cabin. "You're gonna need it."

I made it about ten paces before I heard Ralston ask, "How does he know all that?"

"CJ used to be at LAPD," Wilson muttered. "He's helped me with a couple cases in the last few years. Like who ran into the stop sign on Third and Main."

I rolled my eyes and kept walking. That one wasn't hard to solve. All I did was ask Jason Hardwick about it after school one day and he confessed. I hadn't seen that kid look up from his cell phone once since I'd come to town, which didn't mix well with a new driver's license. All you had to do was keep your eyes open to figure it out.

"You know," the sheriff said, "that gives me an idea."

I stopped walking. I clenched my fists.

Don't do it, Mike. Don't you dare.

"Hey CJ," he called after me. "Think you could give us a hand with—"

"I'll stop you right there, Sheriff." I turned to face them, but I stayed where I was. "The answer's no. Absolutely not. Legally, I can't, and you should know that. I have no jurisdiction here."

The sheriff walked over to me and put an arm around my shoulder. "Come on, CJ. We really need you here." He started walking me back to the ditch. "None of us have experience with this sort of thing. You can just communicate with me while you work the case and let me worry about jurisdiction. It's just paperwork."

I shrugged him off. "I turned in my badge three years ago, Sheriff. I'm done."

The Jonesboro police force stood awkwardly for a moment. "Well," Mike said, "if I can't convince you to help us out, I would still ask that you do us a favor."

"And what would that be?"

"News will get around town quick that Jack died. If you could just say it was a suicide for now, I think that would be best. For the town, you know?"

"I don't plan on saying shit. It's not my job." I jabbed a finger in his chest. "But it is your job to protect and serve and keep the public informed of what's going on. So why the hell wouldn't you be honest that there's a killer in your town?"

"Because if this relaunch doesn't go according to plan, we'll *all* be out of a job." Mike scratched his neck. "Jonesboro won't be able to function anymore if we don't get people coming in to see the winery again soon."

"My girls finally settled in," Ralston said. "They like their teachers, made new friends. I can't move them again."

Catherine took another photo and groaned her agreement. Surely she'd taken enough pictures by now.

"You do realize," I said, but stopped myself. This wasn't going anywhere. My hands tightened into fists again. "Fine. Whatever."

Wilson put a hand on my shoulder again. "Thanks, CJ. It'll be best for everyone if we go about our days as normally as we can and keep this on the down low."

I shrugged him off again. "Just do your damn job, Sheriff."

"Catherine," Mike said, "when can you have an autopsy done?"

Catherine snapped a picture and winced at the image on the display. "I can have preliminary results tomorrow morning."

"All right," Wilson said, "then let's rendezvous tomorrow morning around 9:00. Come on, Jeremy, let's get him in the van."

"Nope," I said. "Fuck no."

"What?" he asked.

I wasn't helping them, but I couldn't help myself. "This is a crime scene," I said. "Don't touch a damn thing."

"Oh," Wilson said. He scratched his head again. "Yeah. Right."

"Ralston," I said, "you get some gloves on. Start documenting and collecting evidence right away. Sheriff, tape off the area and don't touch shit until Ralston's done." Ralston looked at Wilson who nodded silently. Ralston jogged back over to his truck. With one last look at Jack's body, I stormed off down the path back toward the cabin with an uncomfortable silence trailing behind me.

THREE

O'Callaghan's was a cozy little joint. Vertical wood-paneled interior. Nice, long oak bar top with a wall of liquor lining the counter behind it. A few picture frames hung on the wall. One was a picture of the owner, Mick, his ex-wife, and his daughters standing in front of the bar on opening night. The joint's first dollar hung askew in the bottom corner of a glass frame behind the counter. A couple news articles titled "Jonesboro's Hidden Gem" dated nearly a decade ago hung next to the bathroom entrance. The faint smell of whiskey lingered in the air.

The place had character, partly due to the colorful cast I found myself with each night. The usual guys were all there—the Dinsmore twins at the counter watching TV, and Frank Jenkins and Reggie Davis playing chess in the corner booth. I was doing my best to avoid them and any thoughts about Jack. Fortunately, my favorite customer, more of an irregular if anything, was there to keep me occupied.

"So how's the library been treating you, Molly?" I asked her. I was really trying my best to act as normal as I could.

Molly Bauer ran her fingers through her blond hair. "Not too bad," she said. "I help one or two people out at the circulation desk each day. Leaves me plenty of time to work on my dissertation, so I can't complain." She picked up her martini glass and shot a look over it with her radiant blue eyes. "But I wouldn't mind if you paid me a visit sometime, CJ."

The guys had been stealing glances toward her since she walked in, but I felt their attention shift toward me as my face flushed red. Part of me almost felt guilty flirting with a beautiful woman when one of my regulars was literally murdered earlier that day.

I coughed uncomfortably and said, "Yeah, maybe."

"Maybe tomorrow?" she asked and sipped her martini.

I coughed again. The silver bell over the front door jingled as the bar's most recent addition burst through the door.

Thank God.

"You're late again, Abby," I said.

"I know, CJ, I know."

Molly sipped her martini as Abby Smith rushed through the bar, her two large feathery earrings struggling to keep pace with her. Abby's entrance distracted the Dinsmore twins, and they stared as she slipped into the back room. I smacked Ryan Dinsmore with my bar rag, knowing it probably wouldn't do much to deter him or his brother Brian. Yes, their names were Ryan and Brian. I was convinced their parents were sadists.

Molly set the glass on her coaster and rested her cheek in her palm. "So as I was saying," she said, "you could come visit me at the library. Or we could just skip all that if you have something to ask me." She smiled, her metallic bronze lips shimmering in the dim light of the bar. "Do you have something to ask me?"

Abby's entrance wasn't enough of a distraction. The guys weren't even trying to be subtle now. And to top it off, the music in the back suddenly stopped; Abby always changed it when she came in. Every word I had ever learned fell out the back of my mind. I scratched my head, trying to cram the English language back inside.

"Y'know, Molly, I—" I cleared my throat and muttered, "I just wouldn't be good for you."

Molly leaned forward, inches from my face, and ran her fingers through my hair. It took everything in me not to shiver. "CJ," she said, "I'll be the judge of what's good or bad for me."

Green Day's "When I Come Around" started playing over the sound system. Molly sat back on the stool and drank the rest of her martini without breaking eye contact before grabbing her purse and walking to the door. Before leaving, she turned and smiled at me.

"And trust me, CJ Harris," she said, "I would do wonders for you." With a wink, she opened the door and left.

The door to the back office opened and Abby stepped out, readjusting the beanie on top of her long, auburn hair. She looked around the bar and found all five of us staring at the front door.

"What did I miss?" she asked. The guys all started laughing and returned to their business without answering her question, leaving her more in the dark than before.

Abby grabbed the empty martini glass and tossed it in the sink. "Who's the girl?" she asked.

"Molly Bauer," I said. "Works at the library."

"New in town?"

"Eight months, so I guess so. But you're one to talk about being new in town."

She shrugged. "I've seen enough in my two months here. I don't consider myself new anymore." Abby poured a pint of Banquet and immediately drank half of it.

"Long day, huh?" I asked.

"Just like every other day," she said before drinking the other half of the beer. She set the glass on the back counter and turned to the twins. "How's it going, fellas?"

The guys smiled in tandem.

"Better now that you're here," Ryan said. He was always the more vocal of the two.

I smacked him with the bar rag again. "Cut that shit out, man. Seriously."

"It's fine, CJ," Abby said. "I know it's all in good fun. Right, boys?" She leaned across the bar toward them. "We don't want to end up on our ass in the rain like Mr. Jones, do we?"

The twins awkwardly glanced down at their empty glasses and muttered a couple, "Yes, ma'ams." Abby gave them an approving nod and poured them each another beer. Abby was the only person in town willing to cut the owner of the Jonesboro Winery and Vineyards down to size. No one was surprised when Albert Jones tried to pinch her backside when she brushed past him a week earlier, but everyone in town was amazed when she sent him sprawling out the front door shortly after. Two months in town and she already had a reputation. She was proud of it.

"Hey CJ," Frank Jenkins called from the corner. "Put another tally on the board for me."

Lost in thought, I stared blankly into space, not even hearing what Frank said.

Abby looked at me, then back at him and said, "I gotcha, Frank." She wrote another tally on Frank's side of the chalk board the daily specials used to go on. Frank was up to 53 wins to Reggie's 38. She dusted the chalk off her hands and looked at me. "Something on your mind?"

"What?" I looked at her, trying to erase the image of Jack's body from my head. "No, not at all. Why would you think that?"

"Well," she looked at the clock, "it's almost 7:00 and you haven't made Jack's drink yet."

I checked the clock. 6:59. "Right," I said, "Jack's drink."

She rolled her eyes. "I got it." She tossed a couple cubes of ice in a tumbler, poured a double shot of Jack, and topped it off with some Coke before setting it on a coaster in front of Jack's stool.

"Abby," I said, "I don't know if—"

"Oh, stop," Abby said, smiling. "If there's one thing I've learned since moving here, it's that Jack Romero will walk through that door every night at 7:00 sharp."

The bell over the door jingled.

"And there he is now," she said with a grin.

Everyone looked at the door.

Shit.

Sure enough, a Romero walked through that door. Just not the one everyone expected.

FOUR

Robby Romero pulled off his hood. His thick, wavy hair was tied up in a bun on top of his head. I was surprised to see him smiling. It wasn't a sad smile, either. It seemed as earnest and goofy as every other time he'd walked into O'Callaghan's in the past three years. He greeted the other guys in the bar with a wave and hung his jacket on the coat rack by the front door. He was still wearing his uniform from the post office.

"How's it going, Seej?" he asked.

I forced a smile. "Not bad, Robby."

He sat on the stool next to his uncle's and said, "Come on, Seej, it's Rob now. We've been over this."

"Whatever you say, Robby," I said. I gave him a cautious look. "What about you? How are you doing?"

He shrugged. "Pretty good. Could be worse."

My gut clenched. Goddammit, I thought, he doesn't know. And it's not my job to tell him, especially in front of all these people. I looked at the Jack and Coke in front of his uncle's usual stool, condensation forming on the glass. It was only a matter of time.

I did my best to act normal and set a coaster in front of him. "Can I get you anything?"

"Mind getting me a beer?" he asked with a grin.

"Mind showing me an ID?"

We'd had the same exchange hundreds of times, ever since the first time he'd bellied up to the bar with a fake California license three years ago. I could spot that shit a mile away, but his little peach fuzz mustache didn't help his case. He was still the same old Robby, but the facial hair had at least grown in better.

Robby whipped out his ID and slapped it on the counter. "Look there, man, you can't say no to me for much longer." His 21st birthday was coming up on July 3rd and he wouldn't let me forget it.

"Oh, you misunderstand, kid. I run this joint." I slid his ID back toward him, leaning over the counter as I did so. "I can say no to whoever I want."

He punched me in the shoulder and laughed. "Bullshit, man. You wouldn't refuse service to your old buddy Rob Romero."

"We'll see, Robby. We'll see." I absently glanced at Jack's drink and gave the bar a couple raps with my knuckles. "The usual?"

"For sure, man." As I reached into the mini fridge for a can of Coke, Robby turned up the dial on his New York accent and said, "How you doin,' Abs?"

"Oh, I'm doing just fine, Robby. How 'bout yourself?"

She set an empty pint glass on his coaster with a lime wedge on the rim as I set the can in front of him.

"I keep telling you all, it's Rob now," he muttered, cracking open the soda. "Oh, Seej, want an update on what I heard around town today?"

"Sure," I said, thankful for the distraction. Jack had always been my primetime anchor, but Robby was a reliable man in the field. "Lay it on me."

Robby poured the Coke in his glass, squeezed the lime into it, and pulled a Zippo lighter out of his pocket. "Nothing too special," he said. "But there's been stuff happening around town this week." He thumbed the lighter's cap open and sparked the flame to life in one fluid movement, then extinguished it by snapping the cap back shut with a flick of his wrist. Then he flipped the cap open again and repeated the motions, all without breaking his concentration in our conversation.

"I made a delivery by the pawn shop today," he said. "Reggie's new business means I can actually fit some of his packages in my bike bag, but he says he has a new business strategy coming down the pipe. Isn't that right, Reggie? Yeah, that's right." He snapped the lighter shut as he leaned forward and said with a hushed tone, "Mostly because the shop isn't doing well—surprise, surprise—so he might scrap the whole electronics thing. And you know about the Fosters' new dog? Well, apparently it pounced on the Robertsons' kid at the supermarket the other day. Mrs. Robertson was pissed, said something about suing the Fosters over it.

"And I'm sure you've heard about the whole Jenkins' girl pregnancy thing." He glanced back to where Mr. Jenkins stared at the chess board with bourbon in hand before flicking the flame to life. "Well, their neighbors apparently hear a bunch of shouting over at their house almost every night, fighting about what to do about the whole thing."

Robby and I went back and forth as we always did while Abby made the rounds checking on the boys. I could hardly focus on what he was saying. After a few minutes, Abby tapped me on the shoulder and asked the question I'd been dreading.

"Hey, where's Jack?"

I looked at the clock. 7:12. The ice in Jack's "Me and Coke" had started melting. I scratched my head and said, "Probably just late, right?"

"Actually," Robby said, "that's partly why I came by tonight." He rubbed his nose and looked at me. "No one's seen Uncle Jack since yesterday morning. We called the cigar shop, and it looks like he never showed up last night. I came by to see if you guys had seen him."

"We haven't seen him since Monday," Abby said. She turned to me. "CJ, you were going to say something about Jack earlier when I was making his drink. Do you know where he is?"

Abby and Robby looked at me expectantly. I could tell the twins and the chess players had tuned in to our conversation, as well. Dammit, I thought, the sheriff should have taken care of this hours ago. This isn't my damn job.

I took a deep breath. "Yeah, Robby. I know where your uncle is. I found him on my run this morning."

Robby cocked an eyebrow.

He was murdered, I thought.

"He...he killed himself," I said.

I almost expected there to be a record scratch in the bar, but punk music continued playing through the sound system as everyone failed to process what I said.

Robby's eyes welled with tears. "No, he didn't. He wouldn't." He shook his head. "That's not a good joke, Seej. It isn't funny."

I looked at Abby, whose hand was pressed over her mouth, her eyes shimmering. I said, "It isn't a joke, Robby."

"But how—" Tears were running down his cheeks now. "Where?"

Mangled in the bottom of a ditch.

"That's not important right now," I said. I circled the bar and walked to him. "Hey, Robby, look at me. Look at me." When he finally did, there was so much pain in his eyes. So much sorrow. I'd seen that look hundreds of times before. I saw it every time I looked in the mirror.

"Robby, I don't know why he did it." I took a breath and bit my lip. Hard. "We might never know why. I wish I had answers for you. All I know is that he's gone."

The tears kept coming. "Bullshit, man. It isn't true. Can't be."

"Robby." I took him by the shoulders. "I can't imagine what you're feeling. I also don't know what happens next. What I do know is that you need to go home and let your aunt know what's going on. The two of you need to be together right now."

He sniffed and wiped his nose with the back of his hand. He nodded. Without another word, he walked to the door, yanked his jacket off the coat rack and slammed the front door behind him. Abby and the guys stared at me in silence. I walked over to the TV and turned it off.

"Sorry boys," I said. "I think we'll be closing early tonight."

FIVE

It didn't take long to clean up once everyone left. Soon Abby and I had cleared all the tables and started the dishwasher. Everything was cleaned up except for one spot. Neither of us could bring ourselves to dump the Jack and Coke sitting in front of the empty stool at the bar. Abby sat next to Jack's seat, head buried in her hands. She was still, as if someone had carved a contemplative stone sculpture.

I started my wipe down of the counter and asked, "You okay?"

She wiped her hands down her face, as if trying to pull some of the exhaustion with it. "Yeah. No. I don't know."

"You don't have to be."

She rested her head in her palm, looking toward me, but not at me. It was that look people have in an instant when they're recounting all the events in their life that led to the current moment.

"I just can't believe he killed himself," she said.

I froze. Keeping this to myself was going to kill me, and it was only the first night. I looked at the tumbler on the counter, the ice completely melted, the last drops on the outside of the glass soaking the coaster it sat on.

"Abby," I said, "I can trust you, right?"

She blinked. "CJ, two months ago I came bursting into this bar like a tornado in tears begging for a job, and I've been here with you for several hours every night since. You should know by now whether you trust me."

She wasn't wrong. I'd spent more time alone with Abby in the last two months than I had with anyone in the last three years. I threw the rag over my shoulder and leaned against the back counter.

"Swear you won't tell anyone what I'm about to tell you?" I asked.

"Hand me the Jack," she said, gesturing for the bottle of Jack Daniel's on the back wall. I grabbed it as she leaned over the bar and got two shot glasses before taking the bottle from me and pouring two shots. She held one and handed me the other.

"Swear to God," she said. She tapped her glass against mine and threw back the shot. I followed suit. The burn of the whiskey was the only warmth I'd felt since finding Jack's body in the ditch that morning.

I leaned against the bar and took a deep breath. "Jack didn't kill himself. He was murdered."

She held my gaze for a moment before looking down and playing with a ring on her right hand. She inhaled deeply and released a tense, shuddering breath. Her hands started shaking. I grabbed her hand and squeezed it gently. Not sure why, it just seemed like the right thing to do. She knew Jack as well as anybody. Not that she really had an option—Jack shared his life story with everyone he met, even if they didn't ask.

When she finally spoke, her voice was unsteady. "How do you know he was murdered?"

"There was no gun nearby, and the bullet was in the middle of his forehead." I could still feel her hand trembling in mine. "What are you thinking?" I asked.

She shook her head. "I don't know. It's terrible that someone killed him, but it almost feels better knowing that than thinking he did it himself. Do they have any idea who did it?"

"None. Don't think Wilson could figure it out if he tried. He told me to tell people it was a suicide."

"Why would he do that?"

"Something you'll learn about Jonesboro after being here long enough is that all anyone cares about is the winery. Wilson says the town won't survive if the relaunch doesn't go according to plan, and the murder of one of the winery's co-owners three months before the event would be bad for business."

Abby's hand stopped shaking. She looked up at me, her eyes brimming with tears. "So we all just brush it under the rug? We never find out who did this to Jack?"

I squeezed her hand again and leaned against the back counter. "No. I refuse to let that happen."

"What do you mean?"

I rubbed my eyes. I was entering dangerous territory. But looking into Abby's pleading eyes and remembering the grief and rage on Robby's face...

In that moment I made a decision.

I put my hands on the counter behind me to brace myself. "I'm investigating Jack's murder."

"What?" she asked. "You? Why?"

And here we go, I thought. I'd played my cards close to my chest the past three years. I didn't ask my regulars too many questions about their lives and they did me the favor of not asking much about mine. Same went for Abby. Sheriff Wilson was the only person in town I'd told about my past, and the only reason he knew was because he didn't want to listen to me when I'd offered my help with his bullshit investigations before. No one knew I used to be a cop, no one knew where I came from.

And no one knew why I left.

But I trusted Abby enough to get this far. I looked back at her, her hazel eyes glimmering with emotion. I took a deep breath and let it out. "I used to be a detective in LA."

"Bullshit."

I couldn't help but laugh. "No, really. That's what I was doing before I came here."

She searched me, but the truth finally seemed to settle in. "Huh," she said. "Guess that explains why you're so calm." She played with her ring again. "So how did you do it?"

"Do what?"

"When you were a cop. How did you deal with this shit day in and day out?" She pressed her palms against the bar top and looked at her hands. "How did you deal with people dying? How did you see the side of people...you know, the dark side of people that can leave someone dead in a ditch..." She looked up at me. "How did you do it?"

I thought through the question. How *did* I do it?

"Well," I said, "it's a lot easier when the victims are strangers. Nameless, faceless people you don't know. It's easier to distance yourself from it. I guess when you work as much or as hard as I did, you start to grow numb to it. Like you're always walking around in a dream." I shrugged. "Thing about dreams is you have to wake up eventually." I tossed my rag into the bucket under the sink. The rags were piling up, so I grabbed the bucket to take home.

"Sounds more like a nightmare," she said.

No kidding.

"Did you always want to be a detective?"

I set the bucket on the counter and deflected the question back at her. "What about you? What do you want to be when you grow up?"

"*When* I grow up? I'm not much younger than you."

"Oh, please, I've got at least ten years on you. You're what, twenty-two?"

"Twenty-four."

"Okay, so nine years on you. But you still have plenty of time. And I'm sure your end goal isn't working three jobs as the sole provider for yourself and your younger sister in rural Washington."

"What, isn't that every kid's dream? Besides, I grew up a long time ago. Had to." She went quiet. Seemed to be something stirring in the back of her mind.

"So what was it?" I prodded. "What was your dream?"

She rolled her eyes and tried to look at me like I was wrong. As if she never had a dream before. I stared back. I knew I wasn't wrong.

"Okay," she sighed. "But you better not tell anyone."

I poured two more shots of Jack and clinked the glasses together before drinking mine.

She drank hers and sighed, "I wanted to be a dancer."

"A dancer? You?"

"Oh, shut up, don't be a dick." She punched my arm playfully and shifted on her stool. "Yeah, I wanted to be a dancer. I dreamed of being a prima ballerina at the Met, believe it or not." She shook her head. "Stupid, right?" She looked me in the eyes. Her hazel eyes still welled up with something. Whether it was hope or fear, I couldn't tell.

I said, "Not at all." She smiled sadly. Wasn't sure if that was the answer she wanted to hear or not. "So, what happened?" I asked. "What made you give up on it?"

Abby looked away from me, a hesitant silence filling the bar. Then she said, "Well, Mom died. Then Dad started drinking." She looked at me and smiled again. "Fifteen years later, here I am."

We held each other's gaze for what felt like an hour. Several things whirled through my mind. Things I could have said, things I could have done. I didn't act on any of them. Abby wiped her eyes. I poured two more shots of Jack, lifted mine in the air, and said, "To finding new dreams."

We clinked the glasses and threw back the bourbon.

I pulled the keys out of my pocket with the bucket of bar rags balanced on my knee. Abby shuffled back and forth, trying to keep warm in the cool night air while I fiddled with the lock to O'Callaghan's front door. We were closing much earlier than normal, but it always got damn cold as soon as the sun dipped behind the hills.

"What happened?" Abby asked.

"Hm?"

"Being a detective was your dream, wasn't it? And you were living your dream in Los Angeles, but now you're here." She set both feet firmly on the ground, waiting for a response. When I didn't give one, she asked, "Why did you give it up?"

I locked the deadbolt and put my keys back in my pocket. "You really wanna know?"

She nodded.

The church bells down the street rang. 10:00.

"I killed my brother."

SIX

I collapsed into bed ten minutes later, sleep tugging at my eyelids. I stared at the ceiling fan, my eyes following the blades in a circle to clear my mind. Memories of my younger brother Charlie persisted until I finally sat up and swung my legs over the side of the bed. I rubbed my eyes and looked at the old landline phone on the bedside table. I punched the numbers as I had countless times before.

"One saved message."

"Chris? Captain Jameson gave me this number. I tried calling, but your phone goes straight to voicemail." I closed my eyes as Mom took a shuddering breath on the other end of the line. *"I'm sure you need time to...process. And I promise I'm going to give you as much time as you need. I just..."*

Mom and I took a deep breath in unison as I laid back on my pillow. *"I just hope you know that I love you so much. And I'm here whenever you need me."* I started drifting to sleep, the breeze from the fan cool on my bare chest. Mom was quiet, muffled sobs barely audible over the crackle of the landline's speaker.

"I love you, Chris."

SEVEN

My alarm buzzed at 7:00 the next morning. I slapped the nightstand a few times before finding the snooze button. Couldn't remember the last time I woke up before 10, but I needed to get to the station and talk to the sheriff before he fucked everything up. My feet found the floor and stumbled their way into the bathroom where I splashed some cold water on my face, each drop trying its best to get the hell away from me as they fell into the sink. I didn't blame them. I wanted to get the hell away from myself.

I looked in the mirror. Brown hair, flecked with traces of gray, stood up in all directions from another night spent doing a gator roll in bed. Damn PD job. Gray at thirty-three. Dark circles lined the underside of my eyelids. Stubble was back, like every morning.

"You look like shit," I said. If there was one thing I was good at, it was putting down that asshole in the mirror.

As much as I wished I could go for a run to clear my head, I knew I didn't have time. I quickly dressed and made my way downstairs to the kitchen. The rustic decor of Cap's vacation home reminded me of the ones my family stayed at during ski trips we took to Colorado when I was a kid. Only the furnishings in this cabin were covered in golf clubs and golf balls as opposed to moose, wolves, or bears. And there were fewer people yelling at each other.

Cap offered to let me stay in his vacation home as long as I needed, under the agreement that I play a round of golf with him whenever he came to visit. He came out a couple weekends a year, and we always played a round or two. I figured I should give him a call soon, see when he was planning on coming out next and tell him what happened. He'd give me a good lecture if he found out what I was doing.

I finished my meager breakfast consisting of a bruised banana and orange juice and stepped out the front door, the usual Jonesboro Daily at my feet. I tossed the newspaper in the recycle bin on the side of the house and took a deep breath of the cool morning air. Much cooler than it usually was when I woke up. My eyes felt heavy. Everything felt heavy.

Coffee.

I figured I could make a quick detour to Caroline's before heading to the station. Definitely wasn't going to get through this investigation without a pick-me-up. I hopped in my F-150 and drove the short distance down Lakeside to Main Street. Most of the buildings lining Main were empty, with signs reading "For Lease through Westcliffe Real Estate" hanging in the glass storefronts. Only a handful of businesses were still open, namely Jenkins Drugstore, Jonesboro Supermarket, and Reggie's Pawn & Gun.

Jonesboro's downtown wasn't much to look at. Outside of a two-screen movie theater and a video store that somehow managed to stay open, there wasn't anything to do when it came to entertainment. The only places to eat were Howard's Grill, which was owned but not really operated by the Jones family, a Denny's, and Mickey's Pizza. Mickey's shared a parking lot with O'Callaghan's on Main and First, and both were owned by my boss, Micheal O'Callaghan. He owned both businesses, but rarely showed up to either one. Trusted me with his bar and trusted Amanda with his pizza shop.

The only other spot on Main Street worth visiting was Caroline's, a cozy little coffee shop with the best coffee in town. Not that Denny's was much competition. I parked out front and opened the door to the familiar, pleasant aroma of roasted coffee beans. There were a couple people sitting in the cushioned chairs in the storefront working on laptops and talking to people on the other end of Bluetooth headsets. I didn't recognize either of them. Must be on vacation.

I sidled up to the register and was happy to find Abby working behind the counter. She was surprised to see me, and the two golden hoops dangling from her ears wobbled back and forth as she greeted me.

"Hey, stranger!" she said. "What are you doing up this early?"

"Morning, Abby," I said, rubbing my eyes. "Just needed some coffee before heading up to the station."

"What'll it be?"

"A Red Eye. But with two shots of espresso."

"Fun fact," she said as she busied herself preparing my drink. "When it's two shots of espresso, it's actually called a 'Black Eye.'"

"Why is that?"

"I think because of the black circle that appears when you pour the shots into the coffee." She smirked. "Kinda like the circles under your eyes right now."

"Funny. How's work?" I set a crumpled-up five-dollar bill from my pocket on the counter.

She shrugged. "Fine. Just another day of dealing with people. There's always something wrong with something. Spelled their name wrong, drink's too hot, drink's too cold. Can't make anyone happy."

"Caroline treating you all right at least?" I leaned away from the counter and shouted, "Hi, Caroline!"

A muffled response came from a closed door behind the counter.

Abby lowered her voice and asked, "She doesn't come out often, does she?"

"Not at all. Last time I saw Caroline in the flesh was when I needed change for a twenty. Sam couldn't open the register himself, so I had to go knock on the office door to get her out here. As far as I know, she could be rotting away in there."

The door cracked open. "Heard that," Caroline called, without so much as poking her head out. The door shut again.

Abby chuckled, "Yeah, she treats me alright. Well enough, at least. She went off on me when I was late the other day, but—" She raised her voice and directed it toward the back. "It definitely won't happen again."

Another muffled response from the office.

"Wow, you? On time?" I asked. "Wish I could be afforded the same luxury."

She rolled her eyes and smacked me in the chest. Abby was honestly the best co-worker I could ask for. She brought a certain welcome energy to the bar, even got the guys to start tipping again. After spending hours together just the two of us over the last two months, a sort of kinship developed between us. We were both outsiders. We didn't belong in Jonesboro, yet here we were, each of us for our own reasons, with our own pasts that we mutually had an unspoken agreement to keep to ourselves.

Well, until last night anyway.

"No run today?" she asked.

"No time today unfortunately, but I try to run every morning. It's always good to start the day with some consistency. Helps set the tone for the rest of the day."

"Huh," Abby said with a curious smile.

"What?"

"Oh, nothing. That's just very..." She paused, looking for the right word. "I don't know, wise, I guess. For you, I mean."

"Yeah, well, I can't take all the credit for that one. One of the few things my old man taught me."

"Not close with your dad?"

"Nope. Haven't talked to him since Charlie died."

"Charlie?"

"Yeah, my—" I bit my tongue. I'd opened up to Abby a bit the night before, but I'd left the story there. I don't know why I'd even shared my reason for leaving LA in the first place. Must have been the exhaustion of the day, but I didn't share any further details. I honestly didn't want to say anything more, but I was in too deep at that point.

I took a breath and said, "Charlie was my brother."

Her expression changed. "Oh." She hesitated, then said, "Actually, I wanted to ask you about that."

Goddammit.

"What about it?" I asked.

She swallowed. "What happened exactly?"

I shrugged as apathetically as I could and said, "I was just doing my job. But I'd rather not get into it."

Abby's forehead creased as a frown tugged at the corners of her mouth. She set my coffee on the counter. "Well," she said, "I'm always here to talk if you want."

I picked up the coffee and took a sip. Bitter. Perfect. "I'll keep that in mind," I said.

The front door opened, and Abby changed her demeanor. She said, "Hey, Liz!"

Elizabeth, Abby's younger sister, walked into the coffee shop with a small lavender-colored backpack on. She looked like a younger version of Abby, give or take a couple inches in height. The black beanie on her head really completed the look. She pulled a large pair of over-the-ear headphones off her head and left them hanging around her neck. I could hear pop music of some sort playing through the speakers.

"Morning, sis," she said. "CJ." She extended a fist toward me. I bumped it with mine.

"You a coffee drinker, Lizzy?" I asked.

"Not so much. I mostly just come for the Wi-Fi. And the smells."

Abby said, "You're doing your homework before falling down a YouTube hole."

Elizabeth rolled her eyes. "Yes, Mother. Also, YouTube's not my thing, you know that. Netflix has all my shit."

Abby leaned across the bar and pointed a threatening finger at her sister. "If you watch ahead on *Gossip Girl*, I swear to God, I will *end* you."

"Yeah, yeah," Lizzy said. "Trust me, I learned my lesson last time." She filled a plastic cup from a small water cooler sitting on the counter. "You pumped to help us move a couch on Saturday, CJ?"

"Do what?" I asked.

"Oh, shit," Abby interjected. "I totally spaced. I was going to talk to you about it last night, but—" She paused to think up a story, but for a little too long. Lizzy took a sip of her water, raising an eyebrow as she lifted her cup. Finally, Abby said, "I forgot."

Lizzy shook her head and said, "We're picking up a couch from the Taylors on Saturday after Abby gets paid. But they're leaving to go on vacation Saturday at 9:00, so we need to get it out of there before then. Think you can bring your truck and help us out?"

"Gotta love being the guy with a truck." I chuckled and sipped my coffee. "Maybe. I might be busy."

"Are you kidding me?" Lizzy said. "It's Jonesboro. What the fuck else could you possibly have to do?"

I glanced at the people working on the couches. They continued typing and talking, oblivious to our conversation. What was I supposed to say? *"Yeah, I'm investigating a murder, might be a little busy."* Abby glared at Lizzy and smacked her shoulder with the back of her hand.

"Nothing," I said. "Nothing else to do. I'll be there."

Elizabeth smiled. "Cool. Then I'll see you on Saturday, CJ." She put her headphones back over her ears and sat down on a couch in the front of the coffee shop.

Abby sighed. "Sorry about her."

"No worries. She's a good kid." I sipped my coffee and gestured toward her. "How's she doing?"

"She's doing alright," Abby said, looking at her sister. "From what I can tell. She misses her friends and everything, as any seventeen-year-old would, but she seems to be taking things in stride. She isn't a huge fan of doing school online, which isn't surprising. She's always been the social one. But she's a tough kid. Tougher than me, anyway."

I smiled and shook my head. "I don't think that's possible, Abigail Smith." Even as I said her name, it sounded so generic. So down-home American. From the day she came blazing into town, I had a suspicion that wasn't her actual name, but I didn't ask. Not my business.

She smiled and her face flushed. Flustered, she asked, "So what are you doing today? With the—" She looked around and whispered, "With the investigation."

I took another sip of my coffee. God, I was tired. I kept my voice lowered. "Well, first I need to go talk to the sheriff and then head over to the coroner's office to see how the autopsy is going. We'll see what happens from there. I'll be at the station a lot to update Sheriff Wilson on anything I find."

"Why don't you just call him?"

"Don't have a cell phone."

"You don't have a cell phone?"

An image came to mind of my cell phone whizzing through the air out the truck window into a ditch on the side of I-5 three years prior. Didn't feel like talking to anybody once I got where I was going. "Nope. No cell phone."

"Jesus, Chris. Every new thing I learn about you confuses me, but none of it surprises me."

"At least I keep you on your toes, right?" I tossed the change she had given me into the tip jar, thanked her for the coffee and turned to leave. I waved to Lizzy on my way out. Alone with my thoughts and the echoes of Abby's questions, memories of the night Charlie died started to flood back as I got in my truck, wearing thin on the walls I'd built over the years.

EIGHT

The station was quiet when I arrived around 8:30. Door was unlocked, so someone was there, but most of the lights were off. I walked past Catherine's desk in the front lobby and into the offices. Empty desks sat in organized clusters, collecting dust from years without use. All except for Deputy Ralston's desk, the one closest to the sheriff's office. I could see light through the blinds in Wilson's office, but the door was shut. I knocked twice before entering.

"Sheriff?" I said.

Wilson sat behind his desk, staring at his monitor, his face illuminated by whatever was flashing across it. When I poked my head in, he moved suddenly and slapped at the mouse, but not quick enough. The sound of a woman moaning was cut short as he clicked.

"CJ," he said.

"Hard at work, Mike?" I asked.

Wilson cleared his throat and folded his hands on top of his desk. "What brings you in?"

I did my best not to scowl. Partly because he didn't seem to get the joke, mostly because he'd given me reason to tell it. I closed the door behind me and sat in one of the chairs in front of his desk. "I'll investigate Jack's murder."

"You will?" His face lit up. "Oh, thanks, CJ. You're really helping me out here—"

"I'm not doing it for you, Mike," I said. "I'm doing it for Jack."

"Right." Wilson shifted uncomfortably. "Well, I appreciate it either way. What changed your mind?"

Robby, I thought. And Abby. I felt like I owed it to them.

"That sorry display yesterday did," I said. "Didn't sit right with me leaving you to find Jack's killer when you can't even follow basic protocol, so I'm going to make sure the guilty party ends up behind bars."

"Ah," Wilson said. "Well, again, I really do appreciate it." He scratched his head and looked at the time. "Guess we should head over to chat with Catherine, eh?" He stood from his chair, but I raised a hand to stop him.

"I'll take care of it, Mike," I said. "Might get crowded down there with all of us. I'll update you on anything you need to know and let you be the face of this investigation." I stood from my chair. "Just don't broadcast that I'm doing this for you."

The sheriff muttered something compliant as I opened the door. I paused with a foot out of the office and turned back. "How's the wife doing, Mike?"

He glanced at his monitor, then back at me. "She's good."

I gave a huff of disapproval and shut the door behind me.

I hate morgues.

Reality sits heavy, filling any space taken up by our vain attempts to convince ourselves that we'll live forever, that we're above death. Whenever a murder case came around, I would spend as little time in the morgue as I could, just get what I needed and get out. It made me distracted, scared. No time for that shit when I have a job to do.

Catherine, on the other hand, seemed to be in her element in the morgue, contrary to the cringing CSI I'd seen the day before. From the few conversations I'd had with her, I knew she had come from a big city. Chicago or Detroit or somewhere, couldn't remember exactly. One of many wayfaring strangers settling in town, looking for a respite from the realities of the city. She'd gotten the job as Wilson's assistant six months prior, and apparently put her Forensic Science degree to good use learning from Dr. Lancaster in the coroner's office in that time. Up until then she'd just helped handle the old folks that had kicked the bucket around the county. First job she was handling by herself, and it was a murder.

She scurried across the cold floor, dirty blonde hair piled high on her head, white lab coat billowing behind her on top of a light-blue blouse and black pencil skirt. She adjusted her black-rimmed glasses on the bridge of her thin nose as she looked over a set of documents on her clipboard. I stared at the beauty mark on the right side of her upper lip as she spoke to avoid looking down at the autopsy table.

"Jack Romero," she began. "Sixty-four years old, lived here in Jonesboro for nearly thirty years. Found in the golf course drainage ditch on the western edge of Vineyard Lake. Suffered a traumatic brain injury from a single gunshot wound to the head, died almost immediately, if not immediately. Point blank range. He has some rope burns on his wrists from where they were apparently bound, but no rope was found on the scene."

I managed to look down at Jack's body on the cold, stainless steel autopsy table. His eyes were closed; he looked peaceful. The only indication he was dead rather than asleep was the hole in the center of his forehead. A chill wriggled across my back. I hate morgues.

"An execution, then?" I asked.

"Seems to be. If you ask me," Catherine adjusted her glasses, "it looks as premeditated as they come." She handed the clipboard to me, and I looked through the documents myself. The pages of the autopsy report were held together with a purple staple.

"Time of death was sometime between 9:00 am and noon on Tuesday." My eyebrows furrowed. "He was laying in that ditch for an entire day before I found him?"

"Couldn't have been," Deputy Ralston spoke up from behind me. He was a younger guy, at least five or six years younger than me. Budget cuts resulted in most of Jonesboro's police force being let go and majority of the remaining cops resigned shortly after. Ralston stuck around because of the salary increase as the last man standing. He was a hard worker. Had a wife and two daughters to support. When I thought about it, I didn't know if I had ever seen him out of uniform.

He said, "Mrs. Romero called on Tuesday when Jack didn't come home for lunch. I asked around town, nobody had seen him. Spent the whole afternoon driving around town, walked the whole perimeter of the lake, even along that ditch. I sure as hell would've seen him if he'd been down there on Tuesday."

"So someone dumped the body between your search Tuesday afternoon and my run Wednesday morning. Any idea on the gun, Catherine?"

".40 caliber pistol," she said. "The rifling marks are characteristic of Glock, so I'm guessing we're looking for a Glock 22."

I groaned and tossed the clipboard onto the counter. "Of course."

"That's what we're issued here," Ralston said.

"Right," I said. "Remember the arsenal sale Mayor Westcliffe held to cover costs for the station last year?"

"Oh, that's right," Ralston said. "We sold at least twenty of those things, didn't we?"

"I honestly don't even know if that was legal." I rubbed my eyes. "Not to mention half this town is retired military vets and law enforcement and we're talking about one of the most popular pistol models around. Hell, I have one in my truck right now. Who knows how many others are hidden around Jonesboro besides the ones the precinct sold? We're positive there wasn't a gun anywhere on the scene? Any other bullets or shells?"

"Nothing in the surrounding area," Ralston said. "Spent a good couple hours searching around there yesterday like you asked."

I turned to Catherine. "Can you run all the guns still here in the station against the bullet? Can never be too sure."

She nodded. "Way ahead of you, actually. None of the precinct's pistols matched."

Damn, she was good. Pleasant surprise.

"Any gun residue on his hands? Or on him, since it was so close range? How about the rope burns? Any idea what kind of rope?"

"Hold your horses, LAPD," Catherine said. "I said it would take me a couple days."

"Right. Sorry. Thank you." A dozen other questions rattled through my mind, but I managed to restrain myself as I turned my interrogation to the Deputy. "Anything else at the dump site, Ralston? Tire marks?"

He shook his head. "That drainage ditch has two high-traffic routes on either side: the footpath around the lake on one side, and the gravel road of the golf course on the other. It's impossible to get anything off the golf course road. There was that oil stain on the sidewalk near where the body was found, but that doesn't give us much to go on."

I sniffed. The air smelled faintly of formaldehyde.

God, I hate morgues.

"So," I said, "what we've learned so far is that we have a completely unidentified perp, a needle-in-a-haystack murder weapon, and no idea where the body was for an entire day."

"That about sums it up," Ralston said. He clapped me on the shoulder. "Glad we have your help on this one."

I looked at Jack lying face up on the table and muttered, "Jesus Christ." My eyelids felt heavy. "What's your plan today, Ralston?"

"I'm gonna head back to the dump site, search the perimeter, make sure we didn't miss anything. See if anyone's wandering around."

"Fair enough. I'm going to stop by the Romeros' and talk to Clara, see if I can find anything to go on. I'm assuming she's been notified by now, Catherine?"

She was in the middle of scribbling something on her clipboard. "The sheriff offered to break the news and give them his condolences," she said. "He paid them a visit yesterday."

"Great." I asked Catherine if she had a spare notebook lying around that I could use. She pulled a pocket-sized spiral notebook and a retractable pen from a desk in the corner and gave it to me. I jotted down the sheriff's phone number, thanked the two of them for their time, and made my way out of the morgue.

I let the front doors of the coroner's office close behind me and paused at the top of the concrete steps down to the parking lot. I took a deep breath and let it out slowly. Something felt different. Like something in the back of my brain was sputtering back to life. My lungs were drawing deeper from the atmosphere.

Probably just the coffee. Or finally getting out of the morgue.

I hopped in my F-150 and drove south on Main Street through downtown toward the neighborhood. I looked at Jack's Bait & Tackle as I passed it. Robby's bike was leaning against the storefront. Poor kid. Knew exactly what he was going through. I shook off the thought.

It was a shame seeing all the businesses on Main boarded up. I knew from what Jack had told me over the years that most of the business owners in Jonesboro had him to thank for helping them get started. Jack was a businessman, co-owner of the Jonesboro Winery, and had originally been brought on to help with the winery's branding and marketing. What started as a sales job in the wine industry turned into Jack developing an entire town into a tourist trap, wholly reliant on the tourism the winery itself generated. He stepped down from his responsibilities at the winery ten years ago, essentially retiring, which enabled him to spend his time doing the two things he loved: fishing and talking.

Jack was a local icon. He was kind, considerate, and respectful. Kind of an outlier for this little town. No one had a bad word to say about him. Jack's only real flaw, if you could call it that, was that he couldn't shut up. Everyone knew Jack Romero. Everyone loved Jack Romero. He had no enemies.

Which made it difficult to figure out who killed him.

NINE

Talking to the families of recent victims is the most difficult part of the job. The questions are the worst, people pleading to see the body and asking who could have done this to them. The canned answers we have to give during an ongoing investigation don't help. Their loved ones were victims of the most heinous act imaginable. They're looking for anything to quiet the voices echoing in their heads.

I knocked on the Romeros' wooden front door, shifting uneasily on my feet. Nerves were unexpected. Hadn't done this in a while. I looked around uncomfortably while I waited. Robby's bicycle could usually be found on the front porch leaned up against the front of the house under the living room window, but in its place were a dozen bouquets with cards giving condolences. News got around quick.

It was a few moments before Clara cracked open the door. Her gray eyes were puffy and red, marked by a touch of sorrow, but somehow still full of the familiar kindness and compassion she was known for. "Oh, Chris," she said. It was all she could manage.

I did my best to give her a somber smile. "Morning, Clara. I heard the news. I'm so sorry for your loss."

She rubbed her nose with a tissue and nodded. She looked at the flowers on the front porch and said, "What brings you by?"

"I'm actually helping Sheriff Wilson with the investigation and was wondering if I'd be able to ask you a few questions."

"Investigation?" she asked. "The Sheriff said Jack's death was—" She choked up and hid her face behind the door as she sobbed.

I felt the blood drain from my face into my gut. In the rush of the morning, I hadn't connected the dots that she wouldn't be expecting to talk to anyone from the station. That, thanks to Wilson's bullshit, she was under the impression that Jack killed himself. Case closed. All for the good of Jonesboro Winery and Vineyards.

Clara took a deep breath and looked back at me. "With all due respect, Chris, what is there to investigate?"

Fuck you, Mike. And fuck you, Jonesboro Winery.

I cleared my throat. "Mind if I come in, Clara?"

She took a moment to look me over, but I could sense a vague curiosity to her gaze. Though clearly hesitant, she opened the door and allowed me inside. Jack and Clara had me over a few times in the last three years. Their house always reminded me of my grandmother's. She sat down on the pine green-colored leather couch, and I sat down in a matching chair opposite her in the living room.

"So," Clara said, doing her best to keep her voice steady. "What is this about?"

I sat forward in the chair. She stared at me intently. The only sound came from a clock ticking on the wall as she waited patiently. Jack was her husband. She deserved to know what happened. And at the same time, she could have been the culprit for all I knew. This was so much easier in LA when I never knew any of the people involved with the case.

I really wasn't ready for this yet.

I took a deep breath. "Clara, I know I haven't mentioned this before, but I used to be a detective with the LAPD."

She held my gaze.

"And I hate to be the one to tell you this," I continued, "but I'm the one who found Jack's body yesterday. And, in my professional opinion, I can say with all confidence that Jack's death was not a suicide."

Clara pressed a hand to her chest. "What?"

"The injuries sustained and the scene where I found him weren't indicative of suicide in any way." I took a deep breath. "Clara, Jack was murdered."

She stared at me. "So, you mean he didn't..."

I shook my head. "No. Jack didn't kill himself."

Part of the job is informing people their loved ones have died unexpectedly. I've done it dozens of times, and the reactions you get run the gamut. People scream, people cry, sometimes they even faint. Rookie cop mistake is forgetting to sit them down before you break the news. You never know the reaction you're going to get. But Clara had already started wrestling with Jack's death being a suicide, asking herself the million questions about what she could have done differently to change what happened. So, the news that her husband had been murdered, rather than ending his life himself, seemed to go over better than I'd anticipated.

Still didn't make it easy to accept. She grabbed a tissue from a box on the table next to her and began to sob. I sat quietly and gave her as much time as she needed, taking the opportunity to take in my surroundings. It was a typical 80's-looking home, like others in the area. The only things that really stood out in the room were a hand-carved sign on the fireplace mantel etched with "ROMERO – EST. 1972," with a large taxidermized bass hanging on the wall above it. One of Jack's prize catches, I assumed, though upon closer inspection I noticed a red plastic button in the center of the wooden plaque it was mounted on. Not a prize catch, just a novelty Big Mouth Billy Bass. Knowing Jack, it didn't surprise me. Their entertainment center had an old flatscreen TV with a modern game console plugged in next to it, completely out of character with the rest of the room. Robby's, I assumed.

The wall attached to the staircase leading to the second floor was covered in pictures of Jack and Clara in several exotic locations spanning several decades, with pictures of Robby at different ages here and there throughout it. Clara's decorative floral arrangements were placed all around the house: flowers of all different colors and sizes, giving the house a pleasant aroma. A few fishing rods hung on a rack by the front door. I noticed Jack's favorite rod and his tackle box were missing. Odd.

After several minutes, Clara's sobs died down. I knew Clara well enough to recognize the authenticity in her emotions. She loved Jack. There was no way she could have killed him.

I said, "I'm so sorry, Clara. I can't imagine how hard this must be for you and Robby. Jack was a friend of mine, and I want to do anything I can to find who did this. But from what I can tell, Jack didn't have any enemies. So, to do that, I'm going to need to gather as much information on Jack as I can. His past, his time here in Jonesboro, his relationships with people around town."

Clara blew her nose and nodded.

I pulled out my notebook and pen and said, "Any information you can give me will be helpful."

I hated lying to people like that. I knew that most of what she told me would be useless in the long run. But part of the job description was getting down in the river and sifting the pan for even the slightest trace of gold dust. Fortunately, prospecting is one of my strong suits.

Clara dabbed at her eyes and said, "All right. I'll do whatever I can to help. I'll start at the beginning."

Half an hour later, I wasn't much further along than where I'd started. Jack met Howard Jones, Albert's father and previous owner of the winery, on a business trip in Italy. Howard took a liking to Jack and, seeing an opportunity with Jack's business acumen, offered to bring him on as a partner at his struggling winery back home. Jack accepted the offer and moved to Jonesboro with Clara after returning home. Jack helped with the marketing end of the business and, with the aid of his little black book of international contacts, found the investors and publicity that turned Jonesboro Winery into the powerhouse it was. Took it upon himself to breathe some life into Main Street and turn the town into the tourist trap it had become. Howard, as the primary owner, was the face of the company. Juliet Beauregard, Howard's young up-and-coming recruit, was brought on as a third partner, and was responsible for the production end of the business. Jack did all the behind-the-scenes work, putting his time, energy, and finances into making it all come together successfully. He'd given me his life story in bits and pieces over the years, I just hadn't heard it in chronological order. Or without Jack's myriad of tangents, for that matter. That man couldn't finish a story before starting another one.

I flipped back through my notes. Clara sniffled every few seconds, but for the most part sat quietly as I sorted my thoughts. She'd had to stop every couple minutes to regain her composure, and I'm sure she was grateful for the moment of quiet. There wasn't anything particularly noteworthy in what she told me. The only details of any real interest had to do with Jack's experience working at the winery.

At one point during our conversation, she left the room to grab an old photo album. I looked at the photo she'd given me, the edges yellowing with age. The Big Three: Jack Romero, Howard Jones, and Juliet Beauregard with the winery in the background. On the back of the photo was written, "Jonesboro Winery Relaunch, July 1988."

Clara cleared her throat and said, "I don't know if any of that helps, but that's basically our lives here in a nutshell." She pulled a fresh tissue and dabbed at her eyes again.

I smiled at her. "It does help, Clara. Really. I do have a couple quick follow-up questions if you don't mind."

Clara wiped her nose and nodded.

"I know that Jack and Albert were still friendly with each other after Jack retired. They still met at the bar for drinks a couple times a week."

Clara couldn't help but smile. "Until that new girl—Abby, isn't it? —threw Albert out of the bar the other day. Heard he hasn't come back since then. How is she, by the way?"

I smiled again. "She's doing all right, ma'am. She can handle herself well." I looked back at my notes. "Did Jack ever mention any tension between him and Albert?"

She chewed her bottom lip before saying, "No. Not recently, anyway. When Jacky first sold his share of the company back to Albert and retired five years ago, he left Albert to figure out how to do his part of the job, or at least to find someone else who could. He'd been doing both his job and Howard's since he died, so Jack was burnt out. Albert called him relentlessly for a few months, begging him to come back, and Jack always said no. Albert was a bit cross with him for a time, but they've been on good terms ever since they made their little arrangement for Jack's mentorship. Obviously that five percent ownership doesn't pay us much, especially with the state of the business right now, but we don't mind too much. It's not like we need it. We don't even think much of it most of the time."

I flipped to another page of notes. "I know that Howard's death was unexpected, so when he died, was there any disagreement about the settlement of the company? Did Jack have any issues with it?" I knew it was a long shot, but it seemed like it could be a good starting point.

Clara shook her head. "Not at all. Howard had it written in his will that Albert would receive his share of the company. He was Howard's sole heir, so Jack was in support of it. Juliet, on the other hand," she said with a seemingly familiar annoyance, "now that's a different story."

I clicked my pen. "Was Ms. Beauregard upset about the settlement?"

"Oh, very much so. As the winemaker, she felt she had some sort of right to primary ownership. And fair enough, she had been there almost as long as Jack and was one of the main reasons the business got to the point that it did. She wasn't enthusiastic about someone who'd never worked a day at the company and showed no interest in running it having primary ownership. But it made sense to us for the Jones' family business to stay with the Jones family."

I clicked my pen again and tucked my writing materials into my jacket pocket along with the photograph. I shook my head and said, "It's crazy. Seems like your life in Jonesboro has gone by without a hitch until now."

Clara chuckled. "Oh, trust me, Chris, it was a long road to where we are today. We made our sacrifices like anyone else. Jack had several trying times in our first few years." She dabbed at her eyes with her tissue and smiled. "He was always so sweet. I could tell when he was stressed about work, but he never wanted me to worry about it. He always left work at work to come home and be with me."

I smiled. Jack really was a great husband and would have been a great dad. Shame they couldn't have kids of their own. I zipped up my jacket as I stood and said, "Thanks for your time, Clara. I know it's hard to talk about, but I'm going to do my best to find who's responsible. How's Robby doing? He heard the news last night."

"He did?" She shook her head. "I haven't heard from him. He texted me last night saying he was staying at a friend's house."

"I see," I said. "Poor kid. I saw his bike over at the tackle shop on my way here. I'll check on him and send him home."

She nodded. "Thanks, Chris. I really appreciate it."

"It's the least I can do." I walked to the door and turned the knob, but something kept me from leaving. My throat suddenly felt tight. I swallowed and said, "I'm really sorry about Jack, Clara." My grip tightened on the doorknob.

I heard her feet move across the shag carpet, then the wooden floor, and then I felt her hand on my shoulder. She gripped my shoulders in her tender hands and turned me around. Through tearful eyes, she forced a smile and hugged me. The room was quiet, save for the aging creaks of the old wooden house. I allowed myself to be held for a moment before pulling away and walking out the front door.

TEN

I drove back over to Main Street and headed to Jack's Bait & Tackle. My parting exchange with Mrs. Romero replayed in my head, memories overlapping with the last time I saw Mom before leaving for Jonesboro.

It was two weeks after Charlie died. I had turned in my badge that morning, which prompted Cap to offer his vacation home in Jonesboro while I processed everything that had happened. He said my badge would be waiting whenever I came back, but I wasn't sure when that would be. Or if I would ever come back for that matter.

I was packing my things to leave when there was a knock on my apartment door. Mom was standing in the doorway, her eyes welled up with tears. Without a word, she stepped into the room and wrapped her arms around me. I fell to my knees, sobbing, telling her I was sorry, I was so sorry, over and over. She ran her fingers through my hair, reassuring me it was okay.

No time for that. Shake it off. You have a job to do.

I parked in front of Jack's Bait & Tackle. Robby's bike was still leaned against the storefront, and I couldn't help but smile as I read the shop's supposed hours of operation. Jack didn't spend nearly as much time tying and selling flies as he did using them himself. He didn't need to run the shop; it was just a great excuse to spend more time fishing, both for gossip and actual fish.

I flipped the "Open" sign in the front window to "Gone Fishing" as I walked in. Glass display counters lined the perimeter of the shop, filled with an array of different bobs, lures, sinkers, and flies. I assumed they all had different uses, as did the fishing rods of various lengths lining the far wall.

Metal racks laden with shirts, jackets, and waders swamped the middle of the store, and I trudged my way past all of them until I found Robby. He was asleep on a stool behind the glass display cases, his head nestled in the middle of a book on the countertop, his hand clutching a half-full bottle of bourbon, with drool pooled under his open mouth.

"Robby." No response. I slapped his shoulder. "Robby."

He startled awake and wiped his mouth on his sleeve, squinting in the daylight streaming through the front windows. "Seej?" he said. "How many times do I have to tell you? It's Rob now. And—oh God, my head."

"No shit your head. What the hell are you doing?"

"What does it look like, man?" He pressed the bottle against his lips. The whiskey sloshed into his mouth, and he coughed a couple times before saying, "I'm drinking my cares away."

"I told you to go home, Robby."

"Goddammit Seej, it's Rob."

"I don't care what the hell your name is, Romero. I told you to go home."

"And who put you in charge, huh?" He squinted at me, trying to focus on my face. "What makes you so special that you get to boss me around?"

I rubbed my eyes. "I'm working with the police, Robby."

"You? Why would you be working with the police on anything?"

"Because I used to be a cop. I was a detective with the LAPD."

He fluttered his lips in response. "You? No way, man. You're a pushover. Besides, even if you were a cop, why would they need your help figuring out that someone killed himself?"

I took another deep breath.

"Robby, your uncle was murdered."

He sat up straight on the stool. "What?"

I said it without fully thinking through the consequences, but I knew I made the right call. I nodded slowly. "You heard me. I'm supposed to keep it on the down low. I'm only telling you because you deserve to know. I told Clara too."

"Who...who would..." He swallowed and made to try again, but the words wouldn't come.

"I don't know," I said. "That's what I'm trying to find out. But Robby, I told you to go home last night. I told you to let your aunt know what happened. I told you to be there for her. So, I'll ask one more time: what the hell are you doing here?"

"And I told you, man. I'm drinking." He clumsily raised the bottle in front of my face to make sure I saw it. "This is all I have to remember him by." He went to take another swig of bourbon.

"Give me that." I snatched the bottle from him and slammed it down on the countertop. "That's bullshit. Do you even see where you are right now?"

He looked away from me.

"You're in the middle of the town your uncle practically built with his own two hands. You're sitting in the shop your uncle owned and loved. And your aunt, who has done nothing but love and take care of your trouble-making ass, is at home by herself in the house your uncle lived in, worrying about you and how you're doing. And you're telling me you have nothing to remember him by except his goddamn hidden whiskey stash?" My voice raised with every word that came out of my mouth. I could feel the heat rising in my cheeks even though I didn't mean for it to.

He looked down at the counter. "I'm sorry, Seej, I—I just—"

"You just what, Robby?" I shouted.

A tear fell into the book he had open on the counter. He picked the book up and handed it to me. It was full of cursive handwriting, quick little snippets of interactions with people mixed with personal reflections. On the front page in block letters was written: *The Extra-ordinary Life of Jack Romero, Vol. 37.*

"I miss him," Robby said.

I was quiet as several of his tears hit the countertop. A pang of guilt hit my stomach. I shouldn't have yelled like that. My emotions were getting the best of me. I set the journal back on the counter and put a hand on his shoulder. "I'm sorry, Robby. I get it. I know how you're feeling right now."

"The hell you know, man?" He brushed my hand away and looked up. "Don't give me that bullshit. You don't know the first goddamn thing about how I'm feeling right now. Fuck off, CJ." He stood and stomped off, knocking fishing gear off the racks in the middle of the store on his way to the front door.

I bit my tongue and took a breath. Every part of me wanted to scream back at him, but I somehow managed to steady myself. "Yes, Robby," I said as calm as I could manage. "I do. My brother was killed back in LA."

He stopped.

"I know what it's like to lose a family member like that," I said. "He was there one minute and gone the next. Nothing I could do to fix it or bring him back, no matter how much I wanted to. Trust me, I get it."

Robby brushed a strand of wavy black hair from his eyes and sniffed. "Look, Seej, I'm sorry, man. I'm just...I'm on edge, y'know?"

"I understand. I'm just trying to help." I walked to him and put a hand on his shoulder. "Now, please, go home. Get some rest. Spend some time with Clara." I moved past him toward the door.

"I can't."

I stopped and turned back to him.

He clenched his fists. "I can't just sit here with my thumb up my ass, Seej. I have to do something." His fists shook. "I have to do *something*."

I closed the gap between us until we stood toe-to-toe. I could smell the whiskey on his breath. If I didn't tell him what to do, I had a feeling he would take matters into his own hands. When I spoke, my tone was soft, intense: "Okay, Robby, here's what you can do. Go home. Give your aunt a hug. Take a shower and clean yourself up. Then go to work. Run your delivery route. Thank people as they give you their condolences. I don't give a shit if your head is throbbing, you did that to yourself."

He looked like he was about to hit me.

"But," I continued, "as you do that, listen. Keep your ears pricked. Hang on every goddamn word this town says. And at the end of the day, come see me. Tell me everything you hear, especially anything that sounds off. That's how you can help me. And, most importantly," I put a finger in the middle of his chest, "you keep this whole thing to yourself. Even though it hurts. Even though it sucks. I'm expected to keep this secret, so I'm holding you to do the same thing. Can you do that for me? Can you do that for your Uncle Jack?"

I could see his tense shoulders release under my gaze.

"Yes, sir," he said.

"And leave the alcohol behind the damn counter. Your parents shipped you out here to keep you out of this shit. You're goddamn lucky I'm not a real cop anymore or I would have busted your ass, and that's the last thing you or your aunt need right now. You're better than this. Now prove it."

After an intense stare, he said, "Yes, sir. I'll keep an ear to the ground."

I clapped him on the shoulder. "Good man." I walked to the door.

"Hey, Seej?"

I paused.

"Thanks."

I nodded and left Jack's Bait & Tackle.

ELEVEN

The midday sun shined on rows of budding vines as I drove up the hill to the Jonesboro Winery. Tall wrought iron fences lined the road, protecting the grapes from hapless drivers and mischievous teens. The Jones Estate sprawled across a massive acreage north of Jonesboro proper, with two structures atop two of the lush, rolling hills of the vineyard. The winery reached into the gray skies from a hilltop further south, white stone walls intersected by red-tiled roofs. Something about the building always reminded me of a cathedral. On a hill further out, a similarly constructed mansion housed the Jones Estate's only two permanent residents: Albert Jones and his butler. A smaller wrought-iron fence acted as the mansion's primary security.

I parked in an empty spot next to a familiar red Toyota 4Runner at the front of the winery. It was in a designated parking spot with a little signpost in front of it that read "Juliet Beauregard – Chief Winemaker." The parking spots next to it had similar signs. I had seen Juliet Beauregard drive the car in and out of Jonesboro hundreds of times in three years. She lived somewhere outside of town and did her best to keep out of the locals' affairs. Smart woman.

I pulled out the photo Clara had given me. The winery looked the same after thirty years, but Jack had exchanged some height for some extra weight since then. If I didn't know it was Howard in the photo, I would have thought it was a younger Albert. Howard worked until the day he died of a heart attack in his office ten years ago. In the photo, he had a large wedding band on his left hand, which was resting on Juliet's shoulder. Never understood diamonds in men's wedding bands, but Howard clearly liked them.

Juliet was the only person in the picture still alive. I tucked it back into my jacket and stepped out of my truck. I'd been to the winery a couple times with Cap when he came out, so I was familiar with the general layout. I walked up the steps to what I knew to be the main foyer, where tours would gather before setting off into the facility. The foyer was empty, voices sailing in from every direction, echoing off the vaulted ceilings. Jack had given Cap and me a personal tour and shown us his office one time when I came by, so I knew they were up on the second floor. I gingerly climbed the old wooden staircase to the second-floor balcony. No need to attract any unnecessary attention.

As I pushed through the wooden doors of the balcony, previously muffled voices swept through the production facility, the air heavy with grape must and oak. Machines whirred on the floor below me, pumps pushing wine from oak barrels through filters into stainless steel tanks, the bottle filler spinning away on the far end of the floor. Guess I remembered more from Jack's tour than I thought. I was just thankful the noise below covered my footsteps along the observation deck as I made my way to the office space on the other side. I pushed through the far doors into a long hallway and passed a dozen doors with empty placard holders. I didn't know how many people worked in the office when the winery was in full operation, but now the space was all but abandoned.

Pictures hung on the wall between office doors, and one of them caught my eye: The Big Three, smiles on their faces, standing in front of the winery. A caption under it read, "Ten-Year Celebration – July 4, 1994." I looked at Clara's picture. Howard looked the same, save for a missing wedding band. Juliet looked identical in both photos. Jack looked different. In the ten years between photos, his weight fluctuated significantly. His hair was dark in the first picture, but he had nearly finished graying in the second. But there was something else different about him.

It was something in his eyes.

I found Albert Jones' office at the end of the hall. I pressed my ear against the door and lightly turned the knob, but it didn't budge. Directly to my left, easily within shouting distance of Albert's office, was another door. The placard on it read, "Juliet Beauregard – Chief Winemaker." I relaxed my shoulders and let my head roll around on my neck. My muscles felt tight. Cap always compared interviews and interrogations to golf. Took a lot of focus, skill, and relaxation. I took a cleansing breath and did my best to release the tension from my body.

Tee time.

I knocked on Juliet's door.

"Come in," she called.

I cracked open the door and poked my head through.

Juliet Beauregard looked as if she had stepped out of a Renaissance portrait: solemn, refined, beautiful. She was about the same age as Jack. She sat at her desk, lips pursed in concentration as she wrote with an expensive-looking pen, the kind that are given as gifts for a work milestone before being tossed in a box in the closet. The wall behind her was entirely glass with a clear view of the production floor beneath her. Awards from various competitions and publications hung on the wall above her mahogany desk, a reminder to anyone who entered her office of her accomplishments.

She looked over the rim of her glasses, and the crow's feet at the corners of her eyes deepened. "And you are?" she asked.

Holy shit, I thought, she doesn't recognize me.

I flipped out my notebook and clicked my pen. "Afternoon, Ms. Beauregard," I said. "My name's Jimmy Olson and I'm a journalist for The Herald. I was sent down here to ask some folks about the re-opening of the Jonesboro Winery and was hoping to get a statement from you."

Juliet waved a hand, shooing me away. "If you can't tell, I'm very busy. I've had my fair share of reporters this week and I don't have time to waste on you." She returned to her task.

A bit of wind on the course today. We'll have to adjust our shots accordingly.

I plopped down in a chair in front of her desk and spoke before she could protest: "I promise you, ma'am, it won't be a waste. I don't care what anybody says, yours is a success story."

She looked up from her paperwork.

Line yourself up at the tee, get a good look where you're headed. Don't let the distance scare you.

I crossed one leg over the other, eased back in the chair, and said, "I've heard the stories of the young woman hand-picked to usher in what would become a powerhouse in the American wine market. You were legendary before the tasting room shut down. But a winery brought back from the brink of collapse by the woman who started it all in the first place?" I shrugged. "Sounds like a killer story to me."

She considered me. I kept my cool, but I was worried she would remember me. I had met her in passing more than once when she'd made an appearance at local events. But she didn't live in town, and she never came to O'Callaghan's (she was "above it," as Jack had told me), so I took a shot.

Luckily it paid off.

She set her glasses on top of her golden-gray hair with a sigh and looked at her watch. "Five minutes."

"Wonderful."

Take a couple practice swings, loosen up.

I scanned my notebook for imaginary questions I had prepared. "So how long have you worked at the Jonesboro Winery now?"

She swiveled her chair away from me and started rummaging around under her desk. "Going on thirty-three—no, thirty-four years now," she said and swiveled back, setting a bottle of wine and a glass on the desk in front of her. Something French by the looks of it. She removed the foil from the top of the bottle, swiped a corkscrew from a cup filled with pens on her desk, and twisted it into the cork of the bottle.

"Next," she said.

"Wow, thirty-four years. Howard Jones chose you himself, right?"

The cork came loose with a small pop, and Juliet poured herself a glass of the deep red wine. She swirled the liquid in the glass a couple times, held it below her nose, and took a small sniff. "Howard brought me on as a partner right out of my studies in Italy. I've acted as Chief Winemaker and overseen production ever since." She held the glass up to the light and looked through it. "Go on."

"Chief Winemaker seems like a lot of responsibility fresh out of school. What made you decide to take the job?"

She lowered the glass and looked at me, her eyes narrowing. "Do you doubt my abilities?"

"Oh, not at all, ma'am."

She smiled and tilted the glass to her lips, taking the smallest sip of the wine. She silently puzzled through something before setting the glass down. "The offer was too wonderful to refuse," she said. "My own winery. My own private wing in the owner's mansion, all expenses paid. Who wouldn't jump at that kind of opportunity?"

Interesting. Couldn't help thinking about Howard's wedding band disappearing in that ten-year gap. I jotted a note about Juliet's living situation and said, "So tell me a little bit about Howard. What was he like?"

Juliet closed her eyes and took another sip of wine. She let it linger in her mouth, then swallowed. "Howard was an intelligent man. He hired me, after all. He was charismatic, smart, business-savvy. He single-handedly turned this winery into what it is. We wouldn't be where we are today if it weren't for Howard Jones."

Time for the opening drive.

"Interesting," I said. "I've been asking around town today and based on what some of the locals are saying, some guy named Jack Romero is responsible for Jonesboro Winery's notoriety. How does he play into all this?"

Juliet's forehead creased. She drank the remaining wine in her glass. "Next question."

And we're on the fairway.

I changed subjects as Juliet poured herself a second glass of wine. We went back and forth for a few minutes, and every now and then I mentioned Jack. Her frown and apparent frustration intensified every time I said his name.

About halfway through her second glass of wine, I figured it was time for the approach. "What are your thoughts on Jack Romero? Folks around town seem pretty taken with him."

She swirled the wine in her glass. "While Jack Romero did a lot for this company in its early stages, particularly when it came to the marketing and branding end of the business, he spent his days fishing and fraternizing with the locals once the gears began turning on their own. He hardly worked anymore."

"So you, Jack, and Howard owned the company. But Howard, since it was his family's business, was in charge, of course?"

She took another long drink from her glass. "Yes, and then Howard died, and Albert got his father's majority shares. Jack eventually left, leaving his shares to Albert in order to—" She paused and rolled her eyes. "And I quote, 'keep the Jones family business in the Jones family.'"

Good approach. We're on the green.

"Not a fan of the Jones empire's current patriarch?" I asked.

"Next question."

I scratched the side of my head with my pen. "Was there some sort of tension between you and Mr. Romero, then?"

She gripped the stem of her glass with both hands and said, "Young man, I fail to see how any of this is important for your article."

"I just know people are curious how the winery ended up where it is today. Some people thought it was weird that Howard left the business to his son since he didn't have any experience. Especially considering your position in the company and everything."

"My position?" Her volume increased. "Oh, it was more than just my position, young man. It was preposterous that Howard would leave things to his useless son instead of the woman who made this fucking winery what it is today. I was at that man's beck and call until the day he died and saw to his every need in this business. And what did I get in return?"

Only then did she realize she was standing. And shouting. She sat back down and adjusted her hair.

"Damn," I said.

"Excuse me?"

"Sorry, you just sound like my great-aunt after she found out Uncle Larry was cheating on her. That was a fun Easter brunch."

She cleared her throat as a shade of red tinted her already-flush cheeks, then folded her hands in front of her and forced a smile. "Next question."

I flipped to a random page in my notebook. "That reminds me, what role did Howard's wife play in the winery early on?"

Her smile disappeared. "I think we're done here. What did you say your name was?"

I just managed to keep a grin from showing.

"Sorry, last question, then." I closed my notebook and leaned forward. The journalist disappeared as I looked her dead in the eye. "I found Jack Romero's lifeless body in a ditch by the lake yesterday morning. Any idea who may have wanted him dead?"

Juliet paled, looking at me like ten snakes had slithered out of my mouth. She closed her eyes. "Get out. Get the *fuck* out of my office."

Birdie.

I tucked my notebook into my pocket and said, "Thank you so much for your time, Ms. Beauregard. Can't wait to get this article to my editor." I gently closed her office door behind me and moved down the hall before anyone was called to escort me out. I pulled open the door to the observation deck and nearly collided with a familiar face on the other side.

TWELVE

A crooked smile split Piers Clarke's face. "Oh, hello, Mr. Harris." His voice seemed to echo inside his mouth before it escaped. Piers was Albert's butler, and a popular subject in the rumor mill. Piers was former MI6, kicked out of the agency and then hired by the Jones family. Or Piers had been a hitman during the Cold War, offering his services to the highest bidder. Regardless of his past, he attended to many of the needs around the Jones' mansion and handled many of Albert's personal affairs. Followed Albert almost everywhere he went too.

And he creeped me the hell out.

"Funny seeing you here," he said.

"Yep, it definitely is." I circled past him onto the observation deck. "I was up in this part of town, figured I'd try to say hi to Albert while I was up here, but he doesn't seem to be in. Have you seen him?" It wasn't a good lie, but I figured keeping Piers out of my business could only work to my benefit.

Piers chuckled, if you could call it a chuckle. The sound seemed to catch in his throat. "Oh, Master Jones is ill today. I came to retrieve some of his personal effects so he may work from home."

"Sick, huh?"

"Oh, yes, quite. He's been very ill since Monday evening. Hasn't left the house."

Oddly convenient timing. I was curious exactly what time Monday evening that started, but I didn't want to pursue it with this creep. I'd find another way.

"Well, tell him I hope he feels better and to come by the bar whenever he feels like it." I let the door close as Piers called out a "But of course" after me. I didn't look back, but I could feel him watching me.

I shivered and hurried back to the foyer, slipped out the front entrance, and hopped in my truck. The rows of vines sped past once more as I drove south through the wrought iron fence. I wasn't worried about Juliet saying anything to anyone. She didn't want anything to do with Jonesboro or its residents, so I knew she wouldn't talk. She clearly held some sort of grudge against Jack. And the Jones family, it seemed.

I had my suspicions why. I knew Albert's mother was alive from conversations I'd had with him and if Howard's disappearing wedding band was any indication, I assumed they split sometime in those first ten years. If Juliet had something to do with it, that could contribute to her frustration about the winery's ownership. She certainly wasn't happy when I asked about Howard's wife. All speculation, of course, plenty I'd have to ask around to confirm, but things were adding up. Whether or not any of that could drive her to murder I couldn't be sure, but it was all I had so far.

I rolled the window down and let the breeze hit my face. Golden sunbeams poked through the clouds. I felt awake, somehow. Refreshed. Alive. Almost as if I could physically feel the movement and inner workings of each part of my brain as I drove back into downtown Jonesboro.

I also felt hungry. It was nearly 2:00 in the afternoon. I'd had a full day, gotten some good legwork in. Figured it was about time I sat for a few minutes and fed myself. I still had to work the bar that night, after all.

I pulled into the parking lot shared by O'Callaghan's and Mickey's Pizza Shop. I was a frequent patron of Mick's little restaurant. Amanda always knocked a couple bucks off my tab for me. "Employee discount," she always said with a cheeky grin. I always returned the favor with a free first round whenever she popped over to the bar.

Mick had a nice little operation going. The bar didn't serve food, so Mick sent hungry customers next door to grab a slice at his restaurant. Then they'd walk back to the bar and grab a beer to wash it down. I'm no businessman, but it seemed clever to me.

The little silver bell above the glass front door jingled as I walked into the restaurant. It had a very 50's American diner vibe. The brick-walled building had a black-and-white checkered vinyl floor, a couple booths along the walls and a few round tables filling the space in the middle, all of which were empty. I stepped up to the counter and asked Amanda how her day was going.

She brushed a strand of bright purple hair from her face and smiled. "Could be worse. The usual?" I nodded and slapped a ten on the counter as she filled a paper cup with Mick's sweet tea. She snapped a lid on the cup and slid it across to me with a somber look on her face. "I heard about Jack."

I grabbed a straw and stuck it in the lid. "Yeah. It really sucks."

"I don't envy you. I don't know what I'd do if I was the one who found him." She pulled a pair of gloves on and started tossing jalapeños onto a couple slices of pepperoni pizza sitting under a heat lamp. "It came out of nowhere. I just can't believe he really did it."

I took a sip of my drink and let the sticky sweetness dance across my tongue. Amanda and I filled similar roles in town. She was to Mickey's what I was to O'Callaghan's. We both ran Mick's joints for him and attended to our regulars with care and respect. Jack stopped by Mickey's almost as frequently as he stopped at O'Callaghan's, usually just to talk to Amanda. She knew Jack as well as I did.

Still, I needed to keep the number of people who knew he was murdered to a minimum. "I can't believe it, either," I said. "People been talking about it a lot?"

"Oh yeah, of course. I've been listening whenever anyone brings it up, but I haven't been starting the conversation. You know me, CJ. Last thing I wanna do is stress anybody out." She offered a knowing look. "But I wanted to check on you since, you know. It's different for us."

I smiled and nodded. Mick's businesses had a magnetism to them. They were a safe space for the residents of Jonesboro. One of very few places they could go free of judgment, be themselves, and forget the trials and tribulations of their lives, even for a couple hours. Jonesboro was a pleasant escape for many people around the world. O'Callaghan's and Mickey's were that escape for Jonesboro's residents. Mick set that tone, and only hired people he felt could sustain that atmosphere. He wouldn't have it any other way.

Amanda set my food on a paper plate on the counter for me. I thanked her and ate my lunch at a booth in the corner, washing down the savory spiciness with the sticky sweetness of my tea. I lost track of how many times I had done this exact thing.

I only ever really had sweet tea as a kid when we visited Mom's family in Texas. Nothing measured up to Grammy's sweet tea, but the stuff Mick whipped up at his little pizza place came close. The last time I drank Grammy's sweet tea, I was a junior in college. Charlie was a freshman in high school. I had the week off, so I traveled with my family down to Texas for the holiday.

Charlie and I hated the small-town experience, especially when we were greeted by strangers in the supermarket and reminded of how small we were the last time we'd been in town, but we loved visiting Mom's family. We played Phase 10 with our cousins. Granddad told us stories about his time in the Marines. Aunt Shelly always revisited everyone's embarrassing stories at the dinner table. We spent most of the time crying from laughing so hard. That year was the same as any other, except for Mom and Dad, who had several hushed conversations over the week leading up to the holiday. They tried being subtle, but we didn't have to hear them. We knew what they were talking about.

It was Thanksgiving Day, and we were sitting at Grammy's big dining room table. Delicious smells filled the air, creating a mouth-watering aroma that made us excited for every course. But most importantly, over a gallon of Grammy's sweet tea was passed around the table in a big plastic pitcher more reminiscent of a tub. Everyone was enjoying themselves. I was pouring myself a glass of sweet tea when Dad's phone started buzzing on the table. I managed to see the name of the caller before he picked it up: Sylvia.

Dad stood from the table, saying he had to take the call. Mom, lips pressed together so they turned white, stomped after him as he rushed out the back door into the yard. The house grew quiet as their shouts filtered through the crack in the door. My younger cousins crawled into my aunts' and uncles' laps, asking what was wrong. Charlie said nothing. I drank my sweet tea. Minutes passed before they sat back down at the table. Mom's mascara stained her cheeks. Dad didn't talk the rest of the week.

Mom filed for divorce when we got home.

My cup rattled as I sucked down the last of my sweet tea. I threw out my trash, said good-bye to Amanda, and left to prep O'Callaghan's for the night.

THIRTEEN

O'Callaghan's was unlocked, which only meant one thing. The silver bell jingled as I opened the door to find Mick sitting at the bar with a pint in his hand.

Mick looked like if Johnny Bravo had joined a metal band. He always wore a plain black tee shirt that looked way too tight for his huge arms and a pair of jeans that also looked way too tight for his gigantic legs. He had long, jet-black hair he wore in a ponytail and tattoos up and down each muscled arm. How he kept himself in shape with the amount of alcohol he drank and how he squeezed himself into those clothes without tearing them each day was beyond me. He moonlit as a magician at the bar on Friday nights, so I guess it was just one of his magic tricks.

"Mick," I greeted him, tossing my jacket on the bar counter.

"Christopher," he responded. Mick was the only person I'd ever met who called me Christopher. Most people just knew me as CJ, and some people didn't even know my first name. But Mick did a background check on me when I asked for a job; had to make sure I wasn't a felon. He had accidentally hired a felon who was on the run once. Whenever I asked him about it, he just said it was a whole thing he didn't want to get into.

"How are you?" he asked. Mick always asked how I was doing. Always meant it too.

"I've been worse." I flipped a stool from the bartop and sat next to him, running an eye over his tattoos. His favorite tattoo, on his massive right bicep, was of a topless woman riding on the back of a naked mole rat with a banner beneath it that said, "Ride Naked."

He grinned. "Shit, haven't we all?" Mick had some light jazz music playing over the speakers. Said it made the place a bit classier. Abby always changed the music as soon as she walked in, so any class the music provided immediately vanished when she came to work. He patted the bartop. "How's the old girl doing?"

"She's doing well, Mick. I've been taking care of her. What brings you in today?"

He sipped his beer. "Just thought I'd swing by, check in on ya."

I looked at him skeptically. Mick only ever came in for his magic show anymore.

He glanced over at me. "Heard about Jack."

"Yeah," I said. I figured as much.

"How you holdin' up?" he asked.

I scratched my arm. "All right, I guess. I just can't believe he's gone. Suicide, apparently."

Mick returned the skeptical look I had given him before taking a gulp of his beer. "Well," he said, "it's a damn shame. Never would've pegged him for it, but there's nothing we can do about it now." He paused and shifted his weight on the stool. "While I'm here, I wanted to make sure the new girl was doing all right." He cracked a grin. "Heard she put Bert Jones out on his ass the other night."

I sighed. "Yeah, figured you would've heard about that."

Mick gave me an incredulous look. "Hell, Christopher, you know how quick word gets around town? Christ, the old ladies down the street knew what happened before he revved his Mercedes back up the hill to his little mansion that night."

"Sorry, Mick. I can talk to her about it if—"

He put up a hand. "Oh, no, no, don't misunderstand me, Christopher. I can't stand the bastard. This is just one in a long line of piss-poor decisions Bert's made over the years. It's about time someone put him in his place."

He took another sip of his beer. "Just took someone unfamiliar with the hierarchy for it to finally happen."

I rubbed my neck. "Have you experienced any backlash?"

"Oh, yeah. You know how Bert Jones is, always trying to keep his reputation in check. That's learned behavior is what that is. He called me a couple times, I just hung up the phone as soon as I recognized his voice. Had that butler of his call me, what, Pierce? Something like that? Hung up on him, too." He looked me in the eyes. "You keep that girl here, Christopher. In fact, give her a damn raise. Women like her are few and far between. God knows we need 'em."

I smiled. "She'll be glad to know you're in her corner. I'll talk to her tonight."

"You be sure to do that." Another sip. He wiped the foam from his mustache. "You know, son, ever since the wife left, I've always been worried my girls wouldn't have anyone to look up to. No strong female influences, you know? Not that she was a good one to begin with. But my girls are in high school now. About to go out into the world and be their own person. They won't have Dad there to keep an eye on 'em anymore."

He paused to clear the moisture from his eyes. Contrary to appearance, Mick was a big old softy. I could easily imagine him weeping at the sunset on his front porch every night.

He said, "Maybe it's stupid of me, but I'm hoping my girls wind up kinda like Abby. I hope they always know they can defend themselves. That no asshole has the right to touch them without their say-so." He gripped his pint glass. "Shit-hole towns like this one tend to teach girls otherwise." He swallowed the remaining beer in one large gulp.

The sound of an airy saxophone filled the bar. We sat in the serenade, several thoughts spinning through my head. I hopped off my stool, made my way behind the bar and poured two shots of Jameson. I set one in front of him and said, "Mick, believe me. Your daughters are gonna turn out just fine." I lifted my shot glass. "You're one hell of a better dad than my old man ever was."

He suppressed a laugh, toasted my glass with his, and we downed the whiskey. I pointed at his pint glass and gave him a knowing look. He slid the glass toward me. I poured him another cascading pint of Guinness from the tap.

"Nightmares still getting ya?" Mick asked.

Mick was the only person I had talked to about my nightmares. Never told him what they were about. Never told him that I watched my brother die every night. I always had a feeling Mick knew about Charlie and why I left the force. Figured he just did a little extra research when he was doing my background check. Wasn't hard to find, a quick Google search of my name would pull the story up. He never directly asked why I quit my gig as a detective, but he did occasionally ask about the nightmares.

I set the beer back down in front of him. "Yeah," I said. "Same as always."

"Shame," Mick said, taking a sip. "A night of good sleep could do wonders for ya. Tried anything to make 'em go away?"

I shrugged. "Just takes time, I guess."

"Bullshit, son. Time doesn't fix nothin.' Did I ever tell ya about why my wife left?"

I shook my head.

"Because I told her to," he said. "I came home from work earlier than normal one night. Girls were already asleep. I went upstairs to the bedroom and found her with some other fella's dick in her mouth. She'd been railing this guy in my bed once or twice a week for months."

I was surprised. It wasn't an unfamiliar story. I'd heard it a thousand times before. I just had no clue Mick was one of the thousands of people who told it.

"What did you do?" I asked.

"I pulled my wife offa the asshole and threw 'em both out the front door. Told her to find somewhere else to stay 'cause she wasn't welcome in my goddamn house anymore. Filed for divorce the next day, ended up with full custody of the girls after all was said and done. She didn't even want to see them anymore."

He chuckled softly. "I slept on the shitty couch downstairs for the next two years. And even then, I didn't really sleep. I tossed and turned on that couch every night, driving myself crazy trying to think about what I could've done differently and what I did wrong. I didn't even feel comfortable in my own house anymore. Thought that, eventually, the pain would go away, and I'd be all right again. I was wrong."

He drained his second pint and looked back at me. "Ya know the only thing that helped me get past it?"

"I'm guessing it wasn't time."

He slapped the bartop. "Therapy, son!"

He laughed as I poured him another pint of Guinness. Sometimes Mick laughed at things way harder than he should. Most of the time he was the one that made himself laugh. I didn't mind, it was one of the things I loved about the guy.

He settled with a few final giggles. "But really, Christopher. You can't ever really move on if you don't talk about it with someone."

A light cymbal roll brought the song that was playing to an end.

I set the shot glasses we used in the sink. "Are you still sleeping on the couch, then?"

"Nah, I took care of that problem years ago."

"How?" I asked.

Mick chugged the pint I had just set in front of him and slammed the glass down on the counter, empty. He wiped the foam from his mustache with a grin.

"I set the fuckin' mattress on fire."

FOURTEEN

O'Callaghan's was always a little colder than it should have been. Mick didn't feel like investing in a good heater. Drove up whiskey sales, he said. Guess I couldn't argue with him. On particularly chilly nights like that Thursday night, the regulars kept their jackets on, ordered a whiskey neat and found something to keep their minds off the cold. Nothing could keep the regulars out of O'Callaghan's. Not the inevitable heat death of the universe, nuclear war, not even Armageddon itself. Of course, nothing ever happened in Jonesboro, so they had nothing to worry about besides a little cold after sunset.

That evening, Reggie Davis and Frank Jenkins sat at a table in the corner with their chess game, as usual. Frank was already a couple drinks in. He had been drinking a lot more since the rumor mill about his pregnant daughter had started turning. Reggie had even added a few tallies to their running game count. His score had suddenly jumped into the forties.

The twins sat in their usual spot in front of the TV. I'd put *Top Gear* on to keep them occupied, but the two of them kept stealing glances my direction as they sipped their beers. Couldn't completely distract them from ogling Molly when she came by.

"What can I get for you, Molly?" I set a coaster in front of her. "The usual?"

"Sure," she said, settling herself on her stool.

I nodded and started making a martini. "Unusual to see you two nights in a row," I said. "What brings you in tonight?"

"Well, you didn't come by the library today. So here I am, still coming to the bar while you're working since you seem too busy to make it down there." The twins made a noise, and Molly glared at them, which shut them up immediately.

"I'm sorry, Molly," I said. I poured her cocktail into a martini glass. "I was really busy today and just didn't—"

"CJ."

I turned back to her, and her blue eyes pierced me.

She shook her head and said, "My first night in Jonesboro, I came here to get a drink after unpacking all day. I didn't know anyone here yet. You made me a martini and we started talking and didn't stop until we realized it was an hour past closing time. There have been dozens of nights exactly like that since then. I've asked you out and gotten excuses so many times that I gave up. But I keep coming to see you when I can, keep spending hours talking with you, just waiting for you to ask me if you're ever ready. I know you're not busy during the day, but you won't even take time out of your day to come see me at the library where I spend every day by myself."

I bit my tongue. She was right. I'd spent eight months refusing to pull the trigger with the only woman I'd met who completely blew me away. Even though I actually was busy that day, that didn't make up for all the days I hadn't been.

She said, "If I was given any sign that you aren't interested in me, I'd have backed off a long time ago, but every interaction between us proves the opposite. I keep getting all these signals from you, but nothing happens. I feel like I'm going crazy at this point. Like I'm just imagining the whole thing." She shook her head. "I guess what I'm saying is this is my last time coming to see if you have something you want to ask me."

I put an olive in her martini. The silver bell jingled as Abby burst through the front door and made her way to the back room. Ryan nudged his brother and the two of them stared as she walked. I smacked Ryan with my bar rag and set Molly's martini down on her coaster. She took two fingers and tucked them under my chin, lifting my head to look directly into her blue eyes.

"Well?"

Right on cue, the music in the bar stopped as Abby changed to a different station in the office. I could feel the chess game in the corner grind to a halt, every king, queen, bishop, and pawn's eyes burning holes into my skull. The twins openly stared.

"Molly, I..." I didn't have anything else.

She searched my eyes, then stood and walked to the front door. As she opened it, she paused and turned back. There were so many words in her vacant stare, countless thoughts unspoken. She took a deep breath. "You know, CJ, it wouldn't kill you to let something good happen to you for once."

Then she left.

Abby let out a low whistle behind me. "Damn."

Tom Delonge sang "Stay Together for the Kids" in the background of the dive.

Abby looked across the bar with a raised eyebrow and said, "Need something, fellas?"

Reggie and Frank shuffled back to their game and the twins muttered a couple "No, ma'ams," shifting awkwardly on their stools as they looked back at the TV. Abby pulled the untouched martini from the coaster and took a sip, then cringed and dumped it down the drain. She leaned against the bar and smirked, the hoops dangling from her ears wiggling as she shook her head.

"What?" I asked.

"Fucked that one up bad, huh?" she asked.

I grabbed the coaster and set it on the stack on the back counter. "Molly's just a friend who comes by for a drink sometimes."

Abby chuckled. "Yeah, she's thirsty, all right."

"Trust me, it's not like that."

Abby hopped over to me, uncomfortably close to my face, and shouted in the most childish, sing-songy voice I'd ever heard come out of a twenty-something-year-old woman, "Ooh, does CJ have a crush?"

The boys in the bar tried to make their laughter inaudible.

I laughed in turn and said, "Oh, shut up, it's *really* not like that."

"Can't be," Ryan Dinsmore called from the end of the bar. "CJ must be some kind of a homo to turn down a fine woman like that." He nudged his brother with his elbow.

"Really, guys?" Abby spun around and the boys cowered as she closed the distance between them. She leaned over the bar and said, "You wanna call your bartender a homo one more time for me?"

The twins shook their heads frantically as stifled laughter escaped the chess players' corner.

"That's what I thought." Abby plucked their glasses from the counter and started pouring them each another pint from the tap. The boys did their best not to look at her backside as she filled their glasses. It was the least they could do to thank her.

Abby looked over at me and said, "She's right, you know."

"About what?"

"It really wouldn't kill you to let something good happen to you for once." She gave me an inquisitive look, waiting for a response.

I didn't have one, so I just shrugged.

The twins left to have dinner with their sadistic parents and Frank got a call from home and had to leave right away. Reggie followed him out with the chess set tucked under his arm. Out of boredom, Abby and I started taking turns trying to bounce quarters into a double shot glass. Neither of us were much for drinking games, so we weren't very good at it, but we gave it our best effort.

Abby passed the time asking questions. "What," she asked, bouncing a quarter off the counter which flew onto the floor, "is your favorite color?"

"Gray." I bounced another quarter, which chinked off the rim of the glass.

"Gray? That's hardly even a color."

"It's simple. Goes with everything."

"No, it doesn't."

"Name a color gray doesn't go with."

"Okay." She bounced a quarter on the counter. It nudged the glass a couple millimeters as it clinked against the side. "Green."

"Gray would go all right with a muted green."

"Like a pea soup green? Or a vomit green?"

"I mean, with less gross descriptors, but yeah."

"No, I'm talking like, bright green. Like, a super vibrant one."

I bounced my last quarter off the counter and onto the floor. Not even close. "I don't think it's that bad."

Abby circled the bar to retrieve her quarters. "That's just because you have really shitty taste, CJ."

"Oh, come on, I'm not that bad."

"Keep telling yourself that, bud. Speaking of which, I got you something." She set her quarters down on the counter on her way to the back room and returned shortly with a small brown paper gift bag. "Thought this might help."

There was a prepaid cell phone inside the bag. "Where'd you get this?"

"Reggie's pawn shop. Or souvenir shop. Whatever the hell it is. He's doing electronics now, remember? Figured it might save you some leg work if you can just call Sheriff Wilson instead of going up to the station so much. I put my number in there too if you need me for anything."

"Well thanks, Abby." I gave her a grateful smile and she nodded in turn. "Now that you mention it," I said, "I should give Mike a call." I flipped through my notebook and added his number to the cell's contacts. "I'll be back in a sec." I walked into the back office and called him.

It only rang twice. "Sheriff Wilson here."

"Hey Mike, it's CJ."

"Ah, CJ. What's up?"

I figured it best to get business out of the way first, so I gave Wilson the rundown on what I picked up that day. I finished my update by saying, "If you could keep an eye on Juliet, I would appreciate it. I'm sure she'll be back at work tomorrow to ensure no one thinks anything's amiss. And, of course, if she doesn't show up at all tomorrow, we'll ask around and figure out why."

"Gotcha. I'll keep an eye on her tomorrow."

"If she says anything about a Jimmy Olson, that was me."

"Jimmy Olson? Like from *Superman*?"

"You're familiar, huh? It was the first name that came to mind. Figured she'd be more willing to talk to a journalist than a detective."

Wilson laughed and said, "Fair enough. Ralston and I didn't find much today, so I'm glad you at least got something. Let me know if there's anything I can do to help—"

"I'm good for now," I interjected. "Thanks, Mike." I hung up the phone. That was enough of the sheriff for one day. I needed a drink. I tucked the phone into my pocket and walked back into the bar just as the church bells down the street announced it was 7:00. The door's bell jingled, right when Jack would always come in. Of course, Jack wasn't there.

"Robby," I said.

"Seej. Abby. And seriously, it's Rob." He fist bumped both of us and eased onto a barstool, staring quietly at Jack's empty seat next to him. He scratched the back of his head and said, "So, uh, what did you do today, Seej?" He glanced at Abby uncomfortably.

I chuckled. "It's all right, Robby. Abby knows what's going on."

"Oh, thank God." His shoulders visibly relaxed. He laughed to himself. "Sorry, I know I need to work on my poker face."

"Little bit," Abby smirked.

He scratched his head again. "Get any leads today?"

"Possibly."

Abby hopped up and sat on the bartop.

"Ever meet Juliet Beauregard?" I asked.

"Not personally, no," Robby said, shaking his head. "But Uncle Jack told me about her. Said she was a nice enough lady, just has a stick up her ass."

"Your uncle was too nice." I detailed what Clara said about Juliet and Jack's relationship and my conversation with Juliet afterward. Robby nodded intermittently and scratched his stubbly chin. Abby sat with her legs dangling off the end of the bar, ankles crossed, kicking her feet forward and back repeatedly.

Robby shook his head as I finished my report. "Shit man, so you pretended you were a reporter or some shit just to get her to talk to you?"

"Sometimes ya gotta do what ya gotta do, Robby." I motioned for Abby to hop off the bar and grabbed a can of Coke from the mini fridge that was under her feet. I set the soda and a glass on the bar in front of him.

"I keep telling you, it's Rob now," he muttered. Abby rustled his hair as she walked the length of the bar. Robby cracked open the Coke can and poured it into the glass, then said, "What? No lime?"

A lime wedge pelted him in the side of the head, flung from Abby's direction.

I laughed. "Come on, Abby, be nice."

Abby grinned mischievously. These moments of levity were good for all of us. If Abby hadn't been there, Robby and I would have ended up a lot more depressed than we already were.

I grabbed a glass and started polishing it. "Hear anything on your route today?"

Robby wiped the lime juice from his face with a chuckle and squeezed the lime into his glass. "Nothing crazy, no." He took a sip of his drink and pulled his Zippo out of his pocket. "From what I can tell, nothing's been out of the ordinary with Uncle Jack lately. Stopping by all the shops in town, talking to everyone he sees. Nothing weird. I had a couple deliveries over on our street, so I asked a couple of the neighbors if they noticed anything the day he went missing."

"Did they?" Abby asked.

"No, not really. The Robertsons live a few doors down. Uncle Jack always woke up Mrs. Robertson with his whistling every morning on the way to the lake. He walked by that morning. That seems to be the last time anyone saw or heard from him." He snapped his lighter shut, and the only sound in the bar was Joel Madden's voice over the speakers. We were all quiet until Robby sniffed and wiped his eyes before sipping his drink.

"Hey, Abby?" I said. "You're good to watch the bar for an hour or two, yeah?"

She looked at me, then looked at Robby and smiled. "Yeah, I've got it."

I clapped Robby on the shoulder. "Grab your bike and toss it in the back of my truck. I'll meet you out there."

"What?" He rubbed his nose. "Where are we going?"

I walked to the back office and called over my shoulder, "We're going fishing."

FIFTEEN

We had less than an hour of sunlight left when I parked in front of the Robertsons' house. The sidewalk branched off between the Robertsons' and their neighbors, leading down to the docks on Vineyard Lake. It was surreal, taking this little path Jack took every morning to start his day. The water was still and clear, and fish made soft ripples out in the middle of the lake. Jack's rowboat was still tied to the dock. He refused to get one with a motor. Scared away the fish.

"You really don't have to do this, Seej," Robby said.

"I know," I said. I set my rods and tacklebox in the bottom of the boat. I'd learned to keep my gear in my truck after being friends with Jack for three years. I sat between the oars. "Come on, sit down."

Robby situated himself opposite me while I untied the boat from the dock. I rowed out into the middle of the lake. The effort was exhausting. I may have been in shape, but I hadn't worked those muscles like that in a while. I was impressed at Jack's ability to row himself out there every morning. Robby was quiet, looking out over the rippling water as I prepped both rods and handed him one. I cast my line out. Sloppily, I might add. Hadn't been out on the water in a while. Robby stood and swiveled the rod over his head before sending a beautiful cast out over the water.

"You're definitely related to Jack," I said.

He smiled as he slowly turned the reel. "I remember the first time Uncle Jack brought me out here," he said. "I'd been in Jonesboro for a couple weeks maybe. Sheriff brought me home after he found me drinking under the bridge on the golf course when I should have been in class." He reeled the line in and cast it out again. I did the same, though with much less success.

"Uncle Jack wasn't mad," Robby said. "He thanked Sheriff Wilson, and we stood there on the front porch for a couple minutes. I couldn't look at him for a long time. When I finally did, he smiled, grabbed the rods he always had sitting by the front door, and just started walking. He sat down in his boat where you're sitting right now and waited for me to sit across from him before he started rowing. He didn't say anything. We got out into the middle of the lake, he got the fishing rods ready, and he handed one to me. He cast his line out and I just watched. I hadn't fished in years."

Robby and I both reeled our lines in at the same time, and Robby cast his out again. I opted out and set my rod down in the boat.

Robby sniffed. "He didn't say anything. He just set his rod down, came over, and held my wrists as he walked me through the motions. Before long we were both casting our lines out there in silence. Uncle Jack caught and released a couple fish. I didn't get anything, but I didn't really care. We fished until the sun went down, and Uncle Jack rowed the boat back to the dock. He tied the boat to the dock, took his rods and the tackle box, and started walking. I followed him. I still felt bad. Neither of us said a word those several hours. We got back to the house, and he opened the door and set the rods inside. Then he put a hand on my shoulder. He smiled and said, 'We'll try again tomorrow.'"

He reeled his line in and cast it again. "That was it. That's all he said. We went inside and had dinner like nothing happened. It wasn't until I was lying in bed staring at the ceiling that night that I realized he wasn't talking about fishing."

I smiled and looked down at the floor of the boat and noticed Jack's tackle box was wedged underneath Robby's seat. That's weird, I thought. Why would Jack have left his tackle box in the boat? And why would it be under the passenger's seat?

Then it dawned on me.

Oh my God.

"Things were different after that night," Robby said. "I stopped drinking. I started going to class. I even managed to graduate high school on time. Just barely, but still."

I did my best not to let my face show the inner workings of my brain.

I was the last person to see Jack alive.

Jack was murdered in the exact spot Robby was sitting.

Dots started connecting as I remembered that Tuesday morning. I had seen Jack in his boat in the middle of the lake. He was with someone. One of them waved to me. Whoever was in the boat that morning shot him point-blank from the spot I was sitting in. But how could I not notice? I'd easily recognize the sound of a gunshot if it had gone off while I was running that morning.

Robby chuckled. "Y'know, it's funny, if I hadn't gotten caught with weed on me at school three years ago, I wouldn't be here today. I wouldn't have graduated high school. I probably wouldn't even have an honest job."

The gun club. It had become such a normal part of my week that I started to drown it out. Every Tuesday morning a bunch of local guys went to a little firing range on a property nearby. The number of loud bangs I'd heard coming from that direction on Tuesdays was more than I could count. It always happened while I was on my run, in the same window Jack was murdered. If a gun went off while the gun club was in session, I wouldn't have thought twice about it.

Robby reeled his line in and smiled. "I wouldn't have met you, man."

I looked at him.

"You okay?" he asked. "You're kinda zoning over there."

"Yeah." I scratched my head and did my best to avoid looking at Jack's tacklebox. "Yeah, I'm good. I guess it's just really starting to sink in, you know?"

He nodded. "Yeah. Same." He smiled again. "Thanks for doing this, man. You really didn't have to, but I needed this."

I smiled back. "Of course, Robby."

He sat back down and said, "Let's get back. I'm sure Aunt Clara could use some company."

Within a few minutes, we'd rowed back to shore in silence as I continued to ignore Jack's tackle box behind Robby's feet. I gave the boat a quick once over as I tied it to the dock, but the sun was beginning to set and it was impossible to see anything properly. Couldn't go over it right then without looking suspicious, and I figured it would be best for Robby if he didn't know he'd sat in the exact spot his uncle probably died.

As we started back to my truck, lamp lights along the street began to flicker on one at a time, the harsh artificial light creeping toward us. He wrestled his bike out from the bed of my truck and bounced the tires on the asphalt.

"What happens now?" he asked.

"Tonight? Tonight, you go home and spend some time with your aunt. Try to get a good night's sleep, take some Tylenol PM if you need to. God knows you need it."

Robby suddenly looked exhausted. Almost as if he needed permission to show how tired he really was. He yawned. "Thanks, Seej. Let me know if you need anything."

"Hey, actually," I pulled my new phone out of my pocket and handed it to him. "Send yourself a text so you have my number."

Robby laughed. "The hell is this thing, man? This is some caveman shit."

"Just put your goddamn number in the goddamn phone." He couldn't help but laugh again as he sent himself a text from my phone. I snatched it back from him and stuffed it back in my pocket. "Call me if you hear anything, all right?"

"Yes sir, Officer Harris," he said with a mock salute. He started walking his bike back to his house, then stopped. "We're gonna find this bastard, right?"

"Hopefully," I said, thinking about the tacklebox in Jack's rowboat. "Can't make any promises." Robby rubbed his eyes and nodded, then started walking again. I called after him, "Hey, come by the bar tomorrow night. And bring your aunt. It'll be good to have you both there." He threw a thumbs up over his shoulder as he walked away. I smiled.

Good kid.

I looked back down the sidewalk leading to the dock. No one was going to touch the boat at that point, so I figured I'd come back the next day. I hopped in my truck and called the sheriff, but it went to voicemail. "Hey Mike, it's me," I said. "Think I accidentally stumbled upon our crime scene. Pretty sure Jack was murdered in his rowboat. I'm gonna go over it properly when I get the chance in the morning. I'll call you if I find anything."

I hung up and drove back to O'Callaghan's, doing my best not to think about how the sheriff was probably spending his time at that moment. There was laughter coming from inside the dive when I got back. I found the Smith girls sitting alone at the bar, Taylor Swift's "Shake It Off" playing loudly through the speakers. Elizabeth sat in hysterics on her barstool while Abby contorted her face into all manner of expressions with an Oreo balanced on her forehead. The smell of pizza wafted from a Mickey's box sitting on the counter.

Lizzy wiped tears from her eyes as I entered. "Hey, CJ," she choked out through bursts of laughter.

I tilted my head to the side. "What's going on here?"

Lizzy started into another fit and pointed at her sister, who had somehow moved the Oreo from her forehead to her eye. Abby blinked frantically and wriggled her head in several quick spasms until the Oreo fell off her face onto the floor. She shouted in disappointment and started laughing along with her sister.

"Come on, CJ," Abby said. "You should try it."

"Try what?"

Lizzy grabbed an Oreo from a package on the bar and turned her head upward before setting the cookie on her forehead. "Without using your hands," she said, "you have to try and get it from your forehead into your mouth." She started making similar sporadic expressions to the ones her sister had made. The Oreo fell off her forehead onto the floor, which sent the girls into another spurt of giggles. There were nearly a dozen Oreos littering the floor around them.

I smiled and shook my head. "Think I'll pass."

"Aw, come on, CJ," Abby said. "Don't be a party pooper."

"Guess that's just my lot in life." I circled to the other side of the bar. "Isn't it a little late for you to be out, Lizzy?"

"Pffft," Lizzy huffed. "I go to school online, CJ. *On. Line.* I go to school whenever the fuck I feel like it."

Abby slapped the bartop and said, "Oh yeah, Liz, guess what CJ's favorite color is."

"What, it's not something boring like gray, is it?"

Abby pointed at her sister enthusiastically and looked at me.

"What?" Lizzy shouted. "Oh, come on, CJ, how fucking lame can you be?"

I rubbed my eyes and laughed. I had a long night ahead of me.

SIXTEEN

The nightmare always starts the same.

Charlie and I are running around the backyard of Grammy's old homestead, shooting each other with imaginary guns. Laughing, screaming, making what we think are gun sounds like boys are prone to do.

Mom calls us in for dinner and we race to the open doorway, the scent of pot roast wafting into the yard. I make it to the house before Charlie does and turn to rub it in his face that I beat him to the house again. Maybe throw in my usual jab about how he got the shitty middle name. Quentin. What kind of a name was that? I pull out my imaginary gun and shoot at him as he charges the house.

But the sound.

Not the sound of our young imaginings.

The real thing.

I watch as Charlie, a grown man in full military dress, looks down at the hole torn in his belly.

He falls.

I run as fast as my little legs can carry me. I'm still a boy.

As he hits the ground, I slide to my knees and support his head, telling him I'm sorry, it's all right, and that I'm right here. He's fading. Blood spurts from his mouth with each cough. He's trying to say something, but it's a whisper. I lean in close to hear him.

"So much for that Me and Coke, eh, CJ?"

I pull away and see Jack in my arms, blood seeping from a hole in the center of his forehead. He smiles and goes cold as his eyes continue to stare. I feel a hand on my shoulder and turn to see Charlie—pale, blood oozing from his stomach—looking down at me.

"Why, Chris?"

I sat up with a start, my breath labored and heavy, and pressed my fingers into my eyelids, trying to rub the image from my mind. I looked at the clock. 3:23. I leaned over and punched the buttons on the landline, curling into the fetal position as Mom's voice crackles through the speaker.

"I just hope you know that I love you so much. And I'm always here when you need me...

"I love you, Chris."

SEVENTEEN

I shut the back door behind me shortly after 7:00 the next morning. I was goddamn tired getting up that early two days in a row, but I knew a run would do me some good on my way to check out Jack's boat. I couldn't bring myself to run past the drainage ditch again, so after a quick stretch I set off around the lake in the opposite direction.

Running was my routine, my meditation, my morning devotion. Every morning growing up, I would come down the stairs and find Dad sitting in his recliner, reading glasses perched on his nose, writing in a journal on his right knee with a Bible sitting open on his left. A mug of coffee was always steaming on the table next to him. His routine was to wake up before sunrise and read the same scriptures he had read dozens of times before, looking for new lessons to teach the members of his congregation on Sundays.

Never understood how he could stand up there every week after fucking his secretary.

I was seventeen when I found him with Sylvia while Mom was on a business trip. Needed to borrow the car, but I couldn't get ahold of him, so I ended up at the house on a Friday night my senior year of high school, which never happened. There were weird sounds coming from upstairs, so I went to investigate. Fortunately, the two of them were too focused on each other to notice I'd cracked the door open, so I slipped away before they knew I was there. I still needed a car, so I made my way down to the garage. The Corolla's keys hung on the wall, but I grabbed the other set of keys instead and pulled the cover off Dad's pearl white '62 Thunderbird convertible. I sat in the driver's seat for five minutes listening to the creaking of my parents' bed on the floor above me before I finally turned the keys in the ignition, revved the engine a few times, and peeled out of the driveway. My friends were excited when I pulled up in the car, but immediately terrified once they sat in it. We took the Thunderbird for a joyride, sure, but it was in immaculate condition at the end of the night. No one felt like getting killed for ruining my dad's car.

I got in trouble, but I didn't care. Two days later, I sat in service at Dad's church, listening to him speak from the pulpit like he did every Sunday, telling people that Jesus would change their lives and take away their addictions. I never went to Dad's church again.

The wooden slats of the boardwalk on Vineyard's east bank creaked under my feet as I jogged along. The boardwalk was one of the most popular spots for the Fourth of July celebrations, but it had been bare since the Independence Day Incident. Clay Robertson's old pedal boat rental shack hardly got service anymore.

It wasn't much further to the south docks, and I slowed to a brisk walk as I rounded the southeastern curve of Vineyard. The light breeze was cool against my warm skin as I walked the final stretch past Jonesboro's lakefront properties. Several of the houses were empty, and so were the south docks. Only a handful of boats were tied to the dock anymore, including Jack's old rowboat, quietly bumping against the wooden railing with the subtle shifting of the water. Jack's boat was the source of so many happy memories for people in town. I hated knowing it was where Jack died.

Trying to take DNA off the boat would probably cause more problems than it would solve. Jack took everyone out in that boat; I couldn't even guess how many people in town we'd end up finding samples for if we tried. Not to mention that Robby and I had just been out in it the night before. Still, I couldn't help but be careful as I looked around my tiny crime scene, doing my best to avoid touching anything unnecessary.

Jack's tackle box was fully stocked, the latches were tight, and it was comfortably tucked under the passenger seat in his boat. Oddly enough there wasn't any blood in the boat, but there wasn't much blood at the dump site either. There was no rope in the boat, and none of Jack's other belongings. His rod was gone, so whoever was in the boat with him must have taken it but somehow missed the tackle box.

There must be something here, I thought. I checked under the rower's bench and, to my surprise, found a set of keys nestled on the floor of the boat, with a large keychain. I picked them up to look them over. The keychain was a multitool in the shape of a wine bottle with a couple different small blades and, most notably, a couple pieces of metal that unfolded to function as a corkscrew. It had the Jonesboro Winery logo stamped across it, faded from years of wear. Other than that, there wasn't anything special about the keys. Could have been anyone's.

"Morning, CJ."

I tucked the keys into my pocket as I looked toward the voice. "Morning, Clay."

Clay Robertson walked down to the end of the dock where his own sailboat was moored. "Odd seeing you over on this side of the lake. What brings you over here?"

"Just out for a run."

"I see." He smiled and looked out over the lake, the breeze whipping the hair on top of his balding head to stand on end. "Beautiful day, isn't it?"

I looked out over the lake. The sun was out, the light shimmering over the shifting waters of the lake in different sparkling points. "Yeah," I said. "It really is."

Clay looked at Jack's rowboat. "Tough hearing about ol' Jack, isn't it?"

"Yeah." I rubbed my neck. "Could hardly believe it when the sheriff said he killed himself."

"I'm sure." He climbed onto his boat and started prepping the sail. "How's old Mike Wilson doing?"

I tried to pick my words carefully, the sheriff's face illuminated by blue light flickering in the back of my mind. "He's busy. Seems like he spends most of his time tied up in the office nowadays."

"Shame," Clay said. "He's been holed up in that station way more since the budget cuts."

"Really? He's been a desk jockey since I first moved to town when the station was fully staffed. He hasn't always been like that?"

Clay shook his head. "Sheriff's always been one of Jonesboro's best cops. Even when he first became the sheriff, he was always out and about around town checking in with everyone. Always super friendly. Jonesboro's never had much crime, but everyone felt safer knowing he was out on patrol."

"What happened?"

"I don't know for sure. His sister died five years ago. He left town to see her one last time. Wasn't the same when he came back."

I kicked at a rock near my foot and muttered, "Know what that's like." Part of me felt bad for him. I knew the toll losing a sibling took on you. But I also prided myself on my ability to do my damn job at the end of the day.

The breeze picked up a bit and the sails around us started to flutter. Clay continued to prep his boat, but I would have felt weird walking away on that note. The silence started getting uncomfortable, so I said, "How's the kid doing after that run-in with the dog the other day?"

"Oh, Tim's doing all right. He's a tough kid. It scared him more than anything. I don't think the dog was gonna hurt him, it just wanted to play. I'm just glad I was there to get the bastard off him." Didn't skip a beat when I asked him about the encounter. News traveled fast.

"Have you talked to Ms. Foster since the whole thing?"

"Oh yeah, she brought over some cookies the next night, bought Tim a football. He was ecstatic. We tossed it around the backyard the rest of the night."

"Not suing her after all, huh?"

He laughed. "Oh, no, of course not. The wife kinda said that as a reflex in the moment, but she never really meant it." Clay started untying his boat from the dock, then looked at me. "You see, CJ," he said, "something you'll learn about small towns like this one: you know everyone here and everyone knows you. You see each other every day, even if you're trying to avoid each other. You don't really hold grudges. You can't afford to. Life's too short for stuff like that. No time for it."

"Then what do you do?" I asked.

Clay untied his boat and started drifting from the dock. He smiled and said, "You forgive. You forget. You fix it and move on."

I smiled. Nice sentiment. Doesn't work too well in practice.

The church bells rang as Clay maneuvered out onto the water. The keys felt heavy in my pocket. Need to figure out who these belong to, I thought. Guess I'll ask Clara if Jack said anything about going fishing with anyone on Monday. I kicked at another rock on the path and noticed an oil stain on the concrete. Weird. Just like the one where Jack's body was dumped. I jumped when my pocket suddenly started vibrating. Forgot that I brought my new phone with me. I lifted it to my ear. "Hello?"

"Hey there, Harris. Just arrested Ms. Beauregard like you asked."

EIGHTEEN

"What the actual fuck did you do, Mike?"

The sheriff backed away from me, waving his hands in front of himself. "Hey, hey, you told me to keep an eye on her and that's exactly what I did." He pointed through the one-way glass to Juliet Beauregard sitting alone at a table in an interrogation room, angrily tapping her thumb against the table's metallic surface.

I took a moment to catch my breath. I had sprinted back to the cabin and quickly grabbed my jacket before jumping in the truck to drive to the station. Hadn't run so fast in my life. Finally, I said, "Yeah, I wanted you to keep an eye on her. Post up outside the winery and track her movements or something. Not arrest her. What grounds did you even bring her in on?"

Wilson shrank further into himself. "Grounds?"

I wanted to punch him. I could easily let my fist fly into his jaw and level him, try to smack some manner of competence into that dull brain. Instead, I whipped my hand up and smacked the bill of his hat, flicking it off his head onto the floor behind him. Only then did I notice Ralston in the corner of the briefing room, one hand over his mouth, trying his best to keep a straight face. At least someone found this amusing.

"Hey," Juliet shouted. She had crossed to the window and tapped on the glass. "I'd really like to know why the hell I'm here."

"So would I," I whispered. I pressed into my eyes with my fingers. "We don't even have solid proof she's involved with this yet." I took a deep breath, exhaled, and said to Wilson, "Might as well try to ask her a few questions while she's here. Try to fix this mess you made. Give me your badge." The sheriff fumbled his badge out of his jacket and put it in my outstretched hand. With one final glare, I stepped in front of the door to the interrogation room and took a few breaths to clear my mind.

I did my fair share of interrogations in LA. I always saw them as another hole on the course. Asking the right questions with the right inflection, emotion, and volume was a tricky balance to find, but I loved it. Just needed to find the right trigger.

I pushed open the door and shut it behind me. Juliet looked startled but recognized me immediately. "You? What the hell are you doing here?"

I quickly flashed the police badge then flicked it shut. "Ms. Beauregard, my name is Christopher James Harris. I'm working with the police on the investigation of Jack Romero's murder. Can you take a seat for me?"

The wrinkles of her forehead became more pronounced as a puzzled expression crossed her face. "Wait, so you lied to me?"

"Yes, ma'am, I did. Now can you take a seat for me?"

Juliet stormed back to the table and sat opposite me. "I don't know what the hell you want from me or why I'm here."

"I'm sorry for the confusion, ma'am. Unfortunately, Mike Wilson is a complete and total dumbass." I turned and looked at the one-way window as I approached the table. The metal legs of the chair screeched against the concrete floor as I pulled it out and sat down. I felt very uncomfortable in my workout clothes. Didn't feel the part at all.

I said, "All I want to do is ask you some questions. Different ones from yesterday."

She scoffed. "I would assume so, since yesterday you were bullshitting as a reporter from a comic book."

I smiled. "See, I knew you were an intelligent woman. You do your research."

"Oh, shut up. Just get this over with so I can get out of here and call my lawyer."

"As you should." I looked back at the window as I pulled out my notebook. "You sure you don't want your lawyer here now? Wouldn't be surprised if Mike neglected to tell you, but it's your right to have one present."

"I won't be fooled by you again," she said as she brushed some stray hair from her face. "I can assure you that. And I haven't done anything wrong, as you'll soon realize, so I don't see the need to delay my ability to leave any more than necessary." She glared at the one-way mirror. "I'm more focused on putting that idiot in his place."

"Fair enough." I clicked my pen. "Now, Ms. Beauregard, can you tell me where you were Tuesday morning?"

"Well," she said, "I followed my usual routine and went to Caroline's around 8:00 to start my work for the day. I enjoyed my tea and a scone while I took care of some emails before heading up to the office."

"What time did you leave Caroline's?"

"Just before 9:00."

"And you went straight to the office? No detours?"

"Yes."

"How long were you in the office, then?"

"Until around 2:00 when I left, which was later than normal since I had to do Albert's job for him since he was sick that day." She shook her head. "I'm failing to see why any of this is important."

"Jack Romero was murdered sometime between 9 am and noon on Tuesday. Is there any way for you to verify that you were in your office that entire time?"

"There's a security camera in the hallway outside my office. I'm sure you can confirm what I've said if you look at the surveillance video. And I believe there's a camera in Caroline's if you don't believe me about that either."

"And there aren't any other exits from your office?"

She rolled her eyes. "You were there, imbecile. You would know."

Fair point. Not my best follow-up.

"Plus," she went on, "Paul, the custodian, can verify that I was there during those times, as well. I needed him to unlock my office for me that morning and then lock it for me again when I left."

"And why is that?"

"My keys went missing, that's all," she said, nonchalant. "I misplaced them."

No way. I felt the keys in my pocket. Is it possible? I grabbed the wine bottle keychain and pulled out the set of keys, dangling it in front of me as if lulling her into a trance.

"These your keys?"

Her eyes widened. "Where did you find those?"

"Oh, these?" I flipped the keys into my hand. "These beauties were found in the bottom of Jack Romero's rowboat. The exact place I've determined to be where Jack was murdered three days ago."

Her mouth opened and shut several times, like a gasping fish plopped onto dry land. "I—I swear to God I wasn't—" She anchored her jaw. "I want my lawyer."

"Well, Mike?" I turned and looked through the one-way glass once more. "It looks like your stupid mistake somehow paid off." Wilson came into the room and snapped a pair of handcuffs on Juliet's wrists. "Toss her in a holding cell for now, Sheriff. I have some other things to look into."

Wilson wrestled Juliet out of the room and down the hallway, her screams of anger fading further into silence with every footstep. I moved back into the briefing room where Ralston waited for me.

"Impressive," he said. "You really think she did it?"

I tossed the keys in the air a couple times. "Who knows? She could be telling the truth. All I know right now is we might have some solid evidence connecting her to the crime scene. Could be nothing, or she could at least be an accomplice. Either way, it's the best lead we have. For now, I'm going to check out some security footage and see if her story lines up."

Ralston nodded. "Anything else I can do to help out?"

I tossed him the keys. "Put these in evidence lockup for me. And," I pointed a thumb over my shoulder, "make sure that idiot doesn't do anything else to fuck up my investigation."

NINETEEN

"Sure, I can show you the security room," Paul said. I tucked Wilson's police badge back in my jacket pocket.

Paul, with his thick glasses and Santa beard, had worked as the Facilities Manager at the Jonesboro Winery and Vineyards for a decade and now was the only custodian. I followed him across the production floor and down a flight of stairs into an empty hallway. Our footsteps echoed off the cold concrete as we approached a large metal door cut into the wall, labeled with white letters spelling out "SECURITY" that were peeling at the corners.

"We don't actually have anyone working down here right now," he said, flicking through several keys on his keyring. "We've had a lot of people quit and had several lay-offs since traffic's died down in the last couple years." He jiggled a key in the lock and pressed down forcefully on the door handle.

The door swung open to a dark, musty room illuminated by several flickering monitors mounted on the wall above a wooden desk. Most of them displayed blurry live feeds of the various rooms and corridors of the winery in black and white. Other screens were black, the cameras likely either broken or disconnected. Dust hung in the air, a layer of it thick on the desk itself, save for a couple handprints that had disrupted it.

"So no one comes down here anymore?" I asked.

Paul shook his head and sneezed into the crook of his arm. "No, I come by every once in a while to clear the memory on the computer, but that's it." He waggled the computer mouse and woke up a desktop monitor, sending a flurry of dust into the air. "The old security boys set up the computer to compile all of the footage—" He paused and sneezed again. "—into one big folder each day. I come down every couple months to erase all the stuff we don't need so the computer doesn't fill up."

"So everything from this Tuesday should be on that computer?"

"That's right, Officer Harris. If I remember right, it should be..." Paul clicked through a few screens of digital folders. "Ah, right here. Here's everything from this Tuesday."

He expanded the folder and several zipped files labeled with a random assortment of letters and numbers popped up on the screen. The first few numbers of each labeled file were reminiscent of Tuesday's date. I scrolled through the files, trying to make any sense of it.

"Any idea which of these are the office hallway cameras?" I asked.

"No idea." Paul sneezed twice. "The cameras aren't my area of expertise. I just do the cleaning and maintenance."

I scrolled to the bottom of the folder. There were dozens of files in that one folder from dozens of cameras, each video likely several hours long. I didn't have time to sit on my ass and go through all of it.

"Shit," I muttered.

"Language, Officer Harris."

"Sorry." I rubbed my eyes and stooped to look at the computer tower under the desk. An external hard drive sat on top of the tower, a small blue light in its side emitting a steady glow. "Think you can put those files on this hard drive for me?"

Paul sneezed again and said, "Sure, I think I can do that." He fiddled on the computer for a minute. "There you go. I put all the footage from this week on that hard drive. Labeled the days so they'll be easier to find. Just give it a few minutes to copy over and you'll be good to go."

"Thanks, Paul."

"Now, if you'll excuse me—" Paul reared up for a sneeze, but it never came. He shook his head and pulled out his keys. "I have some other things to get to, so I'm gonna lock the door behind you. Just make sure it shuts when you leave."

"Will do."

Paul shut the door and left me in the dark, black-and-white monitors flickering in front of me and a soft blue light flashing near my feet.

A final sneeze echoed down the hallway.

I waved through the front door of Caroline's just as Abby turned off the neon "Open" sign. She greeted me with a smile. "Well, I'm surprised you're so eager to see me after last night." Three sets of eyes looked at me: Abby's and the oversized eyes of the two colorful owls that hung from her earlobes.

"I think I learned more about you and Lizzy last night than I ever wanted to."

"And we won't apologize for that. Welcome to the family."

"Thanks, I guess." It was closer to a question than an expression of gratitude. "I was planning on coming by earlier, but something came up."

"Rough morning?"

"That's an understatement."

"What's up?" We stepped inside and she shut the door behind us.

I scanned the ceiling of the coffee shop until I found the camera mounted in the front corner of the store. "I need security footage from that camera. Juliet says she came here the morning Jack was murdered."

Abby rolled her eyes at the mention of Juliet's name. "Yeah, she was definitely here. God, I hate that woman. Follow me."

I trailed her past the counter into the back office where she spun into a swivel chair in front of the computer crammed in the corner. I had no idea how Caroline could hole herself up in that tiny room all day. Abby said, "Haven't worked here too long, but I think I should be able to find it."

I put a hand on the back of her chair and watched as she maneuvered through the windows of the computer, the two bug-eyed owls wiggling with her movements. Then, seemingly out of nowhere, I sneezed. The dust from the security office finally caught up with me.

"Bless you," Abby said, still clicking away.

"Thanks." I sniffed and rubbed my nose.

"Here we go. Found it. Don't think I can pull it up on this computer, though. Caroline never updates this thing." I handed the external hard drive over her shoulder. "Perfect." She plugged it in and after a few quick clicks, handed it back to me.

"Thanks," I said. "Now I just have to figure out how to go through the countless hours of footage on this thing."

"Wait, really?" she asked.

"Yep. Need to verify Juliet's alibi. But I have a huge folder of unnamed files from a dozen of the winery's cameras."

"When are you going to have time to do that? You don't even have a computer."

"I'm honestly not sure."

Abby leaned back in her chair. "I can't say for sure, but you know who might be able to help you out?"

"Who?"

"Can you think of anyone who sits in front of a computer all day without much else going on?"

I stared at her in confusion and she raised her eyebrows like I was stupid. Then I understood who she meant.

I shook my head. "Uh-uh. No way. Not her."

I rang the bell at the front counter of Jonesboro Public Library, mentally flogging myself for taking Abby's advice. Surely there had to be someone else. I didn't have time for this, even if I wanted time for it deep down. And what if she said no? She was a doctoral student after all, surely she had better things to do with her time.

I hopped on this train of thought as an excuse to bail and turned to leave.

"Christopher James Harris."

I stopped, the scent of yellowing pages, binding, and glue sinking deep into my nostrils as time—and my heart—stopped. I swallowed hard and said, "Molly Bauer."

I turned back to the front desk. Molly stood behind the counter, blond hair in a ponytail, a purple-and-white floral print blouse hidden behind a stack of books she had carried out of the office behind her.

She smiled, displacing the genuine surprise on her face just a moment before. "Well," she said, "to what do I owe the pleasure of your company?" She set the books on the counter and leaned against the stack. "Today's run clear your head enough to make you see things differently?"

I realized for the second time that day I was still wearing my workout clothes. I cleared my throat and stepped back to the front counter, painfully aware of the greasiness of my hair and the scent of sweat leaking from inside my jacket. I could feel the heat in my cheeks as I said, "So—" My voice cracked. I cleared my throat again and said, "So, Molly. As you may have heard by now, Jack Romero died on Tuesday."

Molly's expression changed. "Yes, I did hear about that. The poor family."

"Well, he was actually murdered."

Smooth, Chris. Real goddamn smooth.

Molly raised a hand to her mouth, emotion flickering in her pupils. "Really?"

I cleared my throat a third time. "Yes. The sheriff wants me to keep the fact it was a murder under wraps as best we can, for the winery's relaunch or whatever. I used to be a detective in LA, so I'm heading up the investigation."

She looked puzzled. It was a lot of information to take in at once. She took a second to process it and then said, "Why are you telling me, then?"

The church bells down the street rang. Noon.

"Well," I said, scratching the back of my head, "I could really use your help. If you have time, that is."

"Ah. So you didn't come to see me. You came because you need a favor."

My stomach clenched. "Molly, that's not—"

"Well, as you might be able to tell," she said, looking around the empty library, "I have nothing but time. What do you need?"

"Wait, so you'll help me?"

"Someone in town was murdered, CJ." She moved the stack of books to the side. "I may be disappointed, but I'm not a monster. I'll do whatever I can to help."

"Right. Well, thank you." I set the hard drive on the counter. "I know this is a big ask, but I need to confirm someone's alibi. I have dozens of unlabeled security videos on this thing that are hours long, and I don't have the time to figure out which one I need. Don't even have a computer to do it."

Molly picked up the hard drive and plugged it into the computer behind the counter. "Who and what am I looking for, then?" she asked, sitting at the desk. I described what little I knew about the files on the hard drive and what I was looking for. Molly wrote on a sticky note as I explained and stuck it to her monitor when I finished. "Juliet Beauregard," she said. "Winery office hallway camera between 7:00 and 10:00. Coffee shop between 10:00 and 10:45. Got it. Anything else I should know?"

I grabbed a sticky note and a pen. "Here's my phone number."

"Wow, your phone number?" she asked as I handed her the sticky note. "Are you sure that's a step you're willing to take?" She stuck that sticky note to her monitor as well.

I felt my face flush. "Molly, I'm—"

"No, it's fine. It's fine." She took a deep breath. "Sorry. I'll call you if I find anything. Promise."

I watched quietly as she started clicking through files in silence. "Thanks, Molly," I said. "I really appreciate it."

"In the meantime," she said, "you look like you've been running around all morning. You should go home, clean yourself up, rest for a bit."

"But—"

She waved a hand. "Don't argue with me, CJ, really. You look exhausted. Take a little break. I've got this covered. I'll call you if I find anything."

I sighed. I could feel my eyelids drooping. "Thanks again, Molly." I stood there, the silence only broken up by her frequent clicks, and said, "I'm sorry."

She smiled sadly. "Me too."

———————

I rubbed the towel violently on my head to dry my hair, tossed it in the hamper, and laid down on the bed. The ceiling fan spun lazily as it always did, slowly drying my naked body. My muscles hurt. My eyes felt heavy. But my mind refused to quiet. Amid all the questions plaguing my mind about Jack's murder, my thoughts repeatedly drifted back to my conversation with Clay Robertson that morning. Forgive. Forget. Fix it. Move on. No time for it. I looked at the clock on my nightstand. 12:49. I let my eyes drift shut.

The elevator doors shut slowly, despite my frantic hammering on the button to close it faster. The elevator hums. The doors open. I dart through. Top floor. The penthouse is open. Shouting. Living room. Everything's expensive. Dad's office. "It isn't worth it!" More shouting. "Put the gun down!" All three of us, shouting. Squeeze.

Bang.

I woke with a start. It took a few rotations of the fan to remember where I was. The clock told me it was 3:37. Guess I was more tired than I thought. Molly hadn't found anything yet if my lack of missed calls was anything to go by.

The sound of a gunshot still echoed in my mind, and I shook my head to clear it. Needed to shift gears from detective to bartender. Fridays were always busy.

TWENTY

Everything changes after losing a loved one. The dinner table becomes one of the most uncomfortable spaces, an empty chair the only indication someone is missing. The silence that lingers in those moments is hideous, interrupted only by the occasional sob or vain attempt to lighten the mood.

This silence rested heavy in O'Callaghan's that Friday night.

Ryan and Brian Dinsmore sat in their usual spots, their eyes sunk deep into their beers. Reggie Davis and Frank Jenkins sat together on the corner at the end of the bar, no chessboard between them. It was a Friday, so Mick was there, though I had a feeling he wouldn't be doing any magic that evening. His girlfriend, Rosie, sat on a stool next to him at the bar. Amanda always popped over after her shift on Fridays and that night sat in a booth by herself in the corner, folding her napkin into some sort of origami bird, her White Russian untouched.

I kept looking at Jack's empty seat, each time hoping he would be there. Mick had put on some quiet jazz music which was accompanied by the occasional squeak of my rag against a particularly stubborn pint glass.

I checked the clock. 6:58. I grabbed a tumbler and tossed in a couple cubes of ice. I poured two shots of Jack and topped it off with some Coke, then set it on a coaster in Jack's spot. The room sat transfixed, all eyes on the tumbler, waiting for the familiar smell of fine tobacco.

The bell above the door jingled.

Everyone turned to the open doorway.

Jack wasn't there, of course. But his wife was, along with their nephew.

Clara gave me a soft, sad smile and sat at the bar next to Jack's empty barstool. Robby sat beside her and gave me a somber nod. He set a worn leather journal on the counter next to him, different from the one he'd been reading in the tackle shop the other day. Another volume of *The Extraordinary Life of Jack Romero*, I assumed.

The church bells rang. 7:00. Clara pulled a handkerchief from her purse and dabbed at her eyes. Robby rubbed his nose and sniffed, forcing back tears. The twins drained their beers in unison. The seventh bell faded into silence, and so did O'Callaghan's.

Mick pounded a fist on the bartop. "Fuck this." He stood and made his way behind the bar. "Christopher, line 'em up."

Knew exactly what he wanted.

I nodded and quickly set up ten tumblers along the bar while Mick followed me with a bottle of Jack Daniels, eyeballing a double in each glass. I grabbed a few cans of Coca-Cola from the mini fridge below the bar just as the door jingled and Abby came in. I motioned for her to get behind the bar. She nodded, tossed her jacket on a table, and started cracking cans and pouring Coke into the glasses. She picked up quick.

Before long, the three of us had set a Jack and Coke in front of everyone in the dive, each person now shoulder-to-shoulder surrounding Jack's barstool. I even set one in front of Robby. He picked it up and swirled it around in his hand, then smiled at me sadly. He passed it to Abby, opting for a half-empty can of Coke instead.

Mick centered himself behind the bar and looked at his audience. He closed his eyes and inhaled deeply. "I first moved here about ten years ago," he said, opening his eyes, "with my girls and now ex-wife. We came in a whirlwind. I saw this building listed and we bought it, packed up, and moved here in a week. I didn't know what I was doing. I'd never run a business before." He chuckled to himself and shook his head. "I was stressed out of my damn mind. I felt like I couldn't breathe. I left the house one day and took a walk to clear my head, ended up sitting on a bench by the lake. Don't even remember the walk there."

A flugelhorn crooned over the speakers as we all sat waiting for Mick to continue.

He swallowed. "But there I was, sitting on that bench, looking out over the water. There was a little breeze behind me. It was chilly. I was sitting there, crying, thinking I'm losing it, when I just get hit by this smell. Really nice tobacco. Reminded me of my grandpa. I didn't turn around, didn't say a word, but before I knew it, some stranger is sitting on the bench next to me, smoking a cigar, looking out over the lake." Mick sniffed and ran a hand across his nose. "He didn't say a thing. I didn't either. Then I just feel this little nudge on my arm. I look over and this fat little Italian man has a cigar in his fingers, and he's just prodding me with it."

Gentle laughter passed between us, giving Mick some time to rub his nose again. "I take the cigar and he lights it for me, and we just sit there, smoking these expensive cigars in silence. And I mean silence. We didn't say a word for an hour, blowing little clouds of smoke into the breeze. Then he got up and left. That's how I met Jack."

Everyone along the bar sniffled and rubbed their eyes, even the twins.

Mick clenched a fist on the bartop and said, "Couple years later, my wife and I split up. Day after she left, I wound up on that same bench by the lake. Thinking. Beating myself up over it. Crying. Big surprise, I know." Everyone chuckled, including Mick. "Wasn't there for ten minutes before that same smell hit me. Grandpa's tobacco pipe. I knew Jack well by then, he'd been in the bar almost every night since that day we first met. He sits down next to me again, and I'm expectin' some big spiel about the weather and how it affects fishing or whatever."

The rest of us laughed again, as a tear finally broke from Mick's eye. He cleared his throat and said, "But no. He doesn't say a word. He's completely silent. And soon after, I feel a little nudge on my arm just like that first time and we smoked cigars together on that bench in silence." Mick looked up at us, each with a Jack and Coke clutched in our hands. "Those are the only times I ever saw Jack quiet for longer than ten seconds. I don't know how, but he knew it's what I needed."

Mick paused as the jazz trio continued playing in the background. I scanned the faces on the other side of the bar. Faces I knew so well, all with the same somber expression. These were Jack's friends, his family. And they were devastated.

Mick cleared his throat again. "I went and sat on that same bench today." He paused again. His voice was strained and shaky, and tears began to run freely down his cheeks. He sniffed and said, "I waited for that warm tobacco smell. I waited for my silent smoking buddy. I sat there for three hours, just waiting. But he never came."

I blinked away tears as others along the bar did the same. Mick wiped his eyes and pressed on, his voice steady once more. "But he's not all gone. I know for goddamn sure, every time I have this." He raised his glass. "This fuckin' drink right here. It'll be for my boy Jack Romero. I won't ever forget him. And," he scanned across everyone in the bar, "I know none of you will, neither." He held his glass out in front of him. "For Jack!"

Ten glasses and an aluminum can clinked together.

TWENTY-ONE

The next few hours were filled with tears and laughter as we recounted stories of Jack and his extraordinary life. Over the course of the night, a few other regulars and not-so-regulars popped in and out of O'Callaghan's. Everyone was served a Jack and Coke, and everyone had their own stories of Jack Romero. Even if they had only interacted with him once or twice, everyone in the bar that night had something to say about Jack. Memories of his quirks and compassion, his silly antics, and his generosity.

At one point, Robby opened Jack's journal and read a passage he'd found dated back in 1997, the year Robby was born:

I've realized something these past few years. At the end of the day, family's all that matters. We help each other, support each other, even when the world is beating us down. We make mistakes, but our family's always there. Hell, I've made mistakes. But at the end of the day, when my time's up, I want people to think about me and say "Goddamn, that guy cared about his family. He did everything he could for his family. And his family wasn't just the people he was related to, either." I'd do anything for my family. I hope I can help teach my nephew to do the same.

It took him a few tries, but Robby eventually got through it. There wasn't a single dry eye in the bar that night. Everyone in town knew Jack at some level, and no one could believe he was gone.

Which gave me even more motivation to find whoever killed him.

At closing time, Mick, Abby, and I found ourselves alone in the bar. Abby nursed her third Jack and Coke of the night as Mick poured himself a pint of PBR. Rosie had kissed him goodnight and gone home a couple hours beforehand, and any stragglers shambled out shortly before 1:00 as usual.

I started flipping stools and putting them on the bartop as Mick straddled onto a stool next to Abby. He tapped his pint against her glass and said, "Cheers," before taking a gulp. "How're you doing, Ms. Abigail?"

She rubbed her eyes. "Okay, I guess. It's been a long-ass couple days."

"You're telling me." He took another drink. "How many jobs are you working now?"

"Three, count 'em." She lifted three fingers. "Three jobs. Get off here around 2:00, work the opening shift at the coffee shop at 6:00, work a few hours at the gas station before I come back here. I'm running on about three hours of sleep every night. Sometimes I'm lucky enough to get a nap in during the day."

"Damn," Mick said. He turned to me. "Did you give this girl a raise yet, Christopher?"

Abby looked up.

I shook my head. "Not yet, Mick. I was going to talk to her about it yesterday, but there was a lot going on."

"Well, make sure ya do it. An extra five an hour should do."

Abby looked back at Mick, startled. "What? Really, sir, I couldn't ask—"

Mick raised a hand. "No arguing, Miss. That's what's happening." He smiled. "I own this joint and the one next door. Locals love their pizza and beer. I'm one of the few business owners not struggling in town. Plus, this guy behind the bar is the only one taking a paycheck from this place."

Abby looked at me, then at Mick, then back to me.

I smiled and nodded.

She threw her arms around Mick and started crying into his shoulder. He wrapped her in his big, tattooed arms and patted her on the back. I set a roll of paper towels on the bar in front of her, which she pulled from to wipe her eyes and blow her nose while she regained her composure, saying, "Thank you, thank you so much," repeatedly.

I leaned across the bar, clapped her on the shoulder and said, "Hey, maybe you can quit one of those other two jobs now."

She smiled and nodded, still drying her eyes.

I said, "Which is a good thing, since I might have some busy nights coming up soon."

Abby nodded again.

Mick said, "Investigating Jack's murder, Christopher?"

Abby and I jerked our heads to look at Mick, who casually sipped his beer.

Abby spoke first. "How did—?"

He interrupted and said, "I knew Jack too well, kids. Talked with him every day for ten years. I was one of the closer friends he had in town. Man loved his family and his life too much to take himself out of it."

"But how did you know I was working the case?" I asked.

He grinned without looking up from his beer. "Cause you just told me, Christopher."

Dammit. Rookie move.

"Plus," Mick continued, "Mike's an idiot. And Ralston's a good kid, but he's too green. I know what you did for a living before comin' out here. You're the only man in this town for the job." He lifted his gaze to look at me. "How's it feel to be back on the streets?"

I poured myself a pint of PBR. "Honestly, I didn't realize it before, but I missed it. Something about it just feels right. After all," I looked at Abby. "It was always my dream."

Abby smiled at me, and Mick punched me in the shoulder, which really hurt. "Good for you, Christopher," he said. "I'm glad you're doing something you love. And don't worry." He brought his pointer finger to his lips. "I won't tell a soul."

Abby asked, "How's it all going, by the way? Did you talk to Molly?"

"Yeah," I said. "And that conversation went about as well as I thought it would." I took a few gulps of my beer and pulled my notebook out of my back pocket. I knew these two would keep whatever I told them to themselves. They both wanted Jack's killer found as much as I did. Even though it was only the three of us in the bar, I spoke softly and explained my suspicions of Juliet Beauregard, my initial interview with her, the sheriff's idiotic mistake and the subsequent interrogation, and the keys I found in Jack's rowboat.

"I never liked that old lady," Mick said with a huff. "But I never would have thought she was capable of murder."

I tucked my notebook back into my pocket. "It's still possible she isn't. But she's the only person in town with any sort of bad blood with Jack. I'll just have to wait and see what Molly finds."

"Glad you've found some people to help," Mick said. He sipped his beer. "I don't envy you. I've barely managed to keep from getting tangled up in this goddamn town's affairs in ten years. You're diving straight into the middle of it all."

Abby said, "Oh, it can't be that bad. Nothing ever happens in Jonesboro."

"Wouldn't be so sure," Mick said. "I haven't been here my entire life or nothing, but I've picked up whiffs of somethin' foul in my time here."

"Like what?" I asked.

"Not entirely sure. Sometimes when it was just the two of us in the bar after a night of drinking, Jack would get this look in his eye. Whenever I asked him what was wrong, he would always smile and start talking about something else." Mick himself had a faraway look in his eye for a moment before he returned to us. "Now, mind you, Jack told me everything, and I mean everything. Except that one thing. Got close a couple times, but I never got it out of him."

I thought back to the picture in the hallway of the winery.

There really was something in his eyes.

Mick said, "Something happened up at that winery in its early days. Something you kids'll learn one of these days is that everyone's got a secret. Some sorta dark past." He gestured to the empty barstool. "Even ol' Jacky boy."

Abby looked over to Jack's seat for the thousandth time that night. "How's Rosie doing?" she asked. Probably trying to distract herself.

"She's doing just fine," Mick said. "It took the girls some time to warm to her, but now she's like a regular part of the family. How about you?" He nudged Abby with his elbow. "Ya found a fella yet?"

Abby laughed and said, "No, no, I haven't."

"Oh, c'mon now," Mick egged her on. "There's still a few fine young men out here in Jonesboro. Take Christopher here, for instance."

I gave Mick a threatening glare and shook my head back and forth quickly, subtly.

Abby picked up her drink and said, "Sorry to get your hopes up, Mick, but I don't really do men." She took a sip from her glass.

Mick gave her an inquisitive look and she simply nodded in return.

I'd had my assumptions for a while but didn't bother to confirm them. Figured it wasn't my business. Abby didn't go broadcasting her sexual preferences, so I figured she had her reasons. Probably just nervous about it in a small church-going town like this. No idea what reaction she expected to get out of Mick in that moment.

But I can guarantee Mick's reaction was not what she expected.

"No fuckin' shit!" Mick slapped the bartop and started laughing, which made Abby jump. She ended up giggling nervously in response, and soon the two of them were in hysterics, and I felt as if I had missed a joke somewhere.

Eventually Mick pulled himself together and said through some final gasps, "So sorry to assume, Abigail. But shit, I know some'a these boys have been here week in and week out flirtin' with ya. God, it just makes me laugh."

"Well, I'm glad you're supportive, at least," Abby said.

Mick coughed, putting his last few chuckles to rest. "Completely and totally, Ms. Smith. And don't hesitate to tell any asshole who isn't to get the hell out of my bar. And, sorry if I'm being ignorant, but wouldn't these fellas leave you alone if you said something?"

"Not from my experience, they wouldn't. Assholes are still assholes. Plus, not everyone needs to know. It tends to cause more problems for me than it solves." She took another sip of her drink, then stared deep into it. She said under her breath, "One of the many reasons I'm here in the first place."

"Dad not a fan?" I asked.

She looked up, surprised, and shook her head.

I don't think she meant to say the last part out loud, but I had to ask. Abby bit her lip, seemingly thinking about something, possibly fighting back tears. Whatever it was, she decided to say nothing and finished her drink instead. Mick wrapped an arm around her and hugged her close. He whispered something in her ear, and she smiled and said, "Thank you."

Mick checked his watch and stood to leave. "I'm way too old to be out this late," he said, then guzzled down the rest of his beer before grabbing his leather jacket off the coat rack. "I'll see ya on Sunday, Christopher. Take care of yourself, Abigail. And seriously." He put a hand on her shoulder. "Don't hesitate to ask."

We waved Mick out resumed our closing duties in silence. I felt several questions bubbling up from my stomach but kept swallowing them back down. We left Jack's stool on the floor as we finished cleaning up and before long, we had our jackets on and were walking toward the front door of the dive to head home. I stopped at the door. It had been a long couple days for the two of us, an even longer couple months for her. There were so many things I felt I should ask, so many things I felt I should say.

Abby looked up at me, patiently waiting, holding the straps of her purse in both hands as I tripped over my own feet in my mind. At that point I just figured I needed to say something, so I opened my mouth and just tried to let some words, any words, come out.

Abby threw her arms around me before I could say anything.

I took a surprised step back. Then my brain finally caught up and realized what was happening, so I rebalanced myself and hugged her back. She cried, her head bobbing when sobs escaped. I rested my head on top of hers and squeezed tighter, my dumbass brain still trying to come up with something helpful to say.

Fortunately, I managed to keep my stupid mouth shut.

TWENTY-TWO

I woke up when something hit the floor. I peeked over the side of the bed with half-open eyes and found my cell phone buzzing itself in a circle on the hardwood. I fished for it with one arm hanging off the bed for a bit before finagling it up to my ear.

"Hello?"

"Morning, sunshine!" It was Abby's all-too-cheery voice. "Was starting to think you died in your sleep or something!"

"What is it?" I looked at the clock. "Do you know what time it is?"

"Well, yeah, of course I do." There was something playful to her tone.

"Why are you calling me, then?"

"Not quite awake, huh? We're moving a couch today, remember?"

I rubbed my eyes, trying to figure out what the hell she was talking about. Then it hit me. "Oh. Right. Because I'm the guy with a truck."

"There it is. How soon can you get over here? Just need an ETA for the Taylors."

I swung my legs over the side of the bed and stretched. "Fifteen minutes."

"Rad. I have coffee and donuts for you. See you in fifteen, Chris."

I pulled on a tee shirt and shorts and slathered on some deodorant. Hair was a mess. I ran my fingers through it several times, trying to salvage it as best I could, but it was hopeless. Do I have a hat somewhere? I wondered.

Then I remembered. I did have one hat.

I slid open the closet door and took down the cardboard box stuffed onto the top shelf before setting it on the bed, puffing dust into the air. I stared at the box, two arguments ping-ponging back and forth in my head. It's just a hat, Chris. But it's Charlie's hat. I opened the box. Several of Charlie's belongings sat inside: his journal, an ESV Study Bible, a couple pocketknives, other random items that had been cleared out of his suitcase when he came home from his last tour overseas. I hadn't touched it since I first came to Jonesboro three years earlier. Easier to forget about when it was crammed in the closet. I took Charlie's baseball cap from inside, dusted it off and gave it a good look. Black, with the Marine Corps emblem stitched into the front.

It isn't just a hat. It's Charlie's hat. But Charlie wouldn't mind if I wore it.

I pulled it onto my head. Or at least I tried to, but it squeezed my head too tight. I chuckled. Charlie always did have a tiny head. I readjusted the size and pulled it onto my head backwards before grabbing my essentials and setting out for the Smiths' house.

Jack had set the Smiths up in a nice little part of the neighborhood. They'd been staying at the motel when he knocked on their door and told them he had a place ready for them with the first two months' rent already covered. It was a cozy little condo in a little strip constructed more recently than most of the homes in town. Some of the surrounding condos were used as Airbnb's, but the majority were available for rent through Westcliffe Real Estate.

Abby and Lizzy popped to their feet from their front step and jogged down to the curb when I pulled up, holding a drink carrier and a box from the supermarket. Abby hopped into the passenger seat as Lizzy climbed into the back. They were ready for the day, hair tied up on their heads, with matching headbands to keep their eyes clear.

"Morning, CJ!" they shouted in tandem.

Abby passed me my coffee cup and I gratefully sucked the black nectar through the tiny hole in the lid. "Are you excited? Are you pumped?" Abby asked, playfully punching my shoulder.

I cowered to avoid spilling coffee in my lap and wedged the cup into the cupholder. "How the hell are you two so excited this early?" If the Smith girls hadn't had their seatbelts on, they would have started bouncing off the walls in the cab of my truck. I flipped down my sun visor, shielding my eyes from the morning light as I pulled away from their house.

Lizzy's head popped up next to mine from the back seat. "Maybe it's hard for you to understand, CJ, but you have no idea how stoked we are to not have to sit on the fucking floor to watch *Gossip Girl* anymore."

"We're getting a couch!" Abby shouted.

"We're getting a couch!" Lizzy shouted back.

The two of them screamed in excitement. The cab of my truck was a little small for this level of enthusiasm, but I couldn't help but smile. I was happy to see the two of them happy, even if it did result in hearing loss.

"Where am I going again?" I asked.

Lizzy forced her torso out from the back seat and turned on the radio with an outstretched arm. A morning radio host was detailing the current traffic on I-5. "Seriously, CJ?" she said. I could hear her eyes rolling out of her skull. "How boring can you be?"

I shrugged. "I like talk radio."

"Yeah, so does my grandpa. He's dead."

Abby laughed.

"What?" I asked. "Come on, I'm not *that* boring. Now where am I going?"

Lizzy scoured my stereo, squinting at all the buttons, then flipped open the center console under my arm, shuffling around inside.

"What the hell are you doing?" I asked.

Abby continued laughing as her sister tore my car apart.

"A-ha!" Lizzy shouted. "To the gas station!"

"Isn't that the exact opposite direction of where we're going?" I asked.

"Slight detour," Lizzy said as she plopped back into her seat.

I looked over at Abby, who simply shrugged ineffectually. I turned and headed north on Main Street and pulled up at the gas station a couple minutes later.

"Be right back!" Lizzy shouted, jumping out the door and running into the Corner Store.

I grabbed a donut from the box in Abby's lap. "She's in a good mood."

"It's the little things," Abby said. "She's been wanting to get a couch for a while. To be fair, sitting on the floor to watch TV is killing my spine. We're super thankful Jack got us a place to stay." She looked out the window, her face reflected in the glass. "But it'll be nice to get some comfortable furniture." She took a long drink from her coffee cup.

I washed down half of my donut with some coffee and asked, "How are you so awake and energetic right now?"

"Simple answer: I'm not." She held her cup in both hands in her lap and closed her eyes, and I realized it was taking her effort just to keep them open. She went on, "Liz isn't a child, but she is still a kid. She can handle more than most girls her age could. But she shouldn't have to. She shouldn't have to deal with all the shit that I do. And if she's excited about something, I'm going to be excited with her. I'm not going to let how tired I am ruin that."

Though she was so much younger than me, the admiration I felt for Abby became apparent to me in that moment. She would do anything to take care of her sister, to keep her safe, to give her a good life. She managed to muster up enthusiasm for Lizzy's interests and was always there when she needed her. I couldn't imagine what their lives must have been like growing up, but she was trying to make things different now, in any way she could.

Abby took another sip of her coffee.

I took a bite of my donut and looked into the Corner Store, where Elizabeth was checking out at the counter. "She doing all right?"

"Yeah, all things considered. It's a big adjustment, but she's handling it pretty well."

"Well, that's mostly thanks to you. You're a great sister, Abby."

She smiled. "Thanks." She leaned over to my side of the truck, and I wrapped an arm around her in a hug. I squeezed her tight as Lizzy jumped into the back.

"Finally taking my advice, Abs?" Lizzy asked.

Abigail sat up and looked back at her. "And what advice would that be?"

Lizzy was fiddling with the plastic package of the thing she bought. "Pretending CJ's your boyfriend so all those dick-beaters at the bar leave you alone."

"Jesus," I said. "You two are quite the vulgar pair, you know that?"

Lizzy said, "Oh, chill the fuck out, old man. Here." She leaned forward from the back seat and handed me one end of a black cord. "Plug this into the auxiliary port in that center console."

I did as I was told and plugged the cord into the AUX port.

I wish I had known what I was getting myself into.

I drove back south on Main Street at 7:30 a.m. with Miley Cyrus's "Party in the U.S.A." blasting through the speakers as the Smith sisters sang along, arms waving out the truck's open windows.

TWENTY-THREE

Within an hour, we had moved the couch out of the Taylors' home, loaded it onto my truck, and pulled up in front of the Smiths' house. Lizzy lifted one end of the couch from the bed of my truck while Abby and I maneuvered it safely onto the asphalt. The morning clouds had cleared, and the sun shone down on us, providing some much-appreciated warmth. The three of us shuffled up the front steps and wedged the couch in the doorway; it was just slightly too big. Abby ducked through the doorway from inside and stood next to me, hands on her hips. Her shoulders rose and fell as she breathed in and out.

"Well, shit," she said.

"Gonna have to take the door off," I said, and jogged back to my truck. I always kept a toolbox in the cab, so I grabbed my little electric drill and within a few minutes Abby and I had the door off and resting against the wall inside. Lizzy laid on the couch on the sidewalk, scrolling Instagram.

"Hey," Abby said, "you aren't posting anything about where we are, are you?"

"No, Mother, I'm not," Lizzy sighed, flicking through her feed. "I'm not that dumb."

"Just making sure." Abby clapped once. "Come on, Liz, let's get this thing inside." She grabbed one end of the couch.

"You know," Lizzy said, stretching out her arms, "I actually think I like it out here."

"Guess I'll head home, then," I said.

"Oh, fine." She hopped off the couch and directed us inside, where we set the couch against the wall. After some celebratory high fives, Abby and I reattached the front door. Everything was in its place. The Smiths now had two pieces of furniture in the front room: the couch, and an entertainment center with a TV on top of it on the opposite wall.

Lizzy grabbed a bag of Cheetos from the pantry and sprawled out lengthwise on the couch, kicking her feet up on the back of it with her head against the armrest. "Nice digs, huh?"

"It is nice," I said. "Jack really set you girls up, huh?"

Abby walked into the room from the kitchen with two glasses of water and handed one to me.

"Yeah," Lizzy said, licking cheesy dust off her fingers. "It's better than that shitty motel was."

"Truth," Abby said, plopping down on the far side of the couch.

"We actually have a coffee table but, oh!" Elizabeth threw the back of her hand against her forehead dramatically. "If only we had someone who had time to put it together for us."

Abby smacked her sister.

A large cardboard box leaned against the wall in the corner. I took a sip of water and said, "You know, you could just ask." I set my glass on the floor, opened one end of the box, and started setting wooden pieces on the ground. Abby protested and told me to sit for a little while, but I just smiled and kept pulling pieces out of the box. There were only about a dozen parts, all assembled with an Allen wrench that was packaged in with the bolts and screws. I tore open the bag, sat with my back toward the couch, and started fastening the legs to the tabletop.

"Were you in the Marines?" Lizzy asked.

I'd nearly forgotten about the hat I was wearing. "No, I wasn't," I said. I twisted a bolt into the leg of the table. "But my brother was."

"He still in service?" Lizzy asked. I heard rustling behind me, but no words. I couldn't know for sure, but I was almost positive Abby gave her sister one of those *shut up or I'll kill you* looks.

"No." I grabbed a bolt, stuck it in the hole of the table leg, and started turning it. "He died. Three years ago."

"Shit. What happened?" This time I heard Abby's hand smack against Lizzy's leg. Lizzy whispered, "What?"

I stopped turning the bolt, leaving it stuck halfway out of the wood. I had never talked to anyone about Charlie, not even Molly. Not in detail anyway. I had spent the last three years trying my best to leave it all behind.

Mick's words came to mind: *"Time doesn't fix nothin.'"*

"Chris?" Abby said.

"Yeah?"

"I said you really don't have to talk about it. Liz doesn't need to know."

I closed my eyes, took a deep breath, and let it back out.

"No, it's okay." I twisted the bolt the rest of the way in. "I think it's about time I did." I stood, grabbed the third leg and another bolt, and sat back down on the other side of the tabletop.

"Mom and Dad got divorced when I was in college. Charlie was a freshman and didn't take it well, started acting out and making stupid decisions. Didn't get his shit figured out until I ended up busting his ass when he was trying to break into a car. I talked to him about it, told him he was headed down a bad path. Even made him spend a night in the cell at the station. He hated every second of it, never wanted anything like that to happen again. Decided he wanted to straighten himself out and join the Marines, so a couple years later, he did. Can you toss me that screw? Thanks.

"Charlie came home from a tour three years ago. While he was home, we helped Mom move out of the house we grew up in. It was a long day, and we went to get a few beers at the end of it." I paused to turn a bolt the rest of the way into the table. "Either of you heard of Mark James Harris?"

"Mark James Harris," Abby said thoughtfully. I grabbed the last leg of the table. Then she said, "Wait, isn't he that guy with the huge church in California? He's been in the news for some scandal recently, hasn't he?"

I nodded. "Yep, that's my dad. I've known since I was a kid that Dad always had some shit going on behind the scenes. He took way too many phone calls in front of me to not pick up on it. Frequent negotiations with the church's big financial supporters, stuff like that. Probably just assumed I would always keep it to myself. Typical pastor's kid stuff.

"In the last few years, things had gotten worse. A couple months before Charlie came home, a girl committed suicide. She started working as an intern at Dad's church just six months earlier and was the fourth intern in two years. The other three didn't last very long before leaving. Had a feeling my dad had something to do with it, one way or another, so I started my own secret investigation. I'd never be approved to investigate it if I'd brought it up to my boss. Too close to the situation. Pass me those crossbeams? Thank you.

"Charlie had one too many that night, started getting really fired up about how much he couldn't stand our dad, how terribly he treated Mom and everything. I wasn't as far gone as he was, but I was feeling it enough that I decided to tell him about my investigation. Told him that a girl killed herself and I thought it was Dad's fault. Charlie got real quiet. He finished his beer and went to the bathroom. After half an hour, I realized he wasn't coming back."

I swallowed, the memories flooding back. "I called him. I don't even remember what either of us said, all I remember is the sound of a gun cocking on the other end of the line and Charlie saying 'Dad.' I put my sirens on and drove to Dad's apartment complex as fast as I could. When I got there, Charlie had him at gunpoint. I pointed my own gun at Charlie and tried to calm him down. Tried to explain that I needed Dad alive. That no one would get the justice they deserved if he died. That he couldn't just throw his own life away like this. All three of us were shouting at each other. I swear I saw his finger start squeezing the trigger, so I did what I was trained to do. Sort of."

I could feel their hot stares on the back of my neck. I couldn't look them in the eyes, so I just stood and flipped the finished table right side up, pulled off my hat, and wiped away the sweat beading on my forehead. "Shoot to kill. That's what we're trained to do, but I couldn't bring myself to do it.

At least not on purpose. I hit him in the arm, just trying to make him drop the gun, but it broke an artery. I called an ambulance and tried to stabilize him, but he was gone before we made it to the hospital. As he was laying there, all he said was that he was sorry. He gripped my hand. Smiled at me. Then he died."

I looked over to the couch. Abby and Lizzy had somber expressions on their faces. I pulled my hat back on. "Brother of the century, huh?" My phone rang. Didn't recognize the number, but I answered anyway. "Hello?"

"Hey." It was Molly's voice. "I think I found what you were looking for. Wanna come down to the library?"

"Sure, I'll be over there in ten." I hung up and put my phone back in my pocket.

"Who was that?" Abby asked.

"Molly. I'm gonna head down to the library."

"Oh," Lizzy sat up. "Can I come? I've been wanting to get a new book to read for a while now."

"Liz," Abby said, "I don't know if that's..." She paused and studied me for a moment. I knew that look. She was clearly thinking through something. "Actually, we'll both come." She stood and smirked. "CJ's absolutely hopeless without me."

"What?" I said. "I really don't think—"

The two of them had already walked out the front door. I sighed and followed them.

TWENTY-FOUR

The drive to the library was quiet until Abby started telling her sister about me and Molly. Then I wished it had just been an uncomfortably silent ride. The moment we walked into the library, Lizzy took off to God knows where, leaving Abby and I, still sweaty from our morning's moving activities, to approach the front counter by ourselves.

Abby whispered, "So how are you and Molly doing? Proposed to her yet?"

"Shut up, Abby. It's not like that."

"It totally is. Your face gets so red every time we even talk about her."

"No, it doesn't."

"Totally does. It's red right now."

"I said, shut up. And no, it isn't." It was. I could feel it. But I figured it was due to a combination of couch-moving, coffee table-building, and dealing with the Smith girls' pestering questions on the drive over. At least that's what I kept telling myself. "Besides," I said, "even if there was a chance of something happening, I've completely messed it up this week."

"Then fix it, dumbass."

"And how would I do that?"

"Just take the first step."

"What does that even mean?"

She leaned against the counter next to me, whispering "Chris and Molly sitting in a tree." I rolled my eyes and rang the bell on the counter. Not that I agreed with her by any means, but I couldn't help but mull over her words.

The first step.

"Morning CJ," Molly said as she stepped out from the office. Her usual sunbeam smile was gone; she was all business. "Is this your new wardrobe now or something?"

I couldn't believe I was wearing workout clothes again. "Morning Molly," I said sheepishly.

Molly turned to Abby. "You're from the coffee shop, aren't you?"

"Pleasure to meet you, Miss Molly," Abby said, extending her hand. She was a little too enthusiastic about the whole thing.

"She also works at the bar with me," I said. "Guess the two of you haven't formally met there yet."

Molly shook Abby's hand tentatively. "Nice to meet you too. Anyway CJ, I found what you were looking for if you want to come behind the counter here."

I walked around the counter like a normal person. Abby, on the other hand, hopped up on the counter into a sitting position, spun herself around, and hopped off on the other side. Molly opened her mouth to say something but decided against it.

"Sorry about her," I said. Abby stuck her tongue out at me outside Molly's view. "She knows about everything that's going on," I said.

Molly shook her head. "Here." She sat in the swivel chair and clicked open a video player on the computer. A video of the interior of Caroline's Coffee came up. "This is 7:55 a.m. on the day of the murder." Juliet walked into the coffee shop and gave her order to Abby at the counter, prompting Abby in the video to flip Juliet off as soon as her back was turned. Molly and I both turned to look at her, but she looked at the ceiling and casually started whistling.

Molly then slowly dragged her cursor, fast-forwarding through the rest of the video. "As you can see, she sits in that same spot on her laptop until..." Juliet stood and left the coffee bar. "8:57."

Molly clicked a couple times and pulled up a second shot, and a black-and-white video of the Jonesboro winery hallway filled the screen. "This is at 9:03." The video clearly showed Juliet and Paul walking to her office. Paul unlocked the door, she thanked him, and the door shut behind her.

"Then," Molly referenced a time code written on a sticky note on her monitor and fast-forwarded the video. "This is at 2:14 p.m." The video showed Paul walking back up the hallway and locking Juliet's office for her again as she left.

"Damn," I said.

"So she couldn't have killed Jack, huh?" Abby asked.

Molly looked over at Abby, then turned to me with a confused look.

"Sorry, Abby is…" I paused and then asked, "Why are you here, Abby?"

She shrugged. "Just along for the ride. Curious about what you do."

Molly looked Abby up and down. No idea what was going through her mind, but I figured she was trying to figure out Abby's place in the mess I'd managed to get myself into. "Okay then," she said, then turned back to me. "What's your plan now, CJ?"

"Well, Juliet couldn't have done it. Which kind of puts us back at square one. Her keys were found in Jack's rowboat, so she could still be an accomplice." Then I remembered. "Juliet swears her keys went missing on Monday, but obviously someone had them in Jack's boat. Molly, I hate to ask, but—"

"Got it," she cut me off. "I'll see if I can find anything."

I put a hand on her shoulder. "Thank you. So much. I'll look into some other things in the meantime. No rush or anything, just get to it when you can."

"Of course."

Abby and I stood in silence as Molly started clicking through files on the computer and pulling up new videos. I looked at Abby, who was using one of her hands to mime a person walking on the palm of her other hand as she mouthed, *Take the first step*. I gave her a look trying to get an answer to what that meant, but she just put her hands up and gestured to Molly.

I cleared my throat. "Uh, Molly?"

"Yes?" she asked without looking away from the computer.

"What—I mean..." I scratched the back of my head. "What do you have going on today?"

She looked at me and cocked an eyebrow. "Nothing besides this, really. Why?"

"I don't know. I guess...I just figured if you don't have anything going on, I was wondering..." I looked at Abby, who prodded me along with her eyes. "I was wondering if you wanted to get lunch."

Molly blinked. "You want to get lunch with me?"

"Uh...yes."

She smiled for the first time since I'd stepped into the library. "Well yeah, I'd love to. Let me just grab my purse." Molly stepped into the office while Abby raised her eyebrows repeatedly and silently shot me with finger guns. Molly stepped back out of the office and said, "Where are we going?"

"Well," I scratched my arm, "I figured we could all just go to Denny's or something."

Molly's smile disappeared. "All?"

Abby slapped herself in the forehead.

"Well yeah," I said, "these two rode with me, so they'll be along for the ride."

Molly turned to Abby just as she removed her hand from her face and gave a huge, cheesy smile. The red mark on her forehead helped complete her casual look.

"Wait," Molly said. "Two?"

There was a sudden thud as Elizabeth set a stack of books on the counter. "Hello," she said with a grin. "I'd like to get a library card."

———

"Real smooth, CJ," Abby whispered as we walked to my truck ten minutes later.

"What was I supposed to do? The two of you are here, aren't you?"

"Jesus Christ," Lizzy whispered. "You could have dropped us off at home or something, but no. Now here we are third and fourth wheeling on your date."

"It's not a date," I said.

"Clearly," Abby said.

I whisper-shouted, "Well, you two didn't even have to tag along in the first place."

"Would you have even gotten this far if I wasn't in there just now?" Abby asked.

I stared at the two of them over the hood of my truck, and they gave me an eerily identical expectant look as they waited for my response. I knew Abby was right, but no way in hell was I going to admit it. I opened the driver's side door and said, "Just get in the damn truck."

"See?" Abby said. "Just like I said. You're completely hopeless without me." She looked over at Molly as she stooped into her Prius. "Wait, why is Molly driving there alone?"

"Because cramming more than one person in my backseat is horrible. Plus, she doesn't know either of you."

Abby wrung her hands together mischievously. "She's about to," she said, and sprinted to Molly's car before I could protest. She and Molly had a brief exchange before Abby hopped in the passenger seat and Molly turned to give me a puzzled look. I responded with a shrug, and the two of us pulled out of the parking lot and drove north on Main Street. Lizzy sat in the back seat, taking pictures of something with her phone.

"What are you doing back there?" I asked.

"Posting a picture of my haul," she said. "Gotta keep people updated on the books I'm reading. I have an image to uphold."

"Well, get up here. I'm not a chauffeur."

"What's a chauffeur?"

"You don't know what a chauffeur is? Kind of like a fancy Uber driver, I guess."

"I dunno, I think you'd be a pretty good Uber driver."

"Why do you say that?"

"You don't vomit your life story and political views on everybody you meet. It's pretty nice, actually."

I laughed as Lizzy climbed into the front and sat in the passenger seat. I said, "Your sister's a lunatic, you know that?"

"Oh yeah, I'm aware."

"Not that you're sane, by any means."

"Oh, fuck off."

"Just saying." Lizzy looked out the window, watching the houses go by. Clean, traditional American homes. Most of them empty. I asked, "So how are you liking Jonesboro?"

"Sucks ass."

"Oh, come on. It's not that bad."

"Nah, doing online high school halfway through my junior year in the middle of Buttfuck Nowhere, Washington, populated by old white guys and their submissive little Christian wives sounds like a regular paradise, CJ. Just goddamn peachy." She leaned her head against the window. "But trust me, anything's better than back home."

"Yeah?"

"Yeah."

A couple stoplights went past before Lizzy said, "Sorry about your brother, CJ."

It caught me off-guard. I was taken aback by her sincerity coupled with the lack of profanity. "Oh," I said. "I mean, it is what it is. It's okay."

"It's not okay, though. It fucking blows."

"I mean, yeah. It does. But I can't do anything about it."

I slowed the car to a stop at a red light. I could see Molly and Abby talking in the rearview mirror, both waving their hands around as they spoke. It looked like they were smiling.

Then Lizzy said, "You did the right thing, you know."

I looked at her. She looked at me. The light turned green. I turned back to the road and pulled through the intersection.

Lizzy took a deep breath and said, "So Abby got a scholarship to NYU. Well, first she got a Bachelor's degree at a community college back home in Ohio while working two part-time jobs. She was one of the instructors at a little dance academy and bartended nights. She got her degree, she auditioned for NYU, she got in, she got a scholarship. She was so excited. Partly because it meant she could get out of Canton."

She paused for a moment, and in my periphery, I could see her nervously picking at her fingernails. "She moved to New York last summer and went to NYU for a semester. Dad had been sober for a few years, so everything seemed fine. About a month after she left, I came home from a friend's house late one night. Dad was drunk." She shifted in her seat and planted both feet on the floor. "I wanted to tell Abby what was going on, but I couldn't. I couldn't take that away from her."

Lizzy took a moment as her voice started to break. I kept driving, silent. We passed Jonesboro Community Park, a touch of green in the patchwork quilt of the neighborhood. A couple sat in the shade of a tree, watching their son play fetch with his dog.

"She came home for Christmas break," she said. "This was just a few months ago. I wore long sleeves to cover the bruises, but she found out anyway. That night, we packed our bags with everything they could hold and drove away in the middle of the night. We didn't have a plan. Or even a direction. We just drove. And we kept driving."

She sniffed and rubbed her nose. "For almost two months we just drove around. State lines all blurred together. Some nights we stayed in hotels, most nights we just slept in the car. For three weeks, Abby just cried. She cried and said 'I'm sorry. It's all my fault. I should have been there. I should have stayed. I shouldn't have left you.'"

She took a deep breath, and the shuddering sound she made as she released it sent a wave of emotion crashing over me, blurring my vision with tears. She said, "We cried together. A lot. And every fucking day we woke up in that car, I held her hand and told her that it wasn't her fault. She couldn't have known. It would have happened whether she was there or not. Eventually she stopped apologizing. I still don't think she believes me. She might be tearing herself apart right now. I don't know. I hope not."

I pulled into a parking spot in front of Denny's. Lizzy wiped her eyes with the sleeve of her hoodie. I put a hand on her shoulder. "Your sister really loves you, you know." She nodded. I said, "She's really something."

Lizzy sniffed and said, "Yeah, she is. I'm lucky." She smiled and looked at me. "And so was Charlie. You're a great brother." She opened the door and hopped out of the truck. "And, hey. Don't tell Abby I told you all that, okay?" I nodded, and she shut the door.

I sat alone in the cab with Lizzy's words as my truck's engine rumbled beneath me.

You're a great brother.

I shook my head, took my keys out of the ignition, and stepped out of the truck. Molly and Abby pulled into a spot next to me and got out of the car, laughing together. Lizzy hurried inside the restaurant to the bathroom. I caught the door behind her and held it open for Molly, who thanked me as she walked in.

Before Abby stepped inside, she grabbed my arm and whispered, "I *really* like her."

I rolled my eyes and followed her into the restaurant.

TWENTY-FIVE

"We're good to let her go?" Wilson asked.

"Yep," I answered. I pressed the phone against my ear with my shoulder as I moved stools from the bartop to the floor. "She couldn't have done it. She has an alibi for the entire day."

"What about her keys?"

"I'm having someone look through the surveillance footage to see if they can find anything. Someone had them, and I'm guessing whoever tossed Jack's body in the ditch had them in his rowboat. Juliet could still be an accomplice, so we'll keep an eye on her. For now, we know for sure that she didn't kill Jack."

"All right. I'll drive her back up to the winery then."

"How chivalrous of you."

"I mean, it's the least I can do. Anything else I can do to help you out?"

"You've done enough, Mike." I hung up the phone and pulled the rest of the stools off the counter.

The afternoon had been pleasant, if not confusing. Abby and Molly somehow became best friends in the short drive to Denny's and spent most of our time at lunch talking to each other. Lizzy and I had our own side conversations, some about detective work, others about the books she borrowed from the library, and every now and then the other two acknowledged our existence. I didn't mind. Lizzy and I had both done our fair share of talking that morning, so I figured she was as comfortable coasting through lunch hour as I was.

After lunch, Molly gave Abby a hug, thanked me for asking her to lunch, and said that maybe she and I could do it again sometime just the two of us if I was up to it. She then drove off, leaving me with Abby and Lizzy's harassment on the way back to their house: "Do you like her? She really likes you. You do like her, don't you? You should ask her out for real. You'd have beautiful babies. Do you *want* to die alone?" Those two were relentless. I said as little as I could on the short drive, dumped them on the curb in front of their house, and went home to shower and take a nap before going to work.

Saturdays were always a mixed bag at O'Callaghan's. Even the dedicated regulars often skipped out on Saturday night. I didn't blame them. Speaking from experience, sitting in a chapel on Sunday morning with a hangover is not easy on the conscience. Exactly who showed up on Saturdays was all dependent on who had a shitty week.

The front bell jingled and I was greeted by my first surprise of the evening. Abby, auburn hair freshly washed, dried, and straightened, gracefully floated through the front door, quite unlike the whirlwind she was most days. Her lips were a vibrant red and two oval-shaped pieces of leather, embossed with the pattern of a leaf, dangled from her earlobes. She smiled at me and waved jazz hands to embellish her arrival.

"You're here early," I said.

"Well, I did take work off from the coffee shop today for our couch-moving adventures," she said. "And I quit the gas station gig. After squeezing a nap in after Caroline's every day, I should be here on time from now on."

"You? On time?"

She punched me in the shoulder as she made her way to the back room. "Plus," she called from the back, "I wanted to pester you more about Molly." The music stopped and switched to a 90's punk station.

I coughed dramatically and said, "Hey, I think I'm coming down with a cold. It's all you tonight."

"Fat chance, pal." She stepped back into the bar. "You're stuck with me. Which means I get to bug you about Molly for the next, what? Six or seven hours?"

"I'm not saying shit."

"Oh, come on, Chris. She's perfect for you."

"Sure, she is."

"I'm serious. She's super awesome."

"I'm not disagreeing with you. I'm just not talking about it."

"Why won't you at least give her a chance?"

The front door jingled, and Robby walked in.

"Robby," I said. "Thank God you're here."

"What?" he said with a grin. "You miss your old buddy *Rob* that bad?"

"Sure, let's go with that."

Abby rolled her eyes and grabbed a can of Coke from under the bar.

Robby sat next to his uncle's spot. "Find out what you need to nail Juliet yet?"

"Dude, phrasing," Abby said as she poured the soda into a glass.

I looked at her. "Seriously, Abby?"

Robby chuckled as he set a couple leather journals on the counter. "That was good, Abs. But anyway man, the old lady didn't show up in any of those videos you told me about, right? Your friend didn't find her in them, did they? Juliet did it, right?"

I shook my head. "Unfortunately, Robby, no. Her alibi lines up with the time of the murder."

Abby set the glass in front of Robby with a lime wedge on the rim.

"Shit, man," Robby said, squeezing the lime into his soda. "Then who the hell did it?"

"Still trying to figure that out. I don't have much to go on right now, other than the keys. Molly Bauer's looking through more of the footage to see if she can find anything."

"Aw, Molly's the one helping you? She's hot."

"Right?" Abby chimed in, nudging me with her elbow.

"Jesus Christ," I said, "will you give it up already?"

"Oooh," Robby said, "does Seej have a crush?"

"Goddammit, I'm not dealing with this shit from both of you right now. We have more important things to focus on. Did you get anything today, Robby?"

Robby pulled out his Zippo and began flicking through his usual routine with his fingers. He recounted his day with excruciating detail, even more so than he normally did. He ran the typical route after picking up his deliveries from the post office. The movie theater was getting a new film in next weekend, some slasher flick that had run its course everywhere else. The Taylors had left on vacation. Albert Jones hadn't been seen all week, apparently holed up at home sick, while Piers, his butler, had been out and about running errands all week: to the supermarket, the drugstore, in and out of Albert's office, to the library, to the Romeros' house with flowers. Several people informed Robby that there was a thunderstorm in the forecast next week. The rumor mill about the Jenkins' daughter's pregnancy was still turning, trying to deduce who the father could be. Reggie was thinking about turning his little souvenir-and-electronics pawn shop into an arcade to try and salvage his business. Obviously, he wasn't really with the times when it came to business in general.

"All that to say," Robby concluded as he flicked his Zippo shut, "nothing too important."

"Damn," I said. The chorus of some Green Day song played without a word to interrupt it. I, for one, was running back through everything Robby said, trying to find anything of interest in the events of his day. I assumed the other two were doing the same thing.

"You ever shoot anyone, Seej?"

"What?" I asked, startled.

"When you were a cop," he said. "You ever shoot anyone?"

"Couple times. Only when I had to."

"Could you teach me how to shoot?"

Abby and I exchanged a concerned look. She asked, "Why do you want to learn how to shoot?"

Robby closed one eye and looked down the sights of a gun he made with his fingers and said, "So I can shoot the bastard who killed Uncle Jack right between his goddamn eyes."

I shook my head. "That won't fix anything, kid."

"Sure it would," Robby said. "Because then the bastard would be dead."

I leaned over the counter. I had felt the same way before. I knew where he was coming from. "Look, Robby, things won't come to that. And even if they do, leave any dangerous stuff to me, all right? Your aunt already lost her husband, she doesn't need to lose her nephew, too."

Robby shrugged and sipped his soda.

Abby looked at the journals on the counter. "What are those?"

"These? These are a couple of Uncle Jack's journals. There are almost forty of them on a shelf at home." He thumbed across the pages of one of the journals. "I've just been reading through them. Learning more about his life and everything. It's not the same as him being here, but it helps, y'know?"

Abby nodded. "How's your aunt doing?"

"Not great. She spends most of the day crying. She wants to have a funeral soon, but that Catherine Sinclair lady said she can't release Uncle Jack's body yet, which makes things harder. But she's holding up all right. I convinced her to eat and drink something last night, which is progress at least."

Abby grabbed his hand. "Let us know if we can do anything to help, okay?"

Robby smiled. "Thanks, Abby. You're all right, y'know that?" Abby smiled back. He then gulped down the rest of his soda and let out a huge burp.

"Nice," Abby said.

"Thanks," Robby said with a grin. "Well, I'm gonna head home, keep Aunt Clara company. Call me if you need anything."

"Thanks, Robby. Just keep me posted, okay?" Robby nodded, stood, and began walking to the front door. "And hey," I called after him. "Be careful out there."

"Aw c'mon, Seej. This is me we're talking about." He flashed a grin over his shoulder, the jingling bell singing its goodbyes.

Abby slid a beer in front of me and took a sip out of one she poured for herself. "He's a good kid."

I sipped my beer. "Didn't used to be."

She slid up next to me and got uncomfortably close to my face. "You never answered my question."

"What question?"

"Why won't you give Molly a chance?"

I sipped my beer again. "I'm just no good for her."

"Bullshit. What's the real reason?"

Something by The Offspring played overhead for a while before I finally let out a tired sigh. "Goddammit." I chugged the rest of my beer. "You wanna know the real reason?"

She moved closer and smiled. "I do. I really, really do."

I leaned in and whispered, "I've never been in a serious relationship before."

She took a step back and stared at me with an open mouth. She shoved me with both hands, nearly knocking me to the floor. "Are you fucking serious? You're messing with me right now, aren't you? How? How is that even possible? You're *so old*."

I laughed as I stood upright. "I don't know, it's just kind of a thing growing up a pastor's kid. Purity culture and all that. I went on a few dates or whatever in college, but it never worked out. And by the time I joined the force, I don't know. Just didn't have time."

"No, that's bullshit." Abby waved away my explanation. "There must be another reason. Or you're absolutely pulling one over on me right now. Like, you must literally piss yourself every time you talk to a girl or something."

"Or I just never met the right girl."

"Well, *that's* not an excuse anymore, because Molly's probably the best thing that could ever happen to you. I think you should give it a try. Just one real date."

"Why?"

"Because the one time you asked her to lunch, you brought me and my sister along like a dumbass. Besides, you never know what could happen. Could be good for you."

"I just really don't think it's a good idea right now with everything else going on."

"Come on, Chris," she shouted, slapping my shoulder. "Tell ya what, if you go on one date with her and it doesn't work out, I'll..." She looked up, searching for some sort of inspiration. Then she snapped her fingers. "Steak dinner, my place. Bottle of whiskey, your choice, fifty bucks or less. One hundred percent on my tab. I'll even find a fancy table for you to sit at and everything."

I looked at her.

"*And* Liz and I will wash and detail your truck."

I rolled my eyes.

"And, *and* I'll stop bothering you about it. Promise."

She thrust her hand out, waiting for me to shake it. Really all I was agreeing to was one evening of humiliation, followed by a free steak dinner and car detailing with a bonus of the Smith sisters leaving me the hell alone about Molly. What did I have to lose?

"Deal," I said, and shook Abby's hand.

She hopped in a small circle, pumping her fists in the air repeatedly.

"Think Liz will appreciate you roping her into this without her consent?"

"To get you on a date with Molly? She'd do the whole thing herself. Looks like you're going on a date with my new best friend."

"Best friend? What did you do on that car ride?"

"I'm just that charming." Abby flipped her hair behind her shoulder dramatically, took a long swig of her beer, and burped loudly.

"Nope, that's definitely not it," I said.

She punched me in the arm again. That time it hurt.

TWENTY-SIX

"Juliet Beauregard?" Ryan Dinsmore asked. "Red 4Runner, right? Yeah, she's come into the shop before. Just last week, actually."

"Really?" I set beers in front of the twins. Since Juliet had an alibi, my mind had been spinning trying to latch onto any other leads. The oil stains at the dock and the dump site came to mind. And who better to ask about an oil leak than the only two auto mechanics in Jonesboro? "Did she have an oil leak?"

"Oil leak?" Ryan looked at his brother. "Red 4Runner have an oil leak, Brian?"

"Huh?" Brian pulled his attention away from the house demolition on TV.

"Red 4Runner last week. Have an oil leak?"

Brian took his turn to think. Pretty sure they had to share the single brain between them. "Red 4Runner. Oh, that Juliet lady, right?" He grinned. "She's quite a looker, yeah? Meow."

I smacked him with my bar rag.

He shook his head and said, "Nope, no oil leak. Bad air filter."

"Bad air filter," Ryan relayed to me as if I couldn't hear.

"I'm surprised she lets you two work on her car at all," I said.

"We work on everybody's cars," Ryan said.

"Except for Albert's," Brian sulked.

"Yeah, except for Albert's," Ryan repeated. "He won't let us touch 'em. Pretty sure Piers does all the maintenance on those. We've asked if he'll let us come visit the garage, but he always says no."

"I wouldn't drive the Ferrari," Brian whined. "I just wanna take a picture with it."

"The Ferrari?" Ryan scoffed. "Screw the Ferrari, what about the McLaren?"

I stepped away and left the boys to argue about cars. It was a slow night. The only other person in the dive was Frank Jenkins. He looked tired, his face becoming more reminiscent of Droopy Dog than the sharp-witted chess player who frequented O'Callaghan's other nights of the week. I looked at the chess tally. Reggie's score was quickly catching up to his.

Abby had circled the bar and was sitting next to him with a drink of her own, playing therapist as she was so fond of doing. "S'not fair," Frank slurred. "Wish I could just make it go away." Abby would occasionally nod her head, give a sympathetic "uh-huh," or a reassuring pat on the shoulder.

This wasn't the first time I'd seen one of the guys become a blubbering mess in response to Abby's friendly pointed questions. Hell, I spent three years doing my best Montresor impression, brick-and-mortaring my memories of Charlie to the best of my ability, and Abby had burst through the wall like my own personal Kool-Aid Man in the past week. But these sad saps at the bar told her everything. More than I'd found out about them in three years. Maybe she really cared, maybe she did it because they tipped better when they got some weight off their chest. Regardless, I had learned one thing for sure: Sad people drink. Drunk people talk. Sad, drunk people talk to Abigail Smith.

It was about 9:00 when the front door jingled and in walked Molly Bauer. I nearly dropped the glass I was polishing. Abby leaned her head out of her conversation long enough to give me a childish look that I waved off.

"Evening, Molly," I said.

"Evening, CJ," she said with a smile and sat down at the bar.

Brian, noticing Molly, tapped his brother on the arm and the two of them stared at her. I smacked Brian with my rag and gave him a look, but Ryan didn't take the hint. "Buy you a drink, Ms. Bauer?" he offered.

Molly turned her smile their direction. I'm honestly surprised the boys didn't faint right there. "Thanks for the offer, fellas," she said. "But I have some business to attend to with CJ." The twins frowned, exchanged a glance, and returned their attention to the house remodel on TV.

I grabbed my shaker and began shaking some gin and dry vermouth with some ice. "Didn't expect to see you so soon, Molly. Find something?"

"What, I have to have a work-related reason to come here now?"

In my peripheral vision, I could see Abby, a meerkat on high alert, poke her head out from behind Mr. Jenkins and his sobbing. God knows what look she had on her face.

Molly continued, "No, I haven't found anything yet. Not quite."

I poured the martini into a glass with an olive and set it on a coaster in front of her. "Then what business do we have to attend to?"

Molly chuckled. "You really are clueless, aren't you, Christopher Harris?" She slowly turned her martini glass in small increments, the olive tossed around by the sudden jerks of the liquid's sways. "I never had to have a reason to pop by before, CJ. I just wanted to see you."

"Oh," I said, and scratched the back of my head. "Well, hi."

Molly smiled again. "Hi."

My throat was the Sahara. I coughed and took a sip of water from my glass on the back counter. "Thanks for helping me out with the case and everything," I said. Molly rolled her eyes. A cough came from Abby's direction. "And," I stammered, "it was nice to see you today. Really. It was good to get out of my normal routine."

"The pleasure was all mine." Molly swirled the olive in her glass before taking a sip. "You don't have conversations with women very often, do you, Chris?"

I cleared my throat. "No, I do. You're just..." I searched for the right word.

"I'm just what?"

"Different."

"Different?" She cocked an eyebrow.

I heard Abby's palm smack against her forehead on the other end of the bar.

"That's not what I mean. You're—" I stopped myself. Took a deep breath. "I'm sorry. I'm bad at this."

"I can tell."

"Let me start over."

She rested her hand in her palm with her fingers absently tapping her cheek. A loose strand of her blonde hair fell in front of her eyes, and she blew it back to the side with a puff.

I took another deep breath and said, "There is something special about you, Molly. You're different from everyone else I've met in this town in the last three years. And, you know, I was thinking..." I glanced over toward Abby who, with Mr. Jenkins sobbing into her shoulder, was staring me down with a smug grin. "Maybe we could get dinner sometime. Just the two of us. You know, just see what happens."

Molly's shoulders relaxed as a smile crossed her face once again. I realized how tense my shoulders were as well. She leaned forward and swirled her martini once more. "I'd like that, Chris. I really would."

The elephant I'd felt sitting on my chest finally stood up and I could breathe again. I knew Abby was giving me her usual "I told you so" look, but I didn't give her the satisfaction of glancing her direction.

***

We scheduled a date for the following night. The bar was closed on Sundays and the investigation had basically come to a standstill, so it seemed to make the most sense. She left it up to me to decide where we went and what we did. We started talking about the forecasted thunderstorm and our conversation naturally weaved its way through a myriad of topics and tangents.

I heard the front bell jingle a couple times, but any time I moved to take care of it, Abby would rush behind me, put a hand on my shoulder, and take care of the newcomer herself. When Abby popped into the back office, I realized that all the barstools except Jack's were flipped, and Molly and I were the only people left in the bar.

"Well," Molly said, "I suppose I should get going." She leaned across the counter and kissed me on the cheek, her lips lingering warm on my skin. I missed what happened after that, but the bells of the front door indicated that she'd left.

The iconic opening guitar riff of Marvin Gaye's "Let's Get It On" started playing over the bar speakers, and Abby burst out of the back office, singing, *"I've been really trying, baby!"* For what seemed the hundredth time that day, she punched me in the shoulder. "Look at you. Not the best pilot out there, don't get me wrong. You barely pulled that shit out of a nosedive a couple times. Good thing I'm the best wingman you could ask for."

I tossed the remaining glassware into the sink and said, "Did you tell her to come by tonight?"

"What?" she said, dramatically pressing a defensive hand against her chest. "Me? Interfere in your love life or lack thereof? Never." She smiled. "But actually, no, I didn't say anything to her. The steak dinner was just me spitballing. I had no idea she was going to show up."

She would have told me if she did plan it all; she would have been too proud of herself. "Whatever," I said. "All I know is I'm getting a free steak dinner out of this whole thing."

"Keep telling yourself that, CJ," she said. She bit her bottom lip and started backing away from me, thrusting suggestively as Marvin Gaye repeatedly sang, *"Let's get it on,"* in the background. I chucked a rag at her.

The two of us did our last closing duties: drying dishes, shutting off the sound system, flicking off the lights, locking the doors. My mind was occupied with what exactly I was going to do the following night. I suddenly had a date to plan for, the last thing I ever thought I would be doing.

Especially with a murderer still on the loose.

TWENTY-SEVEN

Jonesboro shut down every Sunday morning. If you were planning on getting a cup of coffee from Caroline's or grabbing a gallon of milk from the supermarket, you would be sorely disappointed. Main Street became a ghost town. Every storefront was closed until at least 2:00 in the afternoon. This had been the case since the town was originally founded almost a century before.

Each Sunday morning, the locals congregated inside Jonesboro Community Church. The church itself looked a little strange, with a more modern expansion trying to crawl its way out of the far wall of an historic chapel. While the church used to have a full office with several employees, the only person who even worked there anymore was the pastor, Suzanne Greene.

I liked Suzanne, which is weird for me to say about any pastor anymore. Oddly enough, she and I had plenty of philosophical conversations over vodka-tonics at the bar during my years there. Some crotchety old men got all up in arms about her being a pastor from time to time, pulling their whole "women can't be part of the clergy" bullshit. Whenever it happened, she always offered to let them take over for her. That usually shut them up.

You'd think with my history with church growing up that I'd avoid it at all costs, but I always wound up in church on Sunday mornings along with the locals. Not sure why. Maybe Suzanne's anomalous existence reeled me in after my experience. Maybe I felt the need to validate all the time I wasted sitting in pews as a kid by keeping up with it. Maybe I still believed it all, even if I didn't admit it to myself. Or maybe I was just bored on Sunday mornings since there was nothing else to do. Honestly couldn't tell you why.

Regardless, I sat in my usual spot in the back-right corner of the auditorium that Sunday, waving to Mick and his girls as I sat down. Hushed whispers scattered under the high ceiling as families filed into their maroon-cushioned seats, trying to get their restless kids to focus on the weekly printed-out coloring pages for even one damn minute.

The Jenkins family, who normally sat closer to the front, had squeezed themselves into the back-left corner, like kicked puppies trying to avoid any further abuse. I was surprised they decided to show up at all, what with all the blue-hairs around town who could hardly speak two sentences without using the word "premarital." But I suppose not going to church would have incited even more gossip.

The Romeros always sat in the front row, Jack in the seat closest to the center aisle. When Robby first moved to town, they had to drag him out of bed in the morning to get him there, but over time he stopped fighting it. Robby and Clara walked through the back doors of the sanctuary, the two of them doing their best to smile at everyone. Robby gave me a quick wave. I waved back, and the two of them sat in their usual spots, leaving Jack's seat open next to them.

Just as the regulars had at the bar on Friday, everyone turned and looked at Jack's empty seat. The whispering stopped, save for a few children who didn't quite know how to whisper yet, asking, "What's going on?" and, "Where's Mr. Jack?"

The half-empty auditorium transitioned to uncomfortable silence as Pastor Greene climbed the steps of the stage and took her place behind the wooden podium. She organized some sheets of paper, moved her glasses from the top of her head to the bridge of her nose, and smiled. "Good morning," she said.

"Good morning," the congregation echoed back to her.

Pastor Greene leaned against the podium, seemingly lost in thought. "What do we do," she began. Carefully, gently. "What do we do when life punches us in the gut? When things seem hopeless and it seems like the world, even the people we hold dear, are against us?" She scanned the auditorium, her gaze lingering on the Jenkins' quiet corner before finally resting on Clara and Robby in the front row. "If we are to follow Jesus' example, as he did with his dear friend Lazarus, we weep. We grieve. We don't push away the pain we feel. We feel it completely. And we pray for life beyond that pain. Different, altered, but new."

Several heads turned toward the Romeros in the front row as Clara dabbed at her eyes with a tissue.

Pastor Green continued, "I'm not saying things will get easier. In fact, they may not. They may get worse before they get better." She paused and looked thoughtfully at a spot over everyone's heads. "But what do we do when our life is going well? When ours isn't the one falling apart? When it's our friend, our neighbor, our family member?"

She put her glasses back on her head as she looked at the congregation. "When I was in seminary, one of my best friends came over for dinner, saying he had something important to tell me. He was quiet the entire night, and eventually he told me what was bothering him. He'd tested positive for HIV." Suzanne paused, shifting her weight on her feet. "He didn't know who else to go to. Didn't know what his parents would say. Told me that I was the only person he felt he could tell. Do you know what I said to him? In one of his greatest moments of vulnerability, do you know what words came out of my mouth?"

The auditorium was silent.

"I told him this was God's judgment for being homosexual. Now he had to face the consequences of his actions. He thanked me for my time, stood, and left my apartment." She shook her head. "That's the last conversation I had with him. He died a couple years later."

Someone coughed on the other end of the sanctuary. Suzanne smiled and said, "I could go for hours on a 'Love your neighbor' message, but you've all heard it a thousand times." She shuffled the notes on her podium and went to move her glasses to her nose, but paused, dangling them in the air. "I suppose I'll just say this: regardless of whether you think someone made a mistake or not, we're talking about real people living real lives with real pain. Just love your neighbor. Grieve with them. Care for them. Anything else isn't helpful. No one gives a shit if you think they deserve what happened to them."

A few gasps passed through the crowd and I couldn't help but grin. People in the auditorium shifted uncomfortably as Pastor Greene put her glasses on her nose and said, "Please open your hymnals to page 257."

The congregation stood, pulling hymnals from the pockets on the back of the chairs in front of them. I followed suit, giving myself the vantage point to see an old woman in the row in front of me scrawling on a comment card, "Outraged at pastor's use of the 's'-word."

TWENTY-EIGHT

Church went as church goes. Sang a few hymns. Suzanne spoke about the Parable of the Talents, which I've heard a million times. Sang a few more hymns, and everyone left. The Jenkins family was already gone when I stood to leave. Robby caught me on the way out and asked if there was anything he could be doing to help. I told him to just take his aunt on a walk or something. It was a nice, sunny day. He nodded and met back up with her.

I drove home, my mind filled with hills and valleys, sheep making their way through, up, and over each of them. Inevitably as they reached the top of the final mountain, each sheep was shot in the head with a pistol that was then tossed onto an ever-growing pile of identical police-issued pistols. Goddamn second amendment. Made my job difficult sometimes.

I opened the front door of the cabin to the sound and smell of sizzling bacon.

"Christopher James Harris." Captain Jameson poked his head out from the kitchen, a brilliant white smile peeking out beneath his black chevron mustache. "How the hell are ya?"

I looked back out the front door and saw a black Camaro parked near the curb in front of the cabin. Must have been really lost in thought to miss that. Cap spared no expense on his rentals when he flew out to Jonesboro. Whenever I asked him why, he always responded with "Why not?"

I tossed my jacket on the couch next to Jameson's duffel bag on my way to the kitchen. It always threw me for a loop when he came up to the cabin.

I was used to seeing him in uniform, so seeing him in khaki shorts and a polo always caught me off guard. And the polo shirt he was wearing, a navy blue polo with a pink pattern made up of flamingos, only meant one thing.

"Captain Jameson," I said. "Didn't know you were coming out this weekend."

"Called the cabin phone earlier this week, left a message. Never got a call back. Problematic that I'm here?"

"No, of course not. Not at all. I just had no idea."

Jameson slid a pile of bacon out of the pan and onto an empty plate. He picked up three pieces and set them on a separate plate with some sunny-side-up eggs and toast. He sat down at the table and said, "Help yourself." I sat across from him with a few pieces of bacon and a glass of orange juice.

"Been busy, Chris?" he asked.

"You could say that."

"Mick got you working overtime?"

"No, just have some other stuff going on."

Jameson crunched on some bacon. "Like what? Finally meet someone?"

"No. Well, kind of. Not really. Not sure yet. But probably not."

He raised an eyebrow.

I stammered, "But that's a very recent development. No, I just have some other stuff going on."

"So are you gonna tell me? Or are you gonna keep dodging it?" He took a sip of water and said, "It's fine if you don't want to, just spit it out one way or another."

When Captain Jameson came to Jonesboro, he did so to get away from work, to distract himself from everything he had going on back in the city. To escape how messed up the world was, even for a weekend. The last thing I wanted to do was burden his time off with more of what he dealt with every day. But, at the same time, he had been in my line of work for decades. He was one of the best detectives I knew.

I compromised and said, "I'm helping the police with an ongoing investigation. But the trail's kind of run cold, just waiting for some research to come through."

"Really." It wasn't a question. He mopped up some of the runny egg yolk on his plate with a piece of toast. "Doing some detective work, huh?"

"Trust me, I wasn't planning on it."

"Right." He looked up and smiled at me, like he knew something that I didn't. "What kind of case?"

"Nothing crazy."

He chewed and swallowed the last of his toast. "Sure," he said.

I ate a piece of bacon and drank some orange juice. "When's tee time?" I asked.

Cap checked his watch. "11:00 sound good?"

I nodded, went upstairs, and changed into my golfing clothes. Cap was waiting for me at the front door when I came back down. I pulled the dusty golf clubs he'd given me out of the front closet, and the two of us loaded into the Camaro.

***

"You should give Kyle a call," Cap said as he set his ball on a tee for the first hole.

"I don't know about that, Captain," I said.

"He's still investigating your dad, you know. He hasn't let up on that case since you gave him your case file before you left." He tilted his head to the side and cracked his neck. "Just figured catching up could do you both some good."

There was a light breeze in the air. I watched as he looked down the fairway, letting the wind rustle his salt-and-peppered hair. He considered the breeze before twisting back and forth at the waist, rolling his shoulders back, and taking a few practice swings.

"Your mother stopped by the precinct this week," he said. "Popped into my office. We talked for an hour or so." He paused for a moment, and I knew he was waiting for me to say something. When I didn't, he asked, "When are you going to talk to her?"

I scratched my head and said, "I just don't know if I'm ready for that yet."

"She's your mother, Harris. Nothing to prepare for." I watched in silence as he stepped up to the ball and took a deep breath in and out. The breeze died down. He drew back. Swung. The ball went sailing down the fairway, and he raised a hand to block the sun from his eyes.

"Nice shot," I said.

He clicked his tongue. "Still think you should give your mom a call, Chris."

I laughed. "How do you nail a shot like that and keep a train of thought going?"

"Shot could have been better."

The morning sun turned into an afternoon sun as we chipped our way through the course. Most of our time was spent crouched in the rough, digging through the grass for the balls I had hit. By the time we made it to the eighth hole, I had already dumped sand from my shoes twice and sat on the ground at the tee for the ninth hole to do so a third time. We played out to the northeast and then back south along the perimeter of the vineyard and were about to cross Main Street for the back nine.

Jameson set his ball on the tee and looked out over the fairway once more. Squinting against the sun, he said, "So what about this case you're working on?"

I pulled my left shoe back on and took off my right. "Come on, Cap, you come out here to get away from work. I don't want to bother you with that."

"Not a bother. I'm the one who asked. What made it stall out?"

A light dusting of sand settled on the green as I emptied my right shoe. I figured it couldn't hurt if he was the one asking. "Well, the main thing is this town's lack of resources and tech."

Jameson took a couple practice swings. "Meaning you don't have the resources to easily identify a perp?"

"Right. Plus, the police force is made up of two people now. Jeremy Ralston's a good cop, he's just green. Pretty sure this is his first gig. And don't get me started on Sheriff Wilson."

"Wilson's still in charge?"

"Yessir."

"Christ."

"You know him, huh?"

"I know of him." Jameson put a hand over his eyes and looked down the fairway once more. "I've been coming to Jonesboro at least once a year since I was a kid. I don't know Wilson personally, but I know he has no business running a precinct."

"Apparently, he wasn't always like that. He's changed a lot from what I've heard."

"It's Jonesboro. Everything's changed a lot. Ever since Jack Romero showed up, this town has done nothing but change. Not that the change is unwelcome." He turned and gestured to the golf course. "This, for instance. Great little addition."

I stood, both shoes cleared of sand. "Not a fan of Jack?"

"Exact opposite. I love Jack. He's a good guy. I always get a drink with him when I come to town. How's old Jack doing?"

My heart sank. "Well," I said, "not great, if I'm being honest."

"What?" Jameson asked. "Something happen with the business again?"

Again? I thought.

"Hey Cap," I said, "you're not the first person I've heard mention something happening with the business. From what I can gather, something big happened in the winery's early years. Any idea what it was?"

Jameson lined himself up near his ball and said, "Not really, no. I met Jack shortly after he came to town. Impossible not to meet him, right? He always recognized me and remembered my name, and we always got a drink whenever I came to town. But there were a couple times I came out when he was super stressed about the winery. Couldn't get what was wrong out of him either time. For how much that man talks, he sure can keep a secret when he wants to." He rolled his shoulders back and looked down at the ball. "But I thought he stepped back from the winery, so what's he so stressed about?"

"Well, that's the thing," I said, as he drew his club back. "Jack was murdered."

The club connected with the ball, sending it sailing off into the vineyard. Jameson turned to me in disbelief. "Jesus Christ. That's what you're investigating?"

I nodded. The breeze kicked up.

"Do you have any suspects?" he asked.

The chirp of a police siren interrupted us. Jeremy Ralston stepped out of his cruiser, parked on the pathway for the golf carts. He looked frantic. "Harris, so glad I found you," he said.

I nodded. "What's going on, Deputy?"

"The sheriff has been trying to call you for hours."

I left my phone charging at home that morning. Stupid.

Ralston lowered his head and continued, "I found Ms. Beauregard dead this morning. Single shot to the head."

TWENTY-NINE

I squinted against the light as I stepped out of Ralston's cruiser. When my eyes adjusted, the crime scene I found myself on confused me. Wilson stood a few paces away from the coroner's van, awkwardly looking over a yellow Corvette as Catherine circled the car, taking pictures from different angles. The car itself was parked on the eastern side of the road, in front of the sign reading "Welcome to Jonesboro." Police tape ran the length of the car and stretched to the sign. The welcome sign was situated at the edge of Jonesboro's city limits, nearly a mile out from where the edge of developed Jonesboro started. We were alone at the crime scene.

Cap got out of the passenger seat and walked alongside me, his flamingo polo paired with the bright sunlight casting a peculiar glow on the grisly scene. He shook hands and introduced himself; Wilson didn't object to him being there. Probably just another excuse for him to stand to the side and do nothing.

Officer Ralston said, "Found her this morning on patrol, around 10:00. Thought it was weird a car was parked over here, especially a nice one like this, so I checked it out."

Juliet sat staring through the open driver's-side window of the car, her head resting limp against the seatbelt still fastened across her shoulders. A trail of dried crimson blood ran down her face and had dripped onto her white blouse, the same one she'd been wearing when Wilson brought her into the precinct. Her hair, in a messy bun on top of her head, seemed to be a last-ditch effort to cover the fact she'd been in a holding cell overnight.

Cap's bushy eyebrows furrowed as he frowned. He did a couple laps around the car, hands in his pockets. "Looks like she's been here since last night. Blood's dried and everything." He stooped and looked in through the passenger window, then looked at Ralston. "Have any gloves in the car, son?"

Ralston popped the trunk of his car, grabbed three pairs of nitrile gloves, and passed them out. Cap pulled off the police tape, popped open the passenger door with a gloved hand, and peeked around inside. "Get all the pictures you need, Ms. Sinclair?" he asked.

Catherine stared at the digital screen of the camera, a look of disgust on her face. Then she realized Cap was talking to her and looked up. "What? Oh, yes. Yes, I did."

Cap sat in the passenger seat next to Juliet, looked forward out the windshield, looked at the driver's side without touching anything. "Keys are still in the ignition," he said. "Car off when you arrived?"

"Yessir," Ralston said.

Cap's frown deepened. "No one just parks like this, but everything about the body looks completely natural. Untouched since she died, which means she parked it here. Someone made her do it, one way or another."

In my time on the force, I had only ever seen Cap behind a desk, so watching him work in the field was more interesting than it should have been. I popped the trunk open to see if I could find anything noteworthy.

Cap stepped out of the car, careful to avoid the ground directly outside it, and crouched low to look at the dirt. He looped to the other side of the welcome sign and looked up to the street. "Well, whoever the bastard was, he parked his car on this side of the sign. Looks like he drove into town when he was finished."

"You mean this guy's still in Jonesboro somewhere?" Ralston asked.

I closed the back of the car and said, "Could be."

I joined Cap in the center of the four clear depressions on the ground where the tires had been. Sure enough, motor oil had stained the dirt where the car had been parked.

Ralston started to speak, more panicked than before, "So what now? Do we question everyone at the winery? Do we start bringing people in? Do we just go door-to-door until someone cracks? Do we—"

"Calm the hell down," Cap shouted. He stormed over to Ralston, slamming the car door shut as he passed it. "You can't just go on a goddamn crusade and raze the village, kid. The second you start that shit is the second this town loses its goddamn mind." He leaned in close to Ralston's face and pressed a finger into his chest. "You're a police officer. So no, you don't do any of that shit you're thinking. You take a deep goddamn breath, you keep your goddamn cool, and you do your goddamn job."

All of us stared at Cap. I'd only seen Vacation Jameson for a few years. It had been a while since I'd really seen Captain John Jameson of the LAPD. Ralston stammered, "I'm sorry, Mister—Captain Jameson, sir. Just thinking about my girls back home and I lost my head."

Cap's expression softened a little. He put a hand on Ralston's shoulder and squeezed. "It's all right, son. I understand. But if you want to keep those girls safe, you need to stay calm and do your job." Ralston nodded and Cap returned to the passenger side of the car.

The biggest question was still bothering me, so I finally asked it: "Whose car is this?"

Cap popped open the glovebox and sifted through it, looking over the insurance and registration. "Looks like it belongs to Albert Jones."

Instead of answering my question, I ended up with several more. "Why was she driving one of Albert's cars? Why wasn't she driving her own car? And where *is* her car?"

"I can answer that," Wilson said, tucking his thumbs through his belt loops and puffing out his chest. "Obviously she couldn't drive her own car. We're keeping her keys as crucial evidence, right?"

"Her work keys," I said. "Her car keys were separate, Mike. Didn't you give those back to her before you took her up to the winery?"

Wilson's puffed-up chest deflated. He ran a hand along his neck and muttered, "Well, someone could have told me they were different sets of keys."

Good old Mike Wilson. Useless as always. I sighed, "Find anything, Captain?"

"Nada," he said, stepping out of the car. "Whoever did this knew exactly what they were doing." He looked at the Jonesboro police force and said, "Ms. Sinclair, you dust for prints and see if you can find anything. Sheriff, get the body to the coroner's office for examination and get the autopsy in Harris's hands as soon as it's done. Ralston, give us a ride up to the Jones Estate. We'll see if we can't get any information out of Mr. Jones."

The three of us piled back into Officer Ralston's cruiser, leaving Sheriff Wilson scratching his neck on the side of the road.

***

The drive to the front gates of the vineyard was silent. I kept running through the evidence I'd gathered so far. What did I miss? Was Juliet an accomplice that needed silencing? Or was she simply another victim? Either way, the only connection Jack and Juliet had was the winery. Juliet hated him for some reason, and I knew for sure the two of them didn't associate outside of work. But now they were both dead. The winery had something to do with their deaths, and I had a feeling it was all connected with whatever happened in those early years.

We stood outside the front gate of Jonesboro Winery and Vineyards, closed along with everything else in town. The giant wrought-iron gate was shut, with no one around to open it. Cap tugged on the gate, which refused to budge. He stepped back and put his hands on his hips, looking up the hill to the winery at the top.

"Either of you have Albert's number?" he asked.

"I didn't even have a phone until a couple days ago," I said.

"Mr. Jones likes to keep to himself," Ralston said. "Doesn't like people bothering him too much, especially on Sundays. He comes to church, then drives up and down Main Street a couple times in one of his collector cars. Makes a big show of it, then drives back home for the day."

"But he wasn't at church today," I said.

Jameson shook his head. "Well, then it looks like we might be done for the day. You'll have to pay him a visit tomorrow, Harris." He turned and walked back to the car. "Deputy, take us back to the golf course so I can get my car. Harris and I have some other matters to attend to."

"You're heading back already?" I asked. Cap pulled my golf clubs from the trunk of the Camaro and handed them to me. "But you just got here."

He walked through the front door and picked up his duffel bag from where it still sat on the couch. He turned to me with a smile. "You know, CJ, when I was your age, I was at the top of my game. You're what, thirty-three? That's how old I was when I caught the SoCal Strangler."

I knew the case well. I read the case files more than once in my time on the force. Young women were disappearing from various points around Southern California, turning up in an alleyway of a different city than they were taken from, strangled to death to top off the other abuses they endured in their time missing.

"I worked that case for eight months," Cap said. "Eight months, Harris. Every couple weeks, a new girl would go missing and a couple days later, the body would turn up in an alleyway. I felt like a beachball getting tossed around the state. I eventually ended up catching the guy after eight months of chasing. Eight months cranking my brain on overdrive. Eight months staring at the red strings and the pins on the wall.

"Once we brought him in and things had settled enough, I took two weeks off work to try and unwind from the whole thing, do what I could to get those poor girls' faces out of my mind." He swung his arm up and slung the duffel bag over his shoulder. "I barely survived it. I was exhausted. Physically and emotionally. I realized I needed to do something different from then on. You know what I did?"

I shook my head.

"Any time there was a lull in a case, any time I was waiting to get info back on evidence, any time the trail ran cold and I had no idea what to do next, you know what I did? I took a nap. I went for a walk. I bought a movie ticket and forced myself to sit down in a theater for a couple hours. I met up with the guys for a beer and shot a round of pool. It was after that case that I bought this vacation home so I could get away from it all when I needed to."

He smiled. "I let myself live my life, Chris. I took work seriously. Dead seriously. But when there was a break, any sort of slow in momentum in a case, I took advantage of it. It kept me sane. It kept me focused. Gave me some time to clear my head. And when things didn't go my way, it wasn't the end of the world. It was a lot better than punishing myself for not solving it right away.

"Before long, I realized when I left work at work and took some time to clear my mind, even for a couple hours, I usually noticed something I hadn't noticed before. You know what I was doing when I connected the dots about the Strangler? I was swimming. Just doing some laps at the pool when a light flicked on. It was like a switch. I wasn't staring at the pins on the wall."

He put a hand on my shoulder and squeezed. I felt like a twelve-year-old boy again, his youth group leader having just finished giving him some sort of wise counsel.

I said, "Then what do I do now?"

Cap smiled again. The sun was beginning to set, casting an orange light through the open door of the cabin. "You're waiting on an autopsy, right? Go ahead and take a goddamn break. You deserve it." He laughed. "Besides, don't you have anything better to do on your only day off?"

My heart stopped. Shit. I ran upstairs and snatched my phone from the dresser. Shit, shit, shit, shit, shit. Ten missed calls from Sheriff Wilson from earlier in the day. Three texts and two missed calls from Molly Bauer. "Goddammit."

Cap called up from the bottom of the stairs, "Everything okay, Harris?"

"Yeah, just...forgot something."

"Gotcha. Well, I'm gonna get moving, get back to Seattle before it gets too late."

I heard his footsteps on the concrete. I ran back down the stairs to the open front door. "Captain," I said.

He tossed his duffel in the back seat and turned to me.

"The girls." I paused, unsure if I wanted to finish the question. "Did you ever get their faces out of your mind?"

He shut the back door of the Camaro and smiled again. Except this smile was different.

"No," he said. "No, I didn't."

THIRTY

Molly didn't answer my calls on the drive to her apartment. She lived a couple blocks over from Abby and Lizzy, where the townhomes transitioned into small apartment complexes. I took the stairs two at a time to the second floor, ran along the balcony to her door, and rapped on it three times. It was only when I was listening for her footsteps behind the door that I realized I was still wearing my golf clothes.

I lifted my hand to knock again, and the door cowered from my knuckles. It stopped a couple inches open by the chain latched to the wall just inside. Molly's right eye was all I could see through the gap, eyeshadow and mascara making the blue pop more than normal.

"What do you want?" she asked.

"Hi. Sorry, I—"

"I asked a question, CJ."

I swallowed. "I want—" My mouth was dry. I swallowed again. "I want to go on that date with you."

"Ha. Really? Could have fooled me. At first, I thought you were avoiding me. Now that you're standing here in your cute little golf outfit, it's obvious you just forgot about me." Her voice started to break. "Which, if I'm being honest, is much worse."

She shut the door.

Sweat crawled down my back. I knocked again. The door opened immediately.

"What?"

"Can I come in?"

"Why?"

"So I can apologize."

"For what?"

I didn't have an answer to that one. She could tell. She shut the door again.

I sat on the ground, leaned against her door, and let my head thud against it. I closed my eyes as the last light of the sun dipped behind the horizon.

Just say it, Chris.

"I'm sorry for being an asshole." Molly said nothing, but I heard movement on the other side of the door as I continued, "I'm sorry for not giving you a chance. Hell, for not giving myself a chance." She was silent.

"For..." I sighed. "For not letting something good happen to me for once."

I waited for some sort of response. Any response.

Nothing.

I stood, brushed the dust from my shorts, and started walking away. Then I heard the chain start to move, ever so slowly. The door cracked open.

"Chris."

I stopped and backtracked to her door, hands in my pockets. She leaned against the doorframe, wearing a knee-length gray skirt with a white shirt tucked into it, a denim jacket on top of that, black boots that stopped halfway up her calf. Her lips glistened bright red, her shoulder-length hair fell in blond waves, her blue eyes looked through me.

"I'm sorry," I said. I looked at the ground and kicked at a lonely rock that had found its way onto the balcony. Molly closed the door behind her and lifted my chin up with her finger. She smiled, kissed me on the cheek, and wove her arm through mine.

"Well?" she asked.

I smiled and led her down the stairs to the truck.

———

"Let me get this straight," Molly said. "Your old police captain, whose little vacation home you live in, came to play a round of golf with you. In the middle of your little outing, your prime suspect, who at this point we thought might have been an accomplice, was found dead in Albert Jones' car, and we have no idea why she was driving it in the first place?"

"That's right," I said. I took a sip of my sweet tea and grimaced. Not as good as Mickey's. "Except they found her this morning. I just didn't have my phone on me so they couldn't contact me."

"Damn." Molly shook her head. "I'm sorry for being so hard on you. If I had known—"

"No, don't." I grabbed her hand. "I should have at least called or something."

She smiled, squeezed my fingers, and said, "Yeah. You should have."

We missed the reservation I'd made at Howard's Grill, but it didn't matter. I got more traffic over at O'Callaghan's on a Friday than the restaurant did in a weekend, so we were able to get a table right away. When it came to drinks, all Howard's had going for it was its wine selection, which appealed to a different crowd than the folks who typically ended up sitting at my bar.

Howard's was the equivalent of a Chili's or a Red Robin in the locals' minds. They didn't dress up much when they went, so fortunately I fit right in. I had only been to the restaurant a handful of times. It was a little too stuffy for me, but I figured it was a more date-worthy location than Mickey's, as much as I would have preferred to be sitting there, right across the street.

Molly sipped her martini. "So how was your day with your old boss?"

"It was good. Nice to catch up."

"Yeah?" She rested her head in her palm. "What did you talk about?"

"Lots of stuff. He caught me up on what's going on back home and everything."

"Back in LA?"

"Yep."

Molly ran a finger along the rim of her martini glass. "Do you want to go back?"

Something artificial was lingering on my tongue from the sweet tea. I took a sip of water and said, "I don't know. I mean, it's home, you know? Mom's still there, I have plenty of friends in the area. My old partner on the force is still working the case I left him."

My thoughts drifted as our waiter set our food in front of us: a ten-ounce sirloin for me with mashed potatoes and asparagus, and a Cajun chicken pasta for Molly. We thanked the waiter and he smiled before rushing elsewhere.

I began cutting into my steak as Molly said, "So what do you think? Would you go back?"

I continued cutting, rhythmically moving the knife back and forth through the sirloin until I hit the black ceramic plate. "I don't know. I have a lot of good memories of LA, but I also have a lot of shitty ones. I left after my brother died."

"You had a brother?"

"Yep, younger brother. Charlie Quentin Harris." I smiled and shook my head. "Shitty middle name."

We ate in silence for a couple minutes before Molly asked, "What was he like? Charlie?"

I was surprised she didn't ask why I never mentioned him before. I was equally surprised she didn't ask how he died, but I was thankful she hadn't. Didn't think I was ready to tell that story again anyway. I wiped my mouth with a black napkin and set it on my lap. "Charlie was a hero. He was brave. Strong. He didn't always make the best decisions, but he was a good kid. He was impulsive sometimes, but only when it came to protecting the people he cared about. He loved his friends. He loved our mom and took good care of her after the divorce. Wrote her a letter every week when he was deployed." I flicked some heads of asparagus around with my fork. "He was a better man than I'll ever be."

A dozen voices carried through the air, conversations blending before they reached my ears, punctuated only by the occasional spurt of laughter. Molly's fingers wriggled their way into my hand and squeezed. She smiled and said, "Sounds like Charlie was a good man. Which is no wonder since he had you to look up to."

I gave her a half-hearted smile and took a drink of water to loosen up my throat again. "What are you doing after this?"

A confused expression crossed Molly's face as she pulled her hand back. Then she took a bite of her pasta and said, "I don't know. You're supposed to tell me."

"Oh. Right." I had originally planned on popping over to the theater and catching the new horror movie they'd gotten ahold of, but it had already started. And, considering the events of the day, a slasher flick didn't seem entirely appropriate. I ran through my options, making a mental map of all the buildings along Main Street.

Then I got it.

"What?" Molly asked.

I realized I was smiling. "Well," I said, taking another bite of steak, "tonight might be a new experience for both of us."

"Are you crazy?" Molly whispered. "We could get in so much trouble."

The restaurant was nearly empty by the time we left. After finishing our dinner, I grabbed a small leather case from inside my truck, took Molly's hand, and pulled her around the side of Howard's onto the empty boardwalk behind it. She was horrified when I proceeded to pick the lock of the pedal boat shack with my lockpick set.

I whispered back, "Who's going to get us in trouble? The police? Which of the two of them do you think is going to care?"

"I don't know, this just doesn't seem right."

"Oh, it'll be fine." The lock clicked, and I pulled it off the metal hasp. "Besides, I'll just pay Clay the rental fee next time he comes by the bar." I pulled the big wooden door of the shack just far enough for the two of us to slip through. I peeked out to make sure no one saw and then shut it behind us.

I walked the length of the dock, stepped into a light blue pedal boat, and held my hand out to help Molly into it. She stood on the dock with her arms crossed tightly across her chest and said, "I'm really not sure about this."

"Trust me," I said, "it'll be fine. Besides, it's just a pedal boat." I extended my hand closer to her. After a moment's hesitation, she slipped off her boots, took my hand, and wobbled her way into the left seat of the pedal boat as I sat down on the right.

"Ready?" I asked. She nodded. We began pedaling our way out through the open side of the shack onto the lake. I cranked the lever between our seats, turning the rudder so the boat veered toward the lake's center.

The lake was empty, the moon and stars reflected on its surface, dancing in the ripples sent out from our boat as we paddled along. Molly's hand gripped my wrist, her fingers squeezed tight. The further into the lake we went, the more her grip relaxed, until finally her hand rested lightly on my arm, our feet pumping little rhythmic circles into the center of Vineyard Lake.

About fifty yards into the middle of the lake, I stopped pedaling and leaned back to look up at the stars. I remembered a Boy Scout camp Charlie and I went to in Wyoming over spring break when we were younger. One night we hiked to the top of a hill in the campgrounds and laid down in the grass with dozens of other boys as one of the camp leaders pointed out all the different constellations. Charlie and I giggled softly to ourselves, making our own inappropriate pictures in the canopy of stars. The only constellation I remembered was Orion, three bright stars glimmering along his belt. Those three lights twinkled in the night sky above Vineyard Lake, our one lonely pedal boat rocking gently in the shifting water.

Molly leaned across and laid her head on my chest, looking up with me. "It's beautiful, isn't it?" she said.

I put my arm around her and grunted in agreement. The boat rocked back and forth, and my eyes started to drift shut. I was tired. "Hm?" I asked. I started dozing off, but Molly had said something.

"I was serious earlier," she repeated.

"About what?"

"You are a good man, Chris."

I said nothing, doing my best to fight the sleep creeping into the back of my brain.

Molly said, "Stubborn, yes. An asshole, yeah, sometimes." I laughed, and her head bounced on my chest. "But good."

"How do you know?"

She sat up to look at me. She stroked a hand across my cheek and said, "Because I've seen it myself." She leaned closer and pressed her lips against mine. I ran a hand along her cheek and kissed her back. She lingered there before pulling away and smiling. She laid her head back on my chest and I wrapped my arms around her again as the gentle rocking of the pedal boat lulled us both to sleep, the stars above us singing their celestial hymn, reflected in the glassy surface of the lake below.

We woke up about an hour later, our backs aching from the hard plastic of the pedal boat. We groggily pedaled back to the shack and moved quickly and quietly back to my truck. I turned the heat up all the way to counteract the chill of the night and rubbed my eyes. We hadn't said a word since we docked, in part to avoid being caught in our less-than-legal act, but also due to being half-awake. We both passed out in that boat; I guess she needed some rest as much as I did.

I pulled up in front of Molly's apartment building a few minutes later. We walked up the steps arm in arm and I leaned against the wall of her building with a yawn as she unlocked her apartment door. She swung it open and leaned against the doorframe, facing me.

"Thanks," I said.

"For what?"

I wrapped her in my arms and kissed the top of her head. We stood in the cold until I heard her teeth chattering. I squeezed her one last time and said, "Go ahead and warm up, get some sleep."

She nodded and smiled, her teeth clicking together noisily as she did so. She kissed me one last time and said goodnight before slipping into her apartment and shutting the door behind her. I walked back to my truck, smiling more than I had in a long time.

THIRTY-ONE

Monday. Another week.

I stretched in the sun on the front porch of the cabin, rolling my sore neck around on my shoulders. I could still feel the tingle of Molly's lips against my own, could still smell her perfume. Cap was right. The break was much needed, and I was ready to get back into the investigation that morning. Figured I'd swing by the coroner's office, see if Catherine had anything for me, then check in with Molly on the surveillance footage.

I walked to the truck just as the Jonesboro newspaper was tossed out the window of a passing minivan onto the driveway. I waved at the car and crouched to pick it up and read the headline, curious as to what they pulled together that week: *Preparations for Winery Re-Launch Continue, Mayor to Speak Today.* Figures.

I tossed the newspaper in the recycling bin and walked to the truck. A manila envelope was taped to the driver's side window. Inside was a small stack of photos and a printed sheet that simply read:

STAY OUT OF THIS.

I felt the blood drain from my face as I looked through the photos. Abby and me locking up O'Callaghan's. Robby with my hand on his shoulder inside the tackle shop. Lizzy wiping her eyes as we drove to Denny's for lunch. Molly asleep on my chest in the pedal boat on the lake.

My heart stopped as I looked at the last picture in the envelope. It was a familiar picture, one I'd seen a dozen times. The last time I'd seen it was three years ago at a military funeral.

Charlie.

———

"Just call me as soon as you get this message, okay?"

I stuffed the phone into my pocket as I raced down the stairs to the morgue, praying to God that Abby was just at work and not dead. Someone was watching me. Whoever it was knew about Charlie, and his photo in that envelope was clearly a threat. Now, thanks to me, everyone I'd gotten close to was involved in this case. Not only that, but now they were in danger of being next.

I couldn't let it happen again.

Catherine was waiting for me in the morgue, writing on a clipboard next to Juliet's pale figure laid out on the autopsy table. She said nothing as I approached her. "Morning," I said gruffly.

She looked up, surprised to see me. "Morning," she said.

"What do we got?"

Catherine nodded. "Juliet Beauregard. Sixty-two. Was dropped off at the Jonesboro Winery by Sheriff Wilson Saturday afternoon after being held at the station overnight. Found dead in a car Sunday morning. Same as Jack Romero, one shot in the middle of her forehead. Both bullets were fired from the same gun. No rope burns on her wrists or anything this time. Happened around 1:00 in the morning."

"Pictures?" I asked.

Catherine handed me a small stack of photos. The scene looked identical to when I had shown up with Ralston. I said, "Well, your crime scene preservation's on point, I'll give you that much. Do we have any idea when she was last seen?" My question went unanswered. I looked up to see Catherine sitting on a stool a few feet away, rubbing her eyes. "Catherine?"

"Hm?"

"You okay?"

"Yeah," she said, and stood up. "Yeah, I'm okay." She looked at Juliet's body. "I moved from the city to get away from all this, you know? When the other guy died, I just figured this would be a one-and-done kind of thing. I wasn't expecting..." She gestured toward Juliet.

I set the photos on the counter. "I get it. I came to Jonesboro for a similar reason."

She sighed. "Guess things are bound to catch up eventually, huh?"

The door to the morgue opened and Deputy Ralston leaned in. "Harris," he said. "Hope I'm not interrupting anything, but Albert Jones is in the sheriff's office. Wants to talk to you."

"He wants to talk to me?" I asked.

"Yessir."

"Why?"

"Not entirely sure, but he's mad."

Albert was always mad about something. He was probably coming to talk to me personally about what happened with Abby at the bar. I thanked Catherine for her time and followed Ralston upstairs onto the short stretch of sidewalk between the coroner's office and the police station.

"You see the paper this morning?" Ralston asked.

"I did. Westcliffe's speaking in front of Town Hall today, right?"

"Yeah, but according to the newspaper, all three co-owners were supposed to say something, too." Ralston opened the door to the station lobby and followed me inside. "The paper mentions that Jack passed away. But according to the article, Juliet's still part of the program."

The two of us stopped, the echoes of our footsteps fading to silence in the empty lobby. I said, "So much for keeping things quiet from the locals, huh?"

"Not sure how we could," Ralston said. He pulled on his shoulder. "The winery's three co-owners were supposed to talk about the winery's re-launch, but only one of them is still alive anymore."

One left alive.

The sole owner of the entire business.

"That's right," I said. I clapped Ralston on the shoulder, and we proceeded into the station in silence. It made sense. Without anyone else to tell him otherwise, Albert now had free reign to do whatever he wanted with the business. According to Clara, he never wanted to run it in the first place. Maybe he wanted to sell it off. Take the money and run. That would also explain the threat I received that morning. He didn't want anybody ruining his plans. But if Albert really wanted to sell the company and be done with it, why didn't he do it sooner? Why now?

I opened the door to Wilson's office. A man sat in one of the chairs facing his desk, and he turned as I entered, a familiar face greeting me with a con-man's smile.

"CJ," Albert Jones greeted me. "It's been a minute. God *damn*, you look like shit."

"Al," I said, sitting in the chair next to him. "What brings you in?"

Wilson cleared his throat. "Mr. Jones was wanting—"

"Shut up," I said. "Didn't ask you." I was flustered enough that morning. Didn't need Wilson's bullshit making it any worse. The sheriff sank back in his chair and I said, "What can I help you with, Al?"

Albert adjusted in his seat, his slicked-back, jet-black hair unmoved. "Well," he said, "I want to talk to whoever's been looking into the whole situation with Jack and Jules."

I glanced at Wilson.

"Oh, I know Jack didn't kill himself," Albert said with a flippant wave. "Sheriff told me about it the other day, so I know he has a guy looking into it."

"You're talking to him," I said.

"Brilliant." He clapped once. "Mostly I want to see where you are with everything."

"What do you mean?"

"Well," he curled his fingers and looked at his nails. "Clearly the two of them didn't just coincidentally die in the last week. Somebody offed 'em." He looked back at me. "So do you have any idea who did it? I'd hope you're close to finding out who's behind this whole thing." Albert spoke confidently, but there was something delicate behind his words. Something seemed shaken.

"Not quite," I said.

He lowered his hand and gripped the armrest of the chair. His expression changed as he said, "What do you mean not quite?"

Suddenly it became clear. Albert Jones was afraid. To ease his fear, I said, "I'm gonna do a couple things today to try and make a break in the case. I'm shaking a couple trees right now, just waiting to see what falls out of them."

Albert's grip loosened a bit. "Well, I would appreciate if you would keep shaking those trees. Cut the goddamn forest down if you have to."

Cut the bullshit, Chris.

"What's going on, Al?" I asked.

"What's going on?" Albert said. His grip tightened on the armrest once again. "What's going on is that the Jonesboro Winery is celebrating its grand reopening in less than three months, a reopening that's only happening because I busted my *ass* for two years to get our license renewed. What's going on is the potential revival of a business. And not just a business, but an entire town. The place where I was raised. What's going on is I'm more stressed than I've ever been in my entire goddamn life. And in the midst of that, what's going on is the two other owners of my company—my family's legacy—were murdered in cold blood in the last week. And not only that, but one of them was murdered in *my* goddamn car."

His knuckles turned white as he leaned forward in his chair and shouted, "What's going *on*, CJ Harris, is that some fucker is trying to steal my company from me. And they're coming for my head next." A vein popped on Albert's forehead, his face red with anger. He sat back in his chair, taking deep breaths, regaining his composure. In an instant, my suspicions that he could have killed the winery's other co-owners all but vanished.

I heard the plastic lid of a water bottle twist open and nearly jumped out of my chair as Piers stepped forward from behind me and handed Albert the freshly opened bottle. I didn't even know he was there. Albert thanked him and drank half the bottle in a few quick gulps as Piers slipped back into the corner behind me. Sneaky bastard.

"Al," I said, "why would someone want to steal your company?"

Albert took a few more deep breaths and said, "I don't know. You're the detective. You figure it out."

I intended to do just that. And I did have some questions for him. "Why did Juliet have one of your cars, Al?"

He looked at the sheriff and said, "Because this asshole didn't give Jules her goddamn car keys back." The sheriff's face reddened as he looked down at his folded hands. Albert said, "She came stomping into my office all pissed off, demanded that I let her borrow a car so she could go home that night. Piers went and grabbed it for her."

From behind me, Piers said, "Precisely, sir. I collected the Corvette for her and brought it back to the winery. She always liked the Corvette."

God, Piers creeped me out. I did my best to hide a shudder and said, "Was there anything weird about Juliet when you saw her last? Anything seem off?"

"She was being a bitch, so no. Same as always. She stayed at work late to get the rest of her shit done, no idea how late she was there."

Not much to go on there. I rubbed my chin a few times to try and think through what I knew so far. If something happened at the winery in those early years, Al likely wouldn't have known about it since he was just a kid at the time. And even if he did know, I had a feeling he wasn't likely to tell me.

Albert tapped his fingers impatiently while I thought, then asked, "Anything else?"

"No," I said. "That's all for now. I'll pay you a visit if I have any other questions."

Albert jabbed a finger at me and said, "You better figure this shit out, CJ. Quick. This town's on the fucking brink of collapse and my company's the only thing to save it. Mayor Westcliffe is talking to the town at 4:00 this afternoon. Jack and Jules were both supposed to be there, so you better have some sort of explanation by then. I'm not losing my company." He tossed the half-full water bottle into the trash can. "And I'm sure as hell not dying for it, either."

He stood and moved to leave Wilson's office, nearly colliding with Catherine as she opened the door with a stack of papers in her arms. She adjusted her glasses and apologized. Albert, a completely different person from mere moments ago, smiled and said, "No worries, Miss. You look lovely today."

Dirty old man.

Catherine blushed and ducked into Wilson's office. Albert walked out of the office and Piers followed him, but not before pausing to give Catherine a curious look. Then he followed Albert and shut the door behind him.

I sank into the chair and heaved a sigh. The pressure was really starting to get to me. The threatening note was making things difficult enough, but now I had until 4:00 to find some sort of explanation for what was going on in Jonesboro. I had a few places to stop by to get things moving. But first I needed a flash drive.

THIRTY-TWO

"Can't say I've sold any guns recently," Reggie said. "Especially any Glocks." The fluorescent lights flickered against the white linoleum floor of his dingy pawn shop. "Come to think of it, I can't remember the last time I sold any guns, even a BB gun. You've been shooting with us before, everyone has their own stuff. Speaking of which, you should come next time. Starting that gun club's the best thing Sheriff Wilson's done for this town. Albert might come again, let us shoot some of Piers' big boys."

"Piers has been bringing stuff to the gun club? Like what?"

"Oh, he has an AK. And a .50 Cal. That fucker could blow your arm off if you aren't careful. No idea what a butler needs those for." He leaned over the counter. "Y'know, I heard Piers used to lead a secret task force in Afghanistan, took out some big names over there."

I wasn't sure about all that, but the rumors about Piers' past did make me curious. "Any idea why the Clarkes have worked for the Jones family for so long?"

Reggie scratched his head with his pointer finger, like a cartoon monkey from the 60's. "Not sure, really. Piers' dad worked for Howard before he did. They've always been the Jones' butlers. The way they go around town, though, you'd think they had ties to the mafia or something."

"Mafia, huh?" I leaned against the counter. "Piers have a Glock that you know of?"

"Really stuck on Glocks, huh?" Reggie scratched his head again. "Piers might have one, but I mean..." He reached behind him and pulled out his own Glock that he had tucked into his waistband.

"Jesus, Reggie," I said, ducking instinctively. "Will you put that away?"

"Sorry, CJ," he said, tucking it into the back of his pants again. "I'm just saying we all have Glocks now, ever since they sold all the extras at the police station. Piers probably has one, but he's got everything. He brought a bunch of different stuff to the club for Albert to shoot. Was nice enough to let the rest of us fire a couple rounds." He shook his head. "I don't have any Glocks if that's what you're in the market for, but I've got some real nice pieces right now. This little Beretta's got your name on it, selling it half-price." Reggie pulled the compact pistol from the back wall and set it on the counter. The last thing I needed was his shitty sales routine.

I pointed at a flash drive hanging on the wall behind the counter. "I just need one of those today." Reggie grabbed the flash drive off the wall and rang it up. I pulled a ten from my wallet and said, "Know anywhere else someone could get a gun around town?"

Reggie handed me the change and said, "Craigslist."

I was getting sick of driving up to the winery. Luckily, Paul was mopping the floor of the foyer when I got there and was happy to let me back into the security office, where he left me to investigate. The winery's surveillance footage was the most technologically advanced evidence at my disposal. I didn't have much option but to use it.

I clicked through the folders Paul had shown me until I found the files for Saturday and Sunday. I dragged everything onto the flash drive just as my phone buzzed in my pocket. It was a text from Robby: *"come to the tackle shop. might have found something."* Figured I'd swing by on my way to the library. Anything I could get would be helpful at this point. I grabbed the flash drive and made my way back to my truck as the day's overcast weather began setting in.

As I stepped onto the asphalt of the winery's parking lot, I noticed Juliet's 4Runner parked in the same spot as the other day. I took a second to walk around it and looked inside. No signs it had been tampered with since Wilson arrested her on Friday, but she apparently had a secret penchant for fast food based on the McDonald's wrappers in the back seat. Was Juliet's killer going for Albert? Did she only die because she was in one of his cars? If Wilson had just given her the keys to her car, would she still be alive?

I looked down at the ground, deep in thought, when I noticed a familiar black stain on the asphalt by my feet. Motor oil, same as the crime scenes. The signpost designating the parking spot read: "Albert Jones – CEO."

The tackle shop was empty when I stepped inside. Made me nervous. "Robby?"

"Over here, Seej," his voice called.

I found him crouched behind the counter, fiddling with something out of view. "Said you found something?" I asked.

He popped up and wiped his forehead with the back of his hand, a screwdriver in his fist. He was wearing his delivery uniform. "Maybe," he said. "I found a hidden compartment."

I circled the counter to see what he was talking about. Sure enough, there was clearly the seam of a cabinet in the wooden part of the counter under the cash register. There was no knob or handle, only a very small keyhole. Easy to miss if you weren't looking for it.

"It's locked tight," Robby said. "Can't get it open. No idea where Uncle Jack might have kept a key that small."

I checked the underside of the counter and opened a few drawers. Nothing taped underneath, no small keys to be found anywhere. "Tough luck,"

I said. "He didn't have anything on him like that when he died either." I put a hand on his shoulder. "It's probably nothing."

"I'm not so sure," Robby said. He dug around in a messenger bag he had sitting on the countertop. Several leather journals were inside, and he pulled one out. "I don't think I would have found this if Uncle Jack hadn't said anything about it." He leafed through the journal and read: *"Was alone in the shop today. Spent some time in the vault. Always a good reminder."*

He handed me the journal. I read over Jack's words and looked back at the hidden compartment. "The vault, huh?" I doubted there would be anything useful inside, but I had nothing. It couldn't hurt. "Give me a sec."

I grabbed my lockpick set out of the truck and started fiddling with the lock in the cramped space under the counter. It took some time, but eventually there was a light click and the wooden panel popped off. There were only two things in the compartment: a leather-bound journal, and an old wooden fishing bobber.

I handed the book to Robby. "Found another one for you." As he leafed through the pages, I looked over the bobber. It was an antique, probably at least forty years old, the red and white paint chipped from age. There were words carved on one side: *"Never forget."* On the other side there were numbers: *"6.5.92."*

"1992," I said. "Hey Robby, what year is that journal from?"

"Looks like it's from 1988," he said. "Weird. I thought Uncle Jack accidentally skipped a number with his journals, but this is the one that was missing."

I handed him the bobber. "June 5, 1992. That date mean anything to you?"

Robby scratched his head. "No, man. That was a few years before I was born." He reached into the messenger bag and pulled a few different journals out of it. He flipped through several and said, "1992, right? Looks like this is the right year." He handed it to me.

I flipped a few pages until I found June 5. There were only two sentences written on that date:

Went fishing today. Piers handled everything.

"Piers, huh?" I handed the book to Robby. "Know much about Albert's butler?"

Robby took the journal back and said, "Not really. I know he's creepy as hell. Uncle Jack said he was a spy or some shit, but I don't know much about him. I see him in weird spots around town a lot, but I haven't even talked to him."

I thought about the envelope on my window. Whoever took those pictures of me knew how to do so without being seen, and I recalled Robby mentioning on Saturday that Piers had been spotted all over town in the last week. Could be something, at least.

"Hey, Seej?"

"Yeah?"

"Why are these things in here?"

My brain was so scattered, the question hadn't yet come to mind. I took the bobber back from him and rolled it around in my hand. "I don't know. Your uncle wanted to hide them for some reason, but I have no idea what that reason is." I looked around the tackle shop. Looked the same as before, except for the clamp on the counter with a half-finished fly in it. Robby must have been working on it for a couple days already.

"What do you think he's talking about?" Robby asked. *"Piers handled everything?"*

I set the bobber on the counter. "I don't know, but I intend to find out. Try not to worry about it too much." I looked him over. "Still need to work today?"

"Yeah man, I just stopped by to check this out before heading out on my route. Why?"

I tapped my fingers on the counter, strategizing what to say. "I need you to be on high alert while you're out today, all right? Text me if you hear anything and call me right away if anything seems off. Make sure you're never alone, don't take any shortcuts or anything. And tell your aunt to stay home, keep the doors locked, and not to answer it for anyone but you and me."

He cocked an eyebrow. "Why? Do you think something's gonna happen to me or Aunt Clara?"

"No. I'd never let that happen." I squeezed his shoulder and circled the counter. I was reminded of the picture of us in the envelope that morning.

"Seej?"

I turned back to him.

"Did my uncle do something..." He stared at the bobber on the counter. "I don't know. Something bad?"

Charlie was eleven years old, sitting in the passenger seat of our old Corolla when he asked me the same question about our dad. I looked him in the eyes and did my best to ignore the image of Dad and Sylvia in my mind. I told him no, our dad didn't do something bad. I lied to him.

Twelve years later, I shot him as he held Dad at gunpoint.

"I don't know," I said. "He might have, Robby. I hope not, but I'm going to find out."

I left the tackle shop, anxiety securing its grip in my mind.

THIRTY-THREE

Something about Robby's question put me on edge. Whoever killed Jack and Juliet was threatening me. I couldn't let what happened to them happen to Robby, or the Smiths, or Molly. They hadn't done anything wrong; they only became targets because they were close to me. I wouldn't let it happen. I'd never forgive myself.

I white-knuckled the steering wheel down to the library, trying to get all my ducks in a row: Juliet's keys. Motor oil. Glock 22. Double homicide. No fingerprints. No witnesses. No suspects.

Whoever did this knew exactly what they were doing.

Hundreds of questions plagued me as I opened the door to the library. I heard voices down a couple different aisles, unlike my previous visits. Molly sat at the front desk, focused on her computer monitor. She looked up as I approached and stood with a smile.

"Hi," she said.

"Hi," I said back.

"I had a lot of fun last night," she said. She tilted her head to the side and smiled.

"Same. Found anything else in that surveillance footage?"

Her expression changed. "Well, no, not yet—"

"Have you been looking through it?"

Her brow furrowed. "CJ, what's going on?"

"I just…" I gripped the edge of the counter. "I really need something. Anything. I need a *fucking* lead, Molly."

"I thought you had some time—"

"Things have changed."

A woman came to the counter with her son, who clutched a copy of *Where the Wild Things Are* in his tiny hands. Molly smiled and greeted them, and I stepped away from the counter. I laced my fingers behind my head and took some deep breaths.

My phone buzzed in my pocket. Abby. "Hello?"

"Hey," she said in her usual cheerful tone. "Do I owe you a steak dinner?"

"Never mind that right now," I said. "Are you and Liz okay?"

"What? Yeah, we're both at home. Why?"

Thank God.

"Just be cautious, all right?" I said. "Keep the doors locked, call me if anything seems off."

"Chris, is everything okay?"

Molly finished checking the book out for the little boy, who began skipping toward the front door ahead of his mom.

"Yes," I said into the phone. "Nothing to worry about. Just stay safe." I hung up the phone and stepped back to the counter. "Have you noticed anything weird? Anyone following you?"

Molly took a step back. "Chris, you're scaring me."

I took another deep breath. "There was an envelope on my car this morning. It had several pictures in it, all of me with people in town. One of them was of us on the lake last night."

"What?" Molly cupped her elbows, wrapping her arms tightly around her waist. "How did they even know we were out there?"

"No idea. That's just one of several questions that's been raised this morning." I closed my eyes and said, "Whoever it is also knows about Charlie."

"Charlie?" Molly said. "What does that have to do with anything?"

"It's a threat, Molly. Charlie died because he got involved in a case I was working. Whoever killed Jack and Juliet wants me to stop looking into their murders, and they're using you—and Robby, and Abby, and Lizzy—as leverage."

She looked me over and rubbed her arms. "Are you sure?"

"Positive. I need you to shut down the library for the day, keep the doors locked, and keep your phone readily available with my number on speed dial. If you have a spare key, I need you to give it to me so I can get in and out." She quickly slipped into the office and returned with a key that I tucked into my pocket.

"I also need you to trust me and stay calm while you look through that footage," I said. "I need something. Anything. The mayor's speaking in front of town hall here in—" I checked the clock on the wall behind her. "Two hours. I'm assuming so they can address everything. I need to have something by then."

She nodded, watching me intently. "What do you need me to do?"

"First," I said, setting the flash drive on the counter, "I need to know Juliet's movements on Saturday after she was dropped off at the winery. She parked Al's car in front of that welcome sign herself, so there must be a reason. Someone talked to her or something. After that, just try to find something in the rest of that footage for me." I spun on my heel and started walking off, then quickly turned back. "Please. And thank you. Call me if anything seems weird. And stay safe." She nodded, and I rushed out to my truck.

I had questions that needed answering, and of the few people that could potentially answer them, there was only one that I trusted at this point.

"A spy?" Clara laughed, easing back on the pine-green sofa. "No, Piers' background isn't anything so glamorous." She looked thin. Pale. Drawn. Much like many of the flowers in her house since I'd last been there.

"What is Piers' role with the Jones family then?" I asked.

"Well," Clara said, cocking her head. "He's more than just the butler, I suppose. One of Piers' primary duties used to be trying to keep Albert out of trouble." She chuckled and shook her head. "He was always a crafty one. He constantly found a way to give Piers the slip."

"Albert became Piers' responsibility?"

"In a sense, yes," Clara said. "Albert loved his mother, and she always took good care of him when Howard was occupied with the business. After his parents' divorce, Albert started acting a little unruly, to put it mildly. So Piers was left in charge of him. If there's one word to describe Piers Clarke, it's loyal. He was at Howard's beck and call until the day he died, running errands for him whenever he needed, doing whatever he asked. Helped him resolve problems on more than one occasion."

"What kind of problems?"

"Oh, nothing you're thinking." Clara waved a hand, shooing away my apparent concern. "Just some disputes with local business owners that would come up now and then. Frank Jenkins' father wasn't happy with Howard one day, something about him stealing his customers somehow, so Howard sent Piers to talk to him about it. He resolved everything peacefully, and the Jenkins family didn't make a fuss after that."

Resolved it peacefully, huh? Maybe it was unfounded suspicion, but something told me things would have been anything but peaceful if Frank's dad hadn't kept quiet. Clara just tried to see the best in people. Now I ended up with more questions than I originally thought. I tapped my notebook with my pen and said, "About Howard's divorce..."

Clara looked at me expectantly.

I tapped a few more times. "When and why did that happen?"

"Oh dear, let's see. We first moved here in 1984. That's when the winery's relaunch happened, and when that picture I gave you was taken. Albert was just starting high school then and they got divorced the year he graduated, so it must have been 1988, I believe."

The year Jack's hidden journal was from.

Clara looked at me, seemingly annoyed and said, "And I have a feeling you might have an idea why they got divorced."

"Juliet?" I asked.

She pointed at me. "Right on the money. I didn't know until a few months after the divorce happened. Nobody did. I just noticed one day that I hadn't seen Laura Jones in a while. The newspaper got wind of it shortly after that and trust me, they had a field day with it. Piers had a talk with the editor and there weren't any more stories printed about it after that."

"I see." Sounded like Piers really was the one doing the Jones family's dirty work. I scribbled a quick note as one last question came to mind. "Clara, I've been meaning to ask, but I've been so busy. Did Jack mention anything about going fishing with anyone on Tuesday morning?"

She tapped her chin a few times. "No, I can't say that he did." She smiled. "But you know Jack. He took people on spontaneous fishing trips all the time. Why do you ask?"

"No reason." Another dead end in the maze. I tucked my notebook away, thanked Clara for her time, and drove back toward Main Street. My stomach did backflips as I parked in front of Town Hall and joined the crowd that was gathering.

I had some vague leads, sure, but I still had nothing.

THIRTY-FOUR

"Hello, everyone," Mayor Westcliffe said. A high, piercing tone filtered through the speakers, and a couple hundred people winced at the noise. Pretty good turnout despite the slight chill from the cloud cover. The mayor took a step back from the podium and whispered to someone operating a mixing board off to the side. He tested the mic a couple times and said, "Ah, that's better. Afternoon, Jonesboro."

The crowd muttered a response of sorts.

Westcliffe cleared his throat and said, "As we all know, here in less than three months' time, the Jonesboro Winery's tasting room is going to have its grand re-opening." A handful of people clapped and whistled, but not enough to justify the hand the mayor raised to quiet the crowd. He continued, "In anticipation of the grand re-opening, I've asked Albert Jones to come and say a few words about the event."

Albert approached the podium to a smattering of applause. By the time he'd shaken Westcliffe's hand and positioned himself behind the microphone, the clapping had stopped completely. I hardly noticed; I was fixated on Piers Clarke, standing off to the side of the stage with his hands behind his back.

"Afternoon," Albert said into the microphone, accompanied by a piercing hum. He leaned away from the mic and aggressively whispered at the person behind the mixing board.

Someone's shoulder brushed against mine. I turned to find Molly standing next to me with her arms folded tightly across her chest.

"Anything?" I whispered.

She shook her head. "Juliet talked to Albert and Piers, then stayed in her office until about 12:30 a.m. The only person to talk to her that entire time was Piers, who poked his head in to give her the keys to the Corvette. When she finally left, she walked straight to the parking lot, got into the Corvette, and drove away."

Dammit. Piers had to have said something to her. Why else would she have parked in front of the town's welcome sign? What other reason could she possibly have?

Albert tapped the microphone a couple times and said, "That's better. Anyway, as you may have heard, I've been busting my ass the last two years to get this tasting room re-opened. And this time, I plan on keeping it open. So, sorry kids, but you'll have to wait until you're legal now."

The crowd chuckled, the sea of heads bouncing up and down. Didn't see what was so funny.

Albert tugged at the sleeves of his black leather jacket. "You might have noticed a couple folks are missing today. Both Jack Romero and Juliet Beauregard were supposed to be up here with me to give some updates on the relaunch. Unfortunately, we all know that our friend Jack passed away last week."

A hushed murmur passed over the crowd.

"In addition to that," he said, steadying himself on the edges of the podium, "I'm sorry to say that Juliet Beauregard, our head winemaker, also passed away just two nights ago."

The murmur grew in volume. I had to admit, I was impressed by Albert's ability to keep his composure after his display that morning.

"I know what this looks like," he said, raising a hand to quiet the crowd. At least that time it was justified. "But I assure you, there is a reasonable explanation for all of this. And here to give that reasonable explanation is Sheriff Michael Wilson."

I took a deep breath and let it out slowly. I'd pulled Mike aside after I arrived and told him exactly what he needed to say. The few leads I had pointed to Piers being our killer, but I needed concrete evidence and a clear motive. I felt one more day was all I'd need to finish his coffin. What I told Wilson to say should have bought me some time at the very least.

Wilson shuffled up to the podium as Albert stepped away. The crowd was silent. "Well," Wilson said. "Uh, we—that is, the police department—have been looking into the recent deaths of a couple people here in town." The crowd started shifting again. Molly inched closer to me.

"So," Wilson began, but then stood there with his mouth agape. The crowd fell silent again. He snapped his jaw shut, scratched his neck, and said, "Well, I don't know if I'm the best one to be talking about this. Actually…" Wilson scanned the crowd until he locked eyes with me.

"Goddammit," I whispered. Molly looked at me.

Wilson pointed and said, "CJ Harris." Every eye in the crowd turned to me. Wilson said, "He's actually been heading up this investigation, believe it or not. Used to be a cop in a big city. He's better suited to explain what's going on. Mind coming up here, CJ?"

Hundreds of eyes stared at me, mixed with anticipation and disgust. My chest felt tight. Blackness started to encroach on the corners of my vision. What the hell was Wilson thinking? This wasn't my responsibility, and I still didn't have any goddamn jurisdiction. He knew that. I wasn't ready to stand in front of all these people and tell them what was going on. I couldn't go up there when someone was threatening the people I cared about.

The crowd started to whisper.

I felt Molly's fingers slip between my own. She squeezed my hand.

I squeezed back and released her grip before weaving my way through the crowd, swearing under my breath every step of the way. Wilson backed away as I approached. I grabbed the sides of the podium with both hands to steady myself and looked out over the crowd. I caught the eyes of several people I knew very well: the Dinsmores, Amanda, Reggie, the Jenkins family, Robby leaning against a light pole toward the back of the crowd. Everyone stared, waiting for me to speak.

I adjusted the microphone and said, "As Sheriff Wilson said, I've been looking into the deaths of both Jack Romero and Juliet Beauregard. Trust me, I'm working my hardest to figure out exactly what happened here. And I, along with Sheriff Wilson and the rest of the police department, will be doing our best to ensure that we get this issue sorted so that the winery's relaunch can go over without a hitch."

I cleared my throat and said, "From my understanding, no one in town bore any ill will against either Mr. Romero or Ms. Beauregard. My investigation has been wholly inconclusive so far." I looked to where Robby stood at the back of the crowd, then averted my gaze. "The evidence I've found so far points to both incidents being suicide."

Nearly everyone started whispering. All of O'Callaghan's regulars started shaking their heads. I hated talking to people like this. Lying. But I needed to buy myself some time and protect the people closest to me.

A woman in the crowd called out, "You expect us to believe that?"

I shook my head and said, "I know how odd that may sound, but the evidence so far is inconclusive of foul play."

Another voice called out, "Then there isn't a murderer in Jonesboro?"

I swallowed as the crowd's chatter increased. "The investigation is ongoing, but the evidence points to both of these deaths being suicide."

"Why should we listen to you?" someone shouted.

"I assure you, the well-being of Jonesboro's citizens is my highest priority."

"How can you prove that?"

"Well, I—"

"Yeah, especially when you killed your own brother!"

My stomach dropped.

The crowd erupted into a roar, any sense of organization lost.

I scanned the crowd, trying to find the voice who'd blurted my secret. This was only a fraction of Jonesboro's population, but by the end of the day everyone in town would know me as the man who killed his own brother. Didn't matter if it was true or not, much less what the story was behind that truth.

The shouts of the crowd crashed over me, sweeping me out with the tide. "No, I...I was just doing my job." No one listened, demanding I answer their questions and asking why I was put in charge of this investigation in the first place. I squeezed my eyes shut and gripped the edges of the podium as their exclamations continued.

"There's a murderer in Jonesboro!"

"Did you kill Jack and Juliet?"

"You're not even from here! You don't care if this town dies!"

"What are you going to do?"

I slammed a fist on the podium and a shrill tone pierced through the speakers as the microphone fed back through them once more. The crowd went silent.

"What am I going to do?" I said. "I'm going to figure out what the hell is going on here in Jonesboro. And after that?" I scanned the crowd and made eye contact with Molly. "After that, I'm getting out of this shit hole."

The crowd began shouting again. As I backed away from the podium, Robby hopped on his bike and rode it south down Main Street. I worked my way around the crowd as the mayor tried to calm everyone down. I rounded the corner onto Main Street just as I heard him say, "Here's Albert Jones again to talk about the winery's relaunch and our Independence Day Celebration."

THIRTY-FIVE

Robby's bike was exactly where I thought it would be, leaning against the storefront of Jack's Bait & Tackle. A familiar scent greeted me when I opened the door, one I hadn't smelled in a while. He sat on a stool behind the counter with a lit cigar in his mouth. Must have picked it out of Jack's humidor. He was gingerly wrapping a thin bit of string around the fly I'd seen half-finished earlier that day.

"Hey," I said.

"Hey CJ," he said. He continued tying the fly without looking up at me. "Did you really kill your own brother?"

I pulled at my earlobe. "Yeah. Yeah, I did. But you have to believe me, I was just doing my job. He was about to kill someone else. I didn't mean for him to die, but I had to stop him. I didn't have a choice."

"I believe you, man. I do." He took a long draw from the cigar, then set it down on an ashtray next to him on the counter. "You don't really think it was suicide, do you?" Smoke billowed from his mouth as he talked, carrying with it the wisps of his disbelief.

"No," I said. "I'm sorry, Robby. I was just trying to buy myself some time. Don't know if it worked, though." He nodded and returned to tying his fly. I leaned against the counter as he wrapped the string around the hook. "You okay?" I asked.

He pulled the thread tight, tied it off, and cut the excess. "They're all looking at me weird," he said. "Everywhere I go, people just look at me. Most of them don't even say anything. I hate it."

His grip tightened on the spool of thread. I could tell there was more.

He threw the spool across the store. "Everyone here, every single person in this goddamn town, they all know me. They all knew Uncle Jack. I can't go anywhere without someone looking at me funny. Like there's something wrong with me. It's like they're sad for me or something, but how do they think I feel? 'Look, there's the kid whose uncle killed himself.' If they knew what really happened..." He ran the back of his hand across his eyes to wipe the tears. "I just want to find the asshole who did this, man." He lowered his head. "I just want my uncle back."

I put a hand on his shoulder as he cried. I knew far too well how he felt, but I also knew that was the last thing he wanted to hear. He sniffed and wiped his nose inside the neckline of his shirt.

"I'm gonna find him, Robby," I said. "I promise you that. I know I sound like a broken record, but keep an ear out for me, all right? I'm gonna need your help to see this through."

He nodded and sniffed. "Actually, I heard something that seemed interesting. Not sure if it's anything really, but hey, better than nothing, right?" He wiped his nose again and pulled out his Zippo. "Apparently you weren't the only reporter to hit up the winery last week. Buddy of mine said there was some lady up there last Monday asking for information about the long-lost heir to the Jones family's estate."

"Heir? But Albert doesn't have any kids."

"Exactly, which is why it stood out to me. Reporter lady was asking about something that happened back in the 80's, claimed she was there for some newspaper, can't remember the name of it. Something Post, or Something Times, but no one knew what she was talking about."

"Anything about her appearance? A name, anything?"

He shook his head. "Sorry, man. Nothing like that. He said she was hot, but obviously that's not much to go on. I didn't think to ask about that."

"Hm." It was something. Albert said someone was trying to steal his company. I had a feeling there was more to his story than he let on that morning. This could have something to do with it. "Thanks for letting me know, Robby. I'll look into it."

He forced a smile, but I could tell there was something he wasn't saying. "What?" I asked.

He looked at the floor, seemingly unsure whether to ask whatever was bothering him. "Were you serious about leaving Jonesboro after you solve this thing?"

"Completely," I said without hesitation. "This town's a shit show." I pushed open the door to the shop. "And I recommend you do the same thing."

I needed a drink.

The bell above the door jingled a brief welcome as I stepped into O'Callaghan's. Abby was already there, wiping down the bartop. All the stools were flipped onto the floor. She smiled and said hi as I walked in. I unenthusiastically raised a hand in greeting without saying anything as I made my way to the back room and unloaded my jacket onto the office couch.

She called through the doorway, "I stayed safe like you asked."

"Uh-huh," I said.

"That all you have to say?"

"Busy day."

"Doing what?"

I stepped back into the bar and stared at her.

"What?" she said.

"You really have no idea what's been going on today?"

She shook her head.

"Juliet Beauregard was murdered yesterday," I said. "This afternoon, the Mayor of Jonesboro held a local press conference where both Jack and Juliet were supposed to speak. I've been running around town like a goddamn lunatic trying to figure out who the hell could have killed both Jack *and* my prime suspect. I didn't have anything substantial by the time the press conference rolled around, so now the entire town's losing their shit because they're worried a murderer's loose in town."

I didn't realize it, but I had approached Abby as I spoke. I stood inches away from her, and she held her breath as she waited for me to finish. She took a couple steps back, exhaled, and said, "Bad day, huh?"

I grabbed a tumbler and a bottle of Jameson. "No shit."

"So," Abby said, putting her hands behind her back. "What are you going to do?"

I threw back the double of Jameson and started pouring myself another.

She watched me pour the whiskey before saying, "Things go all right with Molly?"

"Who the hell cares?"

"Why would you say that?"

I slammed the bottle back down on the counter. It shattered against the countertop and whiskey poured onto the floor, mingled with shards of glass. I paid it no mind.

"Because," I shouted, "while I'm wasting time trying to enjoy my life, other people are losing theirs. And there's a goddamn murderer somewhere in this God-forsaken town and I'm the only asshole with two brain cells who can figure out who it is without the entire thing shutting this town down for good, because apparently that fucking matters. And, as the cherry on top of this shit sundae, *now* every goddamn person in this goddamn town knows that I killed my brother and probably thinks I'm the one behind all this."

Something clicked. "I've only told two people in town about that," I said. "So which one of you two stabbed me in the back?"

Abby's eyes darkened. "Are you serious, Chris? Who do you think we are?" She stared back, unflinching.

She was right. I knew she and Lizzy wouldn't have said anything to anyone, but I didn't feel like admitting it. "Well," I said, "someone figured it out. And it's going to make my job one hell of a lot harder."

Abby's hands were shaking. She looked down at the floor and said, "Is there anything I can do to help?"

"No," I growled. I turned my gaze to the floor and watched as the drops of Jameson dripped off the counter, moisture drizzling off the roof after a storm. "You can't. You need to stay out of this. I'm going to figure this shit out myself. And as soon as I do, I'm getting the fuck out of here."

"What?"

"You heard me. I'm getting out of this hellhole as soon as this shit's sorted."

Abby's hands stopped shaking as she clenched them into fists. "So that's how it's gonna be? That's your plan? You're going to shut everybody out, refuse to let anyone help you? And then once all's said and done, you're just going to run away again?"

I looked up. Three pairs of eyes stared at me; she was wearing the owl earrings again.

"What did you say?" I asked.

"You had your mother, Chris," she said. "You had friends. You had a good life. And when Charlie died, you left it all behind." Tears escaped her eyes. Her voice was unsteady. "You came here. You started over. You escaped. You have new friends. You have a new family. People who care about you. And now that you have that, you're just going to run away and leave it all behind again? Is that what you're gonna do any time there's trouble? Is that what you want?"

I swallowed the Irish whiskey in my glass in one gulp.

Abby said, "Is that what *Charlie* would want?"

I threw the glass across the bar where it shattered against the wall near the front door. She flinched at the sound, but stared at me, awaiting a response. I stormed to the front of the bar and only paused when I grabbed the doorknob. I could hear Abby crying behind the counter as the words "I'm sorry" played at my lips. I snapped. I went too far.

But so did she.

I swallowed back the apology, yanked the door open, and slammed it shut behind me. The church bells rang 5:00.

THIRTY-SIX

Buzzing. So loud. It hurt.

I swiped my hand toward the alarm clock. Something toppled off the nightstand. Shit. I grabbed the open bottle before it could spill any more and forced myself into a sitting position with my toes in a puddle of scotch on the hardwood. My stomach shifted with every movement. My head pounded rhythmically. Probably because the alarm clock was still going off. I ripped its cord out of the wall.

Splashing cold water on my face didn't help. Neither did gulping it straight from the tap. It hurt to blink. I cranked the heat on the shower and let the bathroom fill with steam, the mirror fogging up completely. I rubbed a circle in the glass to get a good look at myself. And I thought I looked bad on Thursday. I stared at the face in the mirror, my pulse thumping behind my eyeballs, then scrawled "fuck you" in the fog of the glass underneath my face.

My stomach churned.

I stood on the front porch of the cabin fifteen minutes later. My head still hurt, but the fresh air helped. Robby's mysterious reporter seemed as good a lead as any. Could have been nothing, like everything else turned out to be, but it was all I had to go on. I pressed my fingers into my eyes. They were throbbing, nearly impossible to keep open.

Coffee.

I don't know which part of my brain I killed the previous night, but before I knew what I was doing, I found myself walking into Caroline's.

"Good morning—" Abby's cheerful customer service greeting was cut short when she saw me. "Oh," she said. "Hi, Chris."

I pinched the bridge of my nose as I approached the counter. I desperately needed coffee and didn't need to waste any more time. "Coffee," I said.

She looked at the floor. "Black Eye?"

I nodded, the motion shooting pain through my head.

She scurried off as I pulled out my wallet. I felt like I was moving in slow motion. She snapped a plastic lid onto the cup and slid it across the counter. "This one's on me," she said.

"You don't have to—"

"I want to."

There was an earnest look in her eyes. Like she ruined my make-believe game with the big kids and just wanted to be included again. I stuffed my wallet back in my pocket, grabbed the cup, and took a sip. It ran across my tongue, down my throat, bitter as all hell. Just what I needed.

"Thanks." I turned to leave.

"Chris." It was nearly a whisper. I almost didn't hear it. Her eyes welled up with tears. "I'm sorry."

"So am I," is what I wanted to say. But I didn't.

"I'm not gonna make it to work tonight," I said. "Hold down the fort for me, will you?"

I fired up the truck and looked at Abby through Caroline's storefront. She looked back at me. There was a pang in my stomach, and it wasn't from the hangover. I wanted to go back in. Apologize. But I had work to do.

I drove north toward the winery.

Albert Jones had five ex-wives and, to my knowledge, didn't have kids with any of them. But based on the stories I'd heard, I wouldn't have been surprised if the number of illegitimates he had out in the world was somewhere in the dozens. Piers could have played a part in keeping them quiet. But why would a scandal like this be coming up now? It seemed a little too convenient with the upcoming relaunch. More like a competitor's attempt at a smear campaign than anything.

Regardless, I still found myself wandering around the winery, asking everyone I ran into about this reporter from last week. The few people who had direct interactions with her all gave me different stories. She introduced herself by different names to different people, each one equally generic for a white American woman. The newspaper she claimed to work for was also different from person to person, and she didn't give anyone any contact info after speaking with them, not so much as a business card. All of this happened in the span of an hour.

The one consistent detail was the physical description: about 5'6," long brightly dyed red hair, late twenties to early thirties. The amalgamation of the rest of their descriptors told me she was young, pretty, and flirty. A younger guy at the winery said she was hot, an older woman said she was showing too much skin. I racked my brain for anyone in town even remotely fitting that description but drew a blank. Besides, someone from the winery would have recognized her if she was a local.

The reporter's presence was confusing at best, so I didn't think much of it. However, I was intrigued to see if there was any validity to Albert having a kid and keeping it secret. If something had set Piers off for whatever reason, this seemed like the most likely cause. It was surely a threat to Albert's reputation, though that still wouldn't explain why two of the winery's co-owners wound up dead. I figured talking to Clara was still my best bet when it came to any of this, so I drove back down to the Romeros' house. Clara and I eased ourselves into our usual seats as she set a glass of water on the table in front of me.

"Thanks for letting me pester you some more," I said. "I just want this whole thing to be resolved as quick as possible."

"Of course," she said. "Anything I can do to help. What were you wanting to know about?"

I set my notebook on my lap. "Based on conversations I've had with several people, it sounds like there were a couple speed bumps with the winery soon after Jack and Howard started working together. But no one seems to know what those issues were. You mentioned Jack always left work at work and did his best not to bother you with it, so you may not know either."

Clara's expression changed, though not to one of stress or anxiety. If anything, she seemed more troubled. Concerned.

"What makes things interesting," I said, tapping my notebook with my pen, "is that a woman showed up at the winery last week claiming to be a reporter, asking around town about the 'long-lost heir' to the Jones' estate. Said something happened in the 80's, back when Jack and Howard first took over. Normally I wouldn't pay attention to something like this, but two of the winery's owners are dead, Albert seems terrified that he's next, and I'm fresh out of leads."

A wry smile touched my lips as I said, "If it's just a competitor's attempt at a smear campaign, it's been very effective."

Clara took a few slow sips from a teacup and set it back on the coffee table. "I always had my suspicions something went wrong in those first few years. I never quite knew what, but I could tell it bothered Jack for years afterward. It wasn't until Robby was born that he really started to be okay again. We never had children of our own, but he loved that boy. Something about him gave him..." She looked up, smiling tearfully. "Hope, I suppose."

"What were your suspicions?"

Clara crossed one leg over and leaned against the arm of the sofa. "It was all around when Howard and Laura got divorced. That's when the rumors started."

I clicked my pen. "What kind of rumors?"

"Well, of course the rumors about Howard and Laura started to spread, but we both know Juliet was the cause of their separation. But even before that, the rumors about Albert's behavior really started getting around."

"You mentioned that yesterday. What kind of 'unruly behavior' are we talking?"

She eased off the arm of the couch and folded her hands in her lap. "Albert became very…lustful, I suppose you could say, after his parents' divorce. Within a few months, Albert had supposedly slept with most of the young women in town. Before long, it was impossible to know which claims were true and which had been completely made up as rumors kept spreading."

"But this started happening before his parents even got divorced?"

"Well no, they were divorced by that point, but that fact wasn't made public until a few months later."

I tapped my notebook. "Any idea how the rumors started?"

Clara picked at her fingernails. "If I remember right, it was big news at first. The newspaper caught wind when it first began, tried to make it some big scandal. Howard had Piers talk to the editor and there weren't any more stories printed about it. But soon after, the town was always abuzz with who Albert's new lady was. Some people even started saying that some of these girls slept with Albert…unwillingly, to put it nicely, though at that point it was impossible to determine fact from fiction. Piers tried to keep everything quiet as best he could, but it soon became too much even for him to contain."

Thing about rumors is that if there's any sort of truth to them in the first place, it all goes back to the source. "Did anyone ever find out where it originated from?" I asked. "A competitor in the industry maybe? One of Albert's ex-girlfriends?"

Clara thought for a moment. "I can't quite recall. The newspaper might have said something in one of those first articles, but I can't remember." She rested her head in her palm and said, "It really is a shame. Albert was such a sweet boy."

"He was?"

"Oh, he really was. He was incredibly kind. He loved his mother dearly. The divorce really affected him. He became a different person almost overnight." She sighed. "It wouldn't surprise me one bit if Albert really does have a child out there somewhere that Piers tried to keep secret."

Something wasn't adding up. If all of this had to do with Albert, it didn't make any sense why Jack and Juliet died. They were co-owners of the winery, but they didn't have anything to do with Albert's sexcapades, so it made zero sense why they were the first people to die. Unless…Clara said something bothered Jack for years. What if he and Juliet knew something they weren't supposed to?

I could tell there was something here, and this "long lost heir" could be the key to it all. I tucked my notebook away. "Thanks again, Clara. You've been a huge help."

"Of course, Chris," she said with a smile.

I peeked up the stairs. "Robby sleeping in today?"

"Oh, no, he was up early this morning. Said he needed to run some errands and stop by the pawn shop today, but he told me he'd come straight home as soon as he was done. Which reminds me, I have a question for you."

"Yes, ma'am?"

Clara frowned. "Robby told me about yesterday. Did you really mean what you said about leaving Jonesboro after all this?"

"Yes, ma'am."

Her frown deepened. "That's a shame."

"I'm sorry, Mrs. Romero," I said. "I know that Robby's been struggling with everything that's been happening, but I—"

"Oh, I'm not worried about Robby, Chris. Robby will be just fine." Her gray eyes stared deep into mine. "I'm worried about you."

THIRTY-SEVEN

What is there to be concerned about? I'm an adult, I can take care of myself. Why is Clara worried about me? I couldn't escape these thoughts as I locked the library doors behind me.

And why do I care so much?

Molly's eyes were glued to the computer screen.

"Hi," I said.

She jumped and pressed a hand to her chest. "Jesus, Chris, you scared me."

"Sorry." I leaned over the desk and peeked at her computer screen to find the surveillance videos still pulled up. "What are you doing?"

She rubbed her eyes. "Still trying to find these stupid keys that I've been looking for."

"Oh." I didn't realize she'd gone back to searching the footage since the press conference. I could tell she was exhausted. And it was my fault. "How's it going?"

She set her palms on the desk to brace herself. "I feel like my eyes are bleeding and my head's about to explode. It's surprising when I look up and things aren't in black and white. I've been staring at this monitor for hours."

"I'm sorry."

"No, it's fine, it's fine." She took a cleansing breath. "It's fine. How are things going on your end?"

"Haven't found anything quite yet, but I was hoping I could sift through some of Jonesboro's newspaper archives."

"Sure," Molly said, pointing to a far corner of the library. "Big filing cabinets, can't miss them."

"Perfect. And if it helps, I actually have something else for you to look for in those videos. Should be easier to find."

"Oh, dear God, yes." Molly leaned back and stretched her arms over her head. "What is it?"

"A woman. Young, late twenties to early thirties, long bright-red hair, not that the color matters in that footage. She was walking around the winery on Monday talking with a bunch of people, claiming to be a reporter for a newspaper."

Molly finished writing the new information on a sticky note and stuck it to her monitor with the others. "Yes," she said with a smile. "That'll be much easier to find."

"Thanks. I appreciate you." I scratched my head. "And hey, I'm sorry for how I acted yesterday. The stress just got to me, and—"

"Chris, it's okay. I get it. Just answer one thing for me, will you?"

"Sure."

She tapped her fingers on her desk a few times. "Are you really going to leave when all of this is done?"

I hesitated. My conversation with Clara was still bothering me.

You're going to run away again?

Abby's voice rang through my memory, and I noticed my teeth were gritted together. I unclenched my jaw and said, "Yes. After all this, I think I have to."

Molly frowned.

"Hey," I said, "let me know when you get hungry. I'll go grab some dinner for both of us. Have a feeling it'll be a long night."

I set off before Molly could say anything and jogged to the corner of the library she'd pointed to. Sure enough, dozens of metal filing cabinets were stacked against the wall. I pulled a random cabinet and found a collection of small boxes covered in a layer of dust.

Goddammit. Microfilm.

I hadn't used a microfilm reader since college. This really was going to be a long night. I slid the drawer back shut and sneezed. Molly shouted "Bless you" from the front desk, and I yelled a "Thank you" back.

Clara said Howard and Laura got a divorce Albert's senior year. 1988. I really hoped Clara had the year right. I grabbed a handful of microfilm reels and loaded them one at a time into the reader on the desk nearby. I assumed a big scandal involving the Jones family would be on the front page if it was anywhere, so I stole quick glances at each newspaper's headline, then quickly skimmed the rest of the paper before switching to the next reel.

I was somewhere in February of 1988 when *6.5.92*, the date from Jack's hidden fishing bobber, popped into my head. I pulled a couple reels from the drawer labeled "Jan-Jun. 1992." Something about the date was important to Jack. The headline for June 1's paper read, *Jonesboro High Graduates Hopeful for the Future.* The following week's paper on June 8 read, *Congratulations, Class of '92!* Two weeks in a row about the graduating class. Really grasping at straws, huh?

I quickly skimmed the papers. More than just the front page was about that year's graduating class. Each of the seniors' photos were printed in the paper with a little blurb on what they planned to do after graduating. A few of the kids had plans to go to college, others had grand aspirations of going to Hollywood or Broadway. After skimming most of the graduates' plans, one of them caught my eye. I zoomed in on the picture and refocused the lens.

Michael Wilson. He was a good-looking guy in his younger days. Looked pretty in shape from what I could tell. I read his post-graduation plans: "Someday, I hope to be the Sheriff of the Jonesboro Police Department." Well, you certainly did that, buddy. Probably didn't know how bad you'd suck at it. Under the section titled *Greatest Inspiration* was written, "My older sister, Jessica."

Reading it in black and white made it more real. It was a shame his sister died so young. Mike was only in his forties himself. If he was anything like me, I knew he missed her. I had a hard time dragging myself out of bed after Charlie died. I lost all sense of purpose, especially when my career, my dream that I had devoted my life to pursuing, ended with him dying by my own hands. I tucked the microfilm reel in the drawer and rolled back over to 1988. Maybe I'd been too hard on Wilson. I figured I'd talk to him next time I saw him. Apologize. Affirm that someone in the world understood how he felt. Never had that myself after Charlie died.

But right then, I had to find something. Any sort of motive for Piers to kill Jack and Juliet.

Paranoid, I checked over my shoulder. Still just me and the occasional clicks of Molly's computer at the front. I returned to the newspapers. Part of me hoped it was Piers who had been following me. That Piers was the person who killed Jack and Juliet. Because if it wasn't, then who the hell was it? Who else would have any reason to kill two of the winery's three owners?

Unless Albert was right, and someone really was trying to steal his company.

His long-lost heir.

At least if things didn't shake out with Piers, I had a solid lead to pursue.

Molly shouted something from the front desk. I walked to the front and sidled up next to her, the scent of her perfume stimulating my senses. "Find something?" I asked.

"Here," she said, pointing at the screen. A figure moved across the winery's main foyer. It was a woman, wearing a white tee shirt with a low-cut V-neck, and carrying a manila envelope. Though the video was in black-and-white, her long hair was a bold shade of gray on the monitor. She was talking to a group of male employees who were on their way to the production floor. Molly paused the video and said, "That your girl?"

"Looks like it," I said. "Keep it rolling for me." Molly pressed play. The woman talked to the group of guys, occasionally scribbling things in a small notebook she was carrying, similar to the kind I used. She then walked out of frame into the tasting room. There was something familiar about her.

"Think you can track her movements now that you've found her?" I asked. "Get a better angle?"

Molly spun in her chair. "Not on an empty stomach."

THIRTY-EIGHT

I walked into Mickey's Pizza a few minutes later, the bell above the door jingling to greet me. The restaurant was surprisingly empty, except for a small group of teenage girls sitting in the far corner, laughing and shouting together.

"Hey, Amanda."

"Oh, hey, CJ," she said hesitantly as she pulled on a pair of gloves.

"Everything okay?"

"Yeah, totally fine."

"Doesn't seem fine."

She shook her head, knocking a strand of purple hair in front of her eyes. "Sorry," she said. "I was there for that press conference yesterday." She brushed her hair out of her eyes and looked at me. "Is it true?"

I swallowed. "Yeah. It is."

Her forehead creased in thought. "I know you pretty well, CJ. I know you're not a bad guy. I'm sure that whatever happened with your brother, there was a good reason for it." She forced a smile. "I still believe in you. And I know you can figure this out."

"Uhh," I said. "Thanks. That's...thank you."

She smiled again, this time more genuine. "The usual?"

I gave her my order and she turned to make it. Amanda's reaction was far from the one I expected, but it gave me a brief sense of relief I didn't know I needed. That relief vanished the second I felt a tap on my shoulder and turned to find Lizzy behind me.

"Hi, CJ," she said.

"Hey, Lizzy." I tried my best to steady myself. Keep it casual. "How's it going?"

She glanced back toward the booth in the corner and said, "Oh, you know, good. Just hanging out with some friends."

"Nice. Glad you've made some friends in town."

"Uh-huh." Lizzy had a blank stare. Amanda set two sweet teas on the counter next to me. I grabbed them, sat at a table, and gestured for Lizzy to sit across from me. She was quiet, looking off into the middle distance.

I felt obligated to ask, "Something on your mind?"

"Well," Lizzy started tentatively. "Abs just seemed really upset about something this morning, but she won't tell me what's going on." She finally looked at me. "Do you know what's going on?"

I wedged a straw into one of my cups and said, "Look, Liz, I just don't know if I—"

"Nobody touched her, did they?" she asked.

I shook my head. "You know I wouldn't let that happen."

Elizabeth crossed her arms and frowned. "And you don't know what's going on?"

I took a big gulp of my tea and sighed. "Last night I told Abby I'm leaving Jonesboro once this case I'm working is sorted."

"What? You're going to leave?"

"I am. Your sister didn't take that news well. And then she crossed a line." I sucked on my straw. "Sprinted across it, if you ask me." Didn't feel like mentioning the part where I crossed a line, too.

Elizabeth sat quietly, staring off to the side with her legs crossed, kicking her dangling foot in the air. Eventually she said, "You're not just some friend to her, you know."

I sipped my tea.

She looked at me. "Abby speaks out of turn sometimes. I know, I'm her sister. But she doesn't do that with just anybody. When she feels strongly about something, she says it. She doesn't hold back. And what I've realized is that when she does that, even if I hate it and it makes me angry, she always says what I need to hear."

My cup rattled as I sucked the rest of my tea out of it.

"You're not just some friend," Lizzy said, and stood from her chair. "She trusts you. She looks up to you. You're like a brother to her. To both of us. Family." Lizzy turned to walk back to her friends and said, "Thought you saw us the same way."

She sat with her friends in the booth, facing away from me. I stared at the back of Lizzy's head until Amanda set a pizza box on the counter. I got a refill of sweet tea, grabbed the box, and drove back to the library, radio static the only sound filling the emptiness of my truck.

The pizza box was almost empty, grease pooling in the craters of the remaining cold slices. I was in June of 1988, about to finish the first drawer of reels. The only sound in the empty library was the occasional click from Molly's mouse. I checked the time. It was nearly 4:00 a.m. I slapped my face a few times to wake myself up. I couldn't believe how late it was. Or early, I guess. But I could believe the time more easily than I could believe that someone—anyone—would ever think of me as a brother again. And not only that, but that they would *choose* to do so.

I blinked a few times and looked at the next reel, the light of the reader's monitor making my head throb. *Monday, June 20, 1988: Local Business Booming Thanks to Jack Romero.* Nope. *Monday, June 27, 1988: Local Man Grows Prize Daisies.* Not what I need. Next drawer. *Tuesday, July 5, 1988: Independence Day Bigger Than Ever.* Guess that week's paper came on Tuesday since that Monday was the 4th. *Monday, July 11, 1988: Vaccines - Do We Need Them?* Yes. Yes, you do. *Monday, July 18, 1988...*

I stared at the box in my hand.

Empty.

I turned the box over and shook it, as if that would jostle the microfilm reel out of the empty box. I stumbled over to the drawer and gave each small cardboard box a quick shake. Every single microfilm reel was in its box in the drawer, except for one: July 18, 1988.

Then the real question became: where did it go?

I heard Molly's voice from the front desk, so I jogged up. She nearly knocked her empty coffee mug over as she swiveled her chair toward me. She rubbed her eyes. "None of the angles are great by any means," she said. "But I found what seems to be the best one."

Her monitor still flickered black and white, paused on a video from a familiar setting: the office hallway. The reporter was walking past the camera near the end of the hall, headed out of Albert's office toward the observation deck. I squinted at the black-and-white pixels. The video quality wasn't great. Still couldn't get a great look at her face. "Think we can go back a little bit?" I asked. "This looks like our best bet, maybe there's just another frame that could be more helpful."

Molly rewound the video a few minutes to when the woman first walked into the hallway and pressed play. I watched as she walked into frame carrying her manila envelope, knocked on Albert's door, poked her head in, and walked into the office before shutting the door behind her. Molly then clicked a button and had the video play at double speed. Several minutes passed in the video. Molly set the video back to normal speed as the woman walked back out of the office and down the hallway, envelope missing from her hands. After she left, Juliet popped out of her office and went into Albert's office, and the door shut once again. Never stood next to anyone we knew for a height comparison, no clear view of her face. But I felt like I saw something else important.

"Wait," I said. "Go back a few minutes. Somewhere in the middle, after she went into the office." Molly dragged the cursor back a few minutes and I leaned toward the screen against the back of her chair. Juliet walked into her office. A few seconds passed, then she reappeared in the doorway, looked at Albert's office door, and scratched her head. She stepped back into her office, leaving the door open so we could see her movements. She lifted folders, shifted papers around, moved everything on her desk.

"She's looking for something," Molly said.

"Exactly," I said. "Go to the start of the day, play it double speed."

Molly started the video over and pressed play. The little movement that happened on the screen was easy to interpret, even at twice the speed. The lights flicked on as Paul moved into frame and then back out. Juliet entered her office unaccompanied, then walked out of her office and out of frame. The hallway was then empty for several minutes until Albert Jones, followed by Piers, approached his office. There was a quick flash of movement, and then they moved into the office. I blinked hard, thinking I imagined it.

"Stop," I said. "Go back to when Albert and Piers first get there."

Molly rewound the video again. Albert and Piers walked to the door of Albert's office, in the middle of a conversation. They stopped in front of the door and Albert patted his pockets. Then Piers went into Juliet's office. He returned to the hallway and unlocked the door, a familiar large keychain dangling from his hand. They entered the office.

"Juliet's keys," Molly whispered.

I couldn't believe it. The case had reached the most cliché possible conclusion.

The butler did it.

THIRTY-NINE

"Piers is behind all this?" Ralston whispered, gun drawn behind me.

I finagled around in the mansion's deadbolt with tools from my lockpick set. "Yes," I said. "He was the last person to have Juliet's keys, the ones I found in the ditch where Jack was left."

"Why do we have to be up here so early? And why are you picking the lock?"

"To catch him by surprise. I don't know what this guy's background is for sure, but he might be former MI6 or something. We want him as off-guard as possible."

Not to mention he'd been threatening me and the people I cared about. The sooner he was behind bars, the better. "I would have had you and Wilson come earlier, but the front gates of the winery don't open until 6:00. I'm just glad I was able to hop the mansion fence and open that gate easily enough from the inside."

A car pulled up behind us and Wilson stepped out.

"Nice of you to join us," I whispered over my shoulder.

"What's going on?" Wilson asked.

"Piers is our guy. Just have your gun ready and we'll arrest him as soon as we find him." The lock clicked. I looked back at the officers and said, "Ready?"

Ralston nodded, his finger braced on the trigger of his Glock. Wilson fumbled around on his belt before finally getting his own gun ready.

I pulled my own pistol from the back of my jeans. My hand was shaking. I swallowed, tightened my grip, and pushed open the front door. An alarm started sounding. Fortunately, it called the Jonesboro Police Department, and the entire police force was already here.

"Spread out!" I shouted, running toward a doorway on the right. Ralston hurried up the stairs while Wilson took the hallway on the left. A long hall stretched in front of me, doors lining either side of the hall. I stepped lightly down the hallway, gun ready. Not sure why I was so cautious when there was an alarm blaring in our ears. Old habits die hard, I guess. I cracked open door after door and found small, empty rooms. Servants' quarters in the past. Guess I was in the right area. Light filtered underneath a doorway at the end of the hall.

I pressed my back against the wall next to the door and gripped the doorknob. This was it.

I twisted the knob and spun through the doorway.

"Police! Put your hands—"

Piers Clarke laid in the middle of a four-poster bed, eyes open, staring at the ceiling, a single dark hole in the center of his forehead. Next to him stood Albert, wrapped in his bathrobe, a look of shock on his face, a Glock 22 gripped in his hand.

The alarm continued blaring.

FORTY

I placed the cardboard box on the table and sat across from Albert. His hands were cuffed through the bar on the metal tabletop. Wilson was gracious enough to let him get dressed before we brought him in. He had thrown on a pair of jeans and a polo shirt. He tapped his foot against the floor in frustration as I sat down. He'd refused to speak to me without his lawyer, a guy he referred to as "Jim," who sat uncomfortably in a chair next to him. I wasn't in a rush. Waiting for Jim to show up gave Catherine some time to verify a few things for me.

"Do you want to start?" I asked. "Or do you want me to?"

"Go fuck yourself," he said.

Jim rubbed his eyes. "Al. Jesus."

"Guess I'll start, then." I said. I pulled a plastic bag holding a Glock 22 out of the box of evidence. "This yours?"

He opened his mouth, but Jim put a hand on his shoulder. He scowled at me instead.

"I only ask because Ms. Sinclair was able to verify it was the weapon used to kill Piers. And, you know." I set the gun back in the box. "You were the one holding it."

"Fuck you," he shouted, trying to stand up. The cuffs jerked him back downward. He winced and sat down as Jim eased him back into his chair. Through strained breaths he said, "I didn't kill Piers."

"Oh, really?" I asked. "Then who do you propose did?"

He wound up to shout something, but Jim pulled him close and whispered in his ear. Lawyers had a habit of spoiling the fun. It didn't matter what Albert said. The gun was registered in his name. After running the rifling marks on the bullet from Piers' body, Catherine was able to match them up with the bullets that killed both Jack and Juliet as well. And to top it all off, Albert's alarm started going off the second we came in. While we didn't find anyone else in the house when we searched it, no one else could have been there anyway.

Jim sat back in his chair. Al took a deep breath and said, "I didn't shoot him."

"Then why were you holding the gun, Al?"

"I—" He stood aggressively, stopped before hurting himself again, then eased back into his chair. Jim rubbed his eyes. Al took another deep breath and said, "I came downstairs for breakfast, but Piers wasn't in the kitchen. I went to his room. When I got there, he was…like that. I walked to the side of his bed and kicked something on the rug, so I picked it up."

A half-hearted laugh escaped my lungs. "Are you trying to tell me you didn't shoot the gun? You just found it on the floor and picked it up?"

"I didn't do it," Albert growled.

"Whatever you say, Al. Let's move on, shall we?" I pulled out my notebook and flipped back through my notes. "Where were you last Tuesday morning between, say, 9 and 11 a.m.?"

"At home, in bed, sick as a dog."

"Really?" I pulled out another plastic bag, this one with Juliet's keys inside. "These keys were found in Jack Romero's boat, where I determined to be the scene of Jack's murder. And the last time these keys were seen, Piers was carrying them into your office Monday morning."

"They went missing pretty soon after that," he said. "Juliet came into my office looking for them and we couldn't find them anywhere. This is the first time I've seen them since then."

"Likely story."

"I didn't kill Jack," he said. "I was in bed, having a goddamn panic attack after that reporter came in."

"It's a panic attack now, huh? Any way you can verify that for me?"

He grinned. "Of course, just ask—" His smile faded.

"Who? Piers? Yeah, he refused our request for an interview."

Albert glared at me. Jim shifted uncomfortably in his chair.

"How about last Saturday night into Sunday morning when Juliet was murdered?"

"I told you, I was—"

"Sick? Still having a panic attack?"

"I didn't kill anyone," Albert said.

"Al," I cooed with a smile. "I think we both know you did. Three people, actually."

"Why?" he said.

"Albert," Jim interrupted, putting a hand on his shoulder. "I really think you should—"

"Fuck off, Jim." Al did his best to swat Jim's hand away and looked back at me. "Tell me why, CJ. Why would I kill three people who worked for me?"

"Why?" I slapped an open palm on the table. "Why? Because thirty years ago, you fucked up. And last week a reporter showed up, threatening to reveal your big mistake before the grand re-opening of your business, threatening your family's legacy. And with Jonesboro in the state it's in right now, that could have completely doomed you and the entire town."

Albert stared. "What are you talking about?"

"Al," Jim muttered.

"Oh, I think you know full well what I'm talking about." I reached into the box and pulled out two more pieces of evidence. One, a manila envelope. The other, the missing microfilm reel from the library. I pulled a stapled packet from inside the envelope and set it on the table. It was a printout of a Jonesboro newspaper dated July 18, 1988. The headline read, *Trouble in Paradise: The Jones Family's Pregnancy Scare.*

Albert scowled at the newspaper and said, "What is this?"

"A perfect example of the garbage that passes for news in this town." I leaned back in my chair. "This envelope was found in your office. Reporter dropped it off for you when she stopped by. The microfilm reel was missing from the library. Little bird told me that Piers was seen at the library last week. I'm assuming he was picking this up for you?"

"Don't answer that," Jim said.

"So what if he was?" Albert sat back in his chair. Jim groaned. Albert ignored him and asked, "What are you implying?"

"This article really helped me connect some dots." I picked up the article and looked over it. "Says here that a young woman, a girl from your graduating class, showed up at the winery and interrupted a meeting with Jack, Juliet, and your dad. Started claiming that you got her pregnant. When the paper asked your dad for comment, he said, 'It's all a lie. Just another girl screaming for attention.'" I looked at Albert over the article.

"And?" he said. "Sounds like it was just another girl screaming for attention."

"Well," I said, looking back at the article, "not only is that misogynistic bullshit, but let's keep reading. Looks like Jack and Juliet were also asked for comment. Jack said, 'It isn't true. She's making it up.' Juliet said, 'Of course it's not true.'" I set the article down and looked at Albert again. "Maybe it's just me, but does that sound a little scripted to you?"

"*Please* don't answer that," Jim said.

Albert shrugged. "Sounds like people trying to defend me."

"But things didn't stop there, as you know," I said. "Over the next few months, countless other girls started claiming you'd slept with them. Most of the town, from what I've heard. Surely you must have gotten at least one of them pregnant with those odds."

"Those were all just rumors. And so what if I did get someone pregnant?" Albert said with a shrug. "Doesn't seem like that big of a deal to me."

"Oh, I agree. At least, I would." I pulled a plastic bag holding a small vial out of the box. "Rohypnol. Roofies."

Albert snorted. "That isn't mine."

"You sure? This bottle was found in your room, covered with your fingerprints." I lifted the bag and dangled the bottle in the air. "You really just keep this shit lying around? Waiting for a pretty girl to come along?"

Albert looked shocked. "You think I—just how big of an asshole do you think I am?"

I tossed the baggie back in the box and leaned forward. "Big enough of an asshole that this girl who busted in on your dad's meeting thirty years ago told them you raped her. Big enough of an asshole that the winery's Big Three—your dad, Jack Romero, and Juliet Beauregard—all felt the need to cover up your mistake to keep their then-struggling business afloat. I think you're big enough of an asshole that when a plucky reporter showed up digging this up from your past, you'd be willing to kill the people who still knew your secret: Jack, Juliet, and now Piers. I think you're big enough of an asshole that, once all was said and done, you would do anything to keep your business, your family's legacy, alive. And if that didn't work out, that you'd sell the entire thing as the sole living owner and skip town when things went south."

Albert sank back in his chair. Jim wiped his hands down his face.

"Well?" I asked, sliding the article toward him. "You want to tell me the truth yet?"

"The truth?" Albert looked down at the paper.

"Well," Jim said, and slapped his hands on his knees. "I think that's enough for today. Now, Al, if we could just—"

"Jim," Albert said, "if you don't shut the *fuck* up, I swear to God." Albert looked me in the eye. "That paper is the furthest thing from the truth. I never got anyone pregnant." He looked at the floor and grumbled something.

"What was that?" I asked.

"I said I couldn't have if I tried."

I cocked my head to the side. "And why is that?"

"Al," Jim said, "I really don't think—"

"No, you know what, Jim?" Albert looked at Jim and jabbed a finger toward him. "Fuck you. Fuck what you think, I think it's high time everyone knew the goddamn truth."

"Albert," Jim said, "this is not the right time—"

"What's the truth, Al?" I interrupted.

Al turned to me and roared, "I'm fucking sterile, you asshole!"

The lights above me buzzed. Sweat beaded on Albert's forehead, and he breathed heavily. Jim buried his face in his palm. Eventually I said, "What?" It was all I could manage to get out.

"You heard me." Albert slumped against the back of his chair and took several deep breaths. "Now you know the Jones family's real secret. You think I haven't tried to have kids? You think I *want* my family's legacy to die with me? You think that's been my goddamn plan the whole time?" He glared at me and said, "Think again."

I sat in silence, processing. The entire story was a lie? There was no pregnant girl in 1988? The light above me continued buzzing. I placed everything back in the box and said, "Well, Al, long lost heir or not, the evidence is still damning. Maybe it really was just to get full control of the company. I don't really care anymore. Sheriff Wilson and Officer Ralston will continue building the case against you."

"What, you won't be?" Albert scoffed.

I shook my head and said, "Nope." I picked up the box. "I finally got you, so I'm packing my bags and getting the hell out of here while I still can."

Albert screamed profanities after me as I walked out, calling me a coward, swearing that he didn't do it and that I was making a mistake. I set the box on the table in the briefing room and rubbed my eyes. I only realized then that I hadn't slept at all that night. It was almost 9:00 a.m. Wilson and Ralston stood side-by-side, watching Albert thrash in the interrogation room as Jim tried in vain to settle him down.

"He seems pretty adamant he didn't do it," Ralston said.

"Of course," Wilson said. "Why would he admit to committing three murders?"

"I don't know," Ralston said, scratching his shoulder. "He just seems so...stubborn."

"Al's always been stubborn," I said. "He'll never admit it. He'll deny it until the day he dies."

"If you say so, Harris," Ralston said. He rubbed his eyes.

Wilson put a hand on his shoulder. "You've been doing good work, Ralston. Go ahead and head home for the day, you deserve it. The town's safe again. I'll keep an eye on this one."

"Yessir," Ralston said, and left the room. Wilson and I watched in silence until Albert finally stopped writhing in his cuffs and laid his head on the table. Jim spoke to him softly, but it didn't look like Albert was listening.

"Thanks for the help, Harris," Wilson said. "I'm glad we finally got him."

"Of course. Glad I could help." I couldn't believe it was finally over. I also had no idea what would happen if something like this ever happened in this town again. If only Wilson could be the cop he supposedly used to be.

"Hey," I said. I honestly didn't even know how I was going to approach it, but I said, "I heard about your sister."

"Oh." Wilson's shoulders slumped and he looked at the floor. "You did, did you?"

"I get it," I said. "I know what it's like when a sibling dies. My brother died three years ago. That's actually why I ended up out here. I'm still not over it."

Wilson kicked at the floor. "I was at her deathbed when it happened. It was the first time I had seen her in, what, twenty years?"

"Yeah?"

"Yeah." He looked through the one-way glass at Albert and Jim. "Last time I saw her she came to town for my graduation. She'd left for college four years earlier. I hadn't seen her that whole time. Thought it was so long." He chuckled sadly. "I was so happy she came home. Then she left a couple days later. Didn't see her again until she died. Hardly heard from her before that. It was hard." He looked at me. "She was tired, you know? Worn out. Sad that was my last memory of her."

"Well, hey." I put a hand on his shoulder. "Hopefully we'll both move past it someday." He smiled and nodded. I reached up in the air to stretch. "I'm gonna poke around a little more, try and help you get a couple more things on him before I leave." Wilson nodded. I grabbed the reporter's envelope and the microfilm reel and left him in the briefing room.

FORTY-ONE

When I walked up the stairs into the office space of the precinct, Catherine was filling a box with things from her desk: pens, notebooks, everything. She looked concerned.

"Moving desks?" I asked.

"What?" She looked up at me suddenly. "Oh, CJ. No, I'm…" She put a purple stapler and a pack of purple staples inside the box. "I just set my resignation on the sheriff's desk."

"Yeah? You getting out of here?"

"I think I have to. I mean, three murders in one week? I came out here to get away from the violence I saw in the city. Clearly I came to the wrong place." She chuckled nervously. "I know that I'm a forensic scientist and all. I love my job, but not that much. It's hard, you know? They were people. They had families, people who loved them. Especially in a place like this. I only knew them in passing, so I can't imagine how everyone here must feel."

"I get it," I said. "I knew Jack well, so I definitely get it. I think you have the right idea. I'm getting out of Jonesboro myself."

She smiled, the beauty mark on her left side traveling ever so slightly. "Good for you. I hope you end up where you need to be."

I smiled back and said, "You, too."

Dark clouds had started to gather, and rain began drizzling from the skies as I walked to my truck. Wasn't common in the Cascade Rain Shadow, but always appreciated when it did. My jacket was still in the back office at the bar. Figured I might as well go grab it before it really started coming down.

I felt like I was floating. I had to tell someone I finally caught the perp. I grabbed my phone from the passenger seat and opened my contacts, leaving it highlighted on the first name. Abby. I hovered over the call button, then stopped myself.

You're going to run away again?

I tossed my phone into the passenger seat and drove south to O'Callaghan's. Something was bothering me. Did it have to do with the case? Or something with my interaction with Catherine? Something seemed off, but I was exhausted and couldn't think straight, so I shrugged it off. I parked in front of O'Callaghan's and walked to the front door. Unlocked.

I hesitated. I didn't know if I wanted to talk to him right then, but I needed my jacket. I stepped inside. Mick sat hunched over a beer. A soft jazz piano ballad played in the background of the bar. "Christopher," he said, without turning around. His tone was cold.

"Mick," I said. "A little early, isn't it?"

He sipped his beer. "I could ask you the same thing."

"Just grabbing something." I walked into the back room, picked up my jacket, and came back. Mick didn't look up from his beer.

"So," he said. "Did you solve it?"

"Yep," I said. I worked my arms into the sleeves of my jacket. "Case is solved. Albert Jones is in custody. Sheriff will take it from here."

"Hm," he said, and sipped his beer again. "So that's it, then?"

"What do you mean?"

"You're leaving now, aren't you?"

I swallowed. "Yeah, Mick. I am."

He finally looked up. His eyes were dark. Sad. "When were you gonna tell me?"

I leaned against the back counter. "I mean, now seems as good a time as any, I guess."

The bell above the front door jingled and a man stepped inside. He had a ruddy face with a mat of gray hair. "Um," he said, "excuse me, I'm looking for Abigail. I was told she'd be here?"

"What?" I said. "Buddy, can't you read the sign? We're closed. She'll be here when we open later."

The man coughed and grumbled something, then stepped back out of the bar.

Mick glanced over his shoulder. "Who was that?"

"I don't know. Never seen him before."

Mick looked back down at his Guinness. The piano player over the speakers finished his solo and passed it over to the bass player. Mick said, "Well. Good luck, then." He sipped from his glass.

I waited for him to say something else. But he didn't.

"Is that it?" I asked.

"Is what it?"

"Is that all you're going to say? Good luck?"

Mick squeezed his glass. "I don't know what else you want me to say, Christopher." He chugged the rest of the beer, then slammed the pint glass on the counter. "Sounds like your mind's made up. I'm not your fuckin' father." He left the bar.

I was left alone in O'Callaghan's, a jazz trio softly playing in the background.

———

I flipped on the light. Albert had more collector cars in the garage than I imagined. The garage was its own building on the Jones' property, lined from end to end with cars. Each one was worth more than I made in a year, and the models spanned several decades. Most were American, though there were several exotic cars as well.

Albert didn't have an "everyday" car. All the vehicles he owned sat in this garage. A few times a week, you could hear the low rumble in the distance as he approached town at high speeds, eventually turning into a roar as he slowly cruised down Main Street, flaunting whatever he happened to be driving that day. I'm sure he did the exact same thing when he was younger.

The rain pattered lightly on the roof as I walked the line of shiny cars. One of these had to be leaking. I stooped low, scanning the floor under each of them. I made it down an entire line without even a single drop of oil on the floor. I stood up straight and stretched my aching back. As I scanned the other line of cars, one of them caught my eye.

I set my hand on the hood of the white '62 Thunderbird. Dad's car. I remembered my little joyride that weekend with my friends, how they all took their shoes off and held them in their laps to keep it clean. How we ordered fast food and didn't even pull a French fry out of the bag while we sat in Dad's Thunderbird, just like this one.

I wanted to key it. Smash the headlights. Tear up the seats. Try to set it on fire or something. Make up for what I didn't do when I was a teenager.

I sighed and crouched to look under the Thunderbird and the rest of the cars along the line. Still not a drop of oil on the ground. All the cars in the garage were well-maintained. Piers did good work. That didn't necessarily mean that Albert didn't have some other car lying around somewhere that he used to commit his crimes. In fact, when I thought about it, he had to. Any of these cars would have stood out driving along the lakeside path or parked next to the "Welcome to Jonesboro" sign. So there had to be another car somewhere else.

There just had to be.

FORTY-TWO

I woke with a start as the light outside was beginning to fade. I checked the time. Just after 5:00. I would have napped longer if the nightmare hadn't woken me up, but I figured an earlier start couldn't hurt. It hadn't taken long to pack my things and get ready to leave. I only brought so much with me when I first came to Jonesboro, so I was able to fit everything in my suitcase. With the front door locked behind me and the key under the welcome mat, I jumped in my truck. I looked at the house as I sat with my hands on the steering wheel. I'd spent three years by myself in that house, doing my best to escape everything I left behind.

You're just going to run away again?

I turned the key in the ignition. "Good riddance," I said. The storm clouds were getting angry as I pulled away from the cabin and headed south on Main Street, with small flashes of lightning in the distance as rain started to pour. I called Robby.

"Hello?"

"Hey, Robby. Everything okay?"

"Yeah man, we're all right. What's up?"

"Just wanted to let you know I got him. Albert was behind everything. We have him behind bars."

"Wait, really?"

"Yeah, really. It's over. Everyone's safe now."

"What about that whole heir to the Jones estate thing?"

"All a lie," I said. "Albert couldn't even have kids. Someone made it up back in 1988. You could probably even figure out who it was if you read through that journal we found."

"Huh," Robby said. The phone crackled in my ears for a few seconds. "Seej?"

"Yeah?"

"Does this mean you're leaving?"

The phone crackled once more. I looked in the rearview mirror at my suitcase in the back seat. "Yeah. I'm leaving. Right now, actually."

Crackle.

"Fine," Robby said. "Real cool of you."

The line went dead. I looked at the phone like it bit me.

Real cool of you.

I tossed the phone into the passenger seat where the microfilm and manila envelope were sitting. I still had one stop to make on the way out.

I knocked on Molly's door and bounced back and forth on my feet. I wasn't looking forward to this. She opened the door.

"Hi," she said. She was wearing sweatpants and a tank top.

"Hi. Well." I paused, thinking of how to phrase it. "Well, case is solved."

"It is?"

"Yep."

"Really?"

"Mmhm."

"You got Piers?"

"Nope. Piers is dead."

"Wait, what? How did that happen?"

"Albert Jones killed him, believe it or not."

She cocked her head to the side. "Albert? What was his motive?"

"Family secrets getting out, something like that. The details are still a bit fuzzy, but I'll let Wilson figure that out."

"How do you know he did it?"

"He was holding his gun when I arrived on the scene. Same gun used for the other murders, so he was behind all of them. Plus, the keys linked him to Jack's murder scene. His house was locked and the alarm was still set, so he's the only one who could have killed Piers."

"All the loose ends are tied up, then?"

"Yep."

She raised an eyebrow.

"Well," I said, "not all of them. There are still a couple things that don't add up quite yet. I figured Wilson and Ralston should be able to figure it all out now that they have their perp."

"And what if they don't?" Her eyes searched mine. She was looking for an answer to a question she wasn't asking.

"Well," I said, "that's not my problem anymore." I handed her the missing microfilm reel and the manila envelope. She looked at them before setting them on a table inside.

She leaned against the doorframe. "You're still leaving, then."

I nodded.

"Did you tell Mick?"

"Bumped into him earlier. He didn't have much to say about it."

"What about Robby?"

"Called him on the way here."

"And Abby?"

I clenched my jaw. I'd had a pit in my stomach all day and it got deeper when I heard her name. Molly waited for an answer. I said, "She'll be fine."

"So that's it, then?" she asked. "You have a perp, so you're just going to leave without saying good-bye to everyone?"

"What do you think I'm doing right now?"

"I'm glad I made the cut, but I'm just one person. And while I appreciate it, I'm still not happy about it. I can't imagine how the rest of them will feel when you're not here tomorrow."

A breeze kicked up. The sun finished setting in the west. Lightning flashed across the sky, thunder crackling in the distance.

"Good-bye, Molly," I said. "It was good to see you. I'll call you tomorrow. Maybe I'll come visit sometime." I started crossing the balcony.

"Chris," she called from her doorway.

I stopped.

"What if Albert's innocent?"

The church bells chimed 6:00. I walked to my truck.

"Thank You For Visiting Jonesboro! We Hope You Enjoyed Your Stay!"

I sped past the sign and continued south. Good-bye, Jonesboro. I certainly didn't enjoy my stay. Rain poured and lightning lit up the sky, flashes mere seconds apart from each other. I flicked on the windshield wipers.

When I thought about it, I really did enjoy my stay in Jonesboro until those last few days. I remembered long nights spent listening to Jack's drunken ramblings. Saturday afternoons fishing on the lake with Robby. Conversations with Pastor Greene about philosophy, religion, the meaning of life. My one date with Molly. The sweet tea at Mickey's Pizza. Bouncing quarters into a shot glass with Abby and discovering my favorite color was apparently wrong.

I tried to forget that last memory. But no matter how hard I tried, it kept coming back.

As I continued down the winding road away from Jonesboro, several questions clawed for my attention. If Albert never had a child—if the whole thing was a lie—why did Jack and Juliet have to die? What role did Jack play in the whole thing? Why did the rumors about Al even spread like that? What happened on June 5, 1992? Why did Juliet park by the welcome sign?

Did Albert really do all of this just to give himself complete control over the company? But if that were the case, why did he kill Piers?

Chris, what if Albert's innocent?

I pressed the gas pedal. "Not my problem anymore."

She just wanted me to stay.

My phone buzzed in the passenger seat. Abby. I hovered over the button to decline the call. I wasn't ever going to see her again. I felt like I at least owed it to her to say good-bye. But that didn't mean I had to be nice about it.

"Hello?"

"CJ?"

"Lizzy?" I could hear shouting in the background. "What's going on?"

"Thank God, Abby told me to call you as soon as she got here. It's my dad. He found us somehow, he showed up at the bar—"

That guy who came into O'Callaghan's earlier.

"—I don't know how, there must have been something in that picture of the library books I posted. She came home as fast as she could, but now he's here and—" There was a loud thump on her end. "Oh my God."

The line went dead.

"Lizzy? Lizzy! Goddammit." I threw the phone down. My tires spun wildly before finally finding purchase on the wet asphalt.

"Welcome to Jonesboro!"

I hardly had time to read the sign as I sped back into town.

I pulled up a few doors down from the Smiths' house. There was a black Jeep Wrangler in front, parked at an angle with one wheel on the curb. Lightning illuminated the street, white light intermittently flooding the strip of condos. There was a man ramming his shoulder against their door, shouting, completely soaked by the rain.

"Abigail Muenzinger, open this goddamn door right now, you ungrateful little bitch!"

I pulled my Glock from its holster on my seat and threw open the door, slipping the gun in the back of my jeans before slamming the door shut. The man's shoulder pounded rhythmically against the door, accentuated by sporadic thunderclaps.

"Hey, asshole!"

He would have heard me if it hadn't been for the thunder. He continued pounding against the door as I approached. I still wasn't happy with what Abby said. I wasn't running away. My time in Jonesboro had come to an end. I solved the case, and everything worked out the way it was meant to. But this guy was here because of me. And he made a huge mistake. No one fucks with my—

I stopped mid-stride in the grass.

No one fucks with my...

Lightning flashed as the lock on the door gave way and the man charged into the house. A scream rang out under the rolling thunder, shaking me from my epiphany. I sprinted the remaining distance to the front door, rain pounding through my jacket and cooling my skin.

Abby was wedged in the corner of their front room, raising her hands in defense as the man sent swing after haphazard swing toward her.

"Hey!" I shouted. The man turned around, gray hair plastered to the forehead of his ruddy face. Lightning flashed behind me. "You stay away from her."

He scoffed, "Who the hell do you think you are? She's my goddamn daughter, you're just—"

I punched him in the jaw. His head spun and he went straight to the floor.

"She is her own person," I said. "And you're just a drunk piece of shit." I grabbed him under the shoulder, yanked him to his feet, and threw him out the front door into the rain. "Now get the hell out of here. And I swear to God if I see you here again, I'll bring you in myself and make sure you never get out."

Abby's father stumbled to his feet in the mud and said, "Bring me in? Who do you think you—"

With one fluid movement, I whipped the gun from behind me and trained it on the center of his chest. He stopped, mouth hanging open, rain dripping from his face. Then he spit on the ground by my feet and backed away from the house to his Jeep, slipping once or twice in the mud on the way. He started the car and drove off.

I tucked the gun away and turned back into the house. Lizzy stood at the top of the stairs inside. We locked eyes for a moment. I could see the remorse in them. I nodded to make sure she knew everything was okay, then hurried to where Abby was sobbing in the corner of the room. I slid to my knees and held her close, cradling her head next to mine. I heard Lizzy's feet rush down the stairs and her head pressed in against ours. The incessant rain beat against the roof and the walls of the house. Thunder clapped overhead. Abby jumped at the sound.

"I'm sorry," I said. "It's all right. I'm right here."

FORTY-THREE

I gradually opened my eyes as the morning sun brightened the master bedroom of Captain Jameson's cabin. I checked the clock. 9 a.m. I had managed to get seven hours of sleep somehow. I stayed at the Smiths'—or, I guess, the Muenzingers'—house until 2:00. We didn't say much. We sat huddled in the corner of the living room for hours. I cried for the first time in three years and didn't really stop until I finally fell asleep to the sound of Mom's three-year-old voicemail coming through the landline.

I stood and stretched, dug into the bottom of my suitcase, and grabbed some shorts and a shirt. I needed to go for a run. After the week I'd had, it would be good to unwind with a nice jog. As I got dressed, I realized it had only been a week since all this started. Christ.

It was a cool morning, the air still damp from the rainstorm. I stretched on the back porch, looking out over the lake as I had every morning for three years. I was happy to have one more run around the lake before I left. I cracked my neck, rolled my ankles around a couple times, and started my last jog around Vineyard Lake.

My mind wandered as I jogged. In the last three years, I hadn't felt more myself than I had in the past week. Staying on the move, bouncing around town, checking in at the station. There was something about detective work's inconsistent rhythm that I thrived on. I wouldn't have been able to solve this case without the friends I'd made in the last three years. Jack and Clara, Robby, Molly, Mick, Abby...

My relationship with Abby was unique. I knew she would always be there for me. And she knew the same was true of me, despite a smashed bottle of Jameson that would say otherwise. I was the first person she called when she needed help. And to my own surprise, I rushed to help without hesitation. I hadn't cared about anyone the way I cared for her and Lizzy. Not since Charlie.

Charlie. I'd spent the last three years trying to forget my own brother. Or at least forget how I killed him.

I remembered his smile. Infectious. Friendly. Forgiving. The same smile he gave me in the ambulance before he died. I remembered his words. *I'm sorry, CJ. I'm really sorry.* He wasn't just sorry for pointing a gun at dad. He was sorry for putting me in the position he did. He was sorry that was how I was going to remember him. He was sorry he wasn't going to pull through it. He didn't blame me for any of it.

Even as he was dying, he still looked up to me.

Clay Robertson was prepping his boat. I waved, then remembered he probably thought of me as a murderer. The guy who killed his own brother. I put my hand down and looked away, embarrassed, but looked back toward him when I caught a slight movement in my peripheral vision.

He was waving back. And he was smiling.

I smiled back, and ran the remaining distance along the boardwalk, around the northeastern corner of the lake, and back to the cabin. I slowed to a walk, then leaned over to catch my breath.

That's when I realized I didn't have any nightmares that night.

"Hey," a voice called. Abby sat on the back porch with a smile.

I sat next to her. "Hey."

"Thought I'd find you out here. Brought this for you." She handed me a cup of coffee. I popped off the lid and inhaled it.

"You work today?" I asked and took a sip of the coffee. Black. Two shots of espresso.

"Yeah," she sighed. "Still need the money."

We looked out over the lake as a man cast a fishing line over the side of his small boat.

"How you holding up?" I asked.

"I'm okay." She rubbed the bruises on her arms. "Well, that's not true. But I'll be fine."

"I'm always here to talk if you want to."

She smiled. "Thanks, Chris." I wrapped an arm around her, and she laid her head on my shoulder. The fisherman reeled in his line and cast it back out into the lake.

"How was your run?"

"It was good. Really good. Almost..." I searched for the right word. "Therapeutic."

"Yeah?"

"Yeah."

The man's rod started to bend, and he began pulling hard and reeling it in frantically.

"Chris," Abby muttered, "about what I said—"

"Don't." She sat up and looked at me. I said, "Don't apologize. The only one who needs to say they're sorry is me. And I am. Really sorry." I sipped my coffee and shrugged. "You were right. I can't keep running away from everything."

She sighed. Not audibly, but physically. "Still, I could have been nicer about it."

I smiled, sipped my coffee, and said, "Yeah, that part still needs some work."

She punched my shoulder.

A fish flopped in the air as the man eased it into his boat.

"So," Abby said, "I'll see you at work tonight?"

"Nope," I said.

She frowned.

"Because you'll be taking a mental health day," I said. "Don't worry, you'll still get paid. But please, for the love of God, take the night off and get some sleep."

She smiled. "You know what? I think I'll do that. I don't know how many more times I can sit and listen to Mr. Jenkins cry about everything going on at home. It's just so sad."

"That bad, huh?"

"Like, I get it. Teen pregnancies aren't an ideal situation or anything. And I get that it's a small town and his family's reputation is at stake or whatever, but he keeps telling me he would do literally anything to make the entire thing go away."

A switch flipped in my brain.

He would do literally anything to make it go away.

"Holy shit."

"What?"

I jumped to my feet. "Thanks for the coffee, Abby. Take the night off, hang out with Lizzy, go see a movie or something. I have something I need to look into." She said something, but I hardly even heard her as I pulled the cabin door open.

"Hey, Chris," she said.

I turned.

She smiled. "Thanks again. For everything."

I smiled and nodded, then rushed into the cabin.

FORTY-FOUR

"Wait, wait, wait," Molly said as she followed me through the library. "Yesterday you said the whole long-lost heir thing was a lie. Now you're saying there actually is a secret kid?"

"Well, yes and no." I sat in the swivel chair at the front desk and pulled the news article out of the manila envelope. "This article says that a young woman, someone from Albert's graduating class, interrupted one of Howard, Jack, and Juliet's meetings claiming she was pregnant. When asked for comment, all three of them said basically the same thing. 'It's a lie, just a girl trying to get attention.'"

"Sounds like a coverup to me," Molly said.

"Exactly. My guess is, whoever this girl was, her claims were a hundred percent true, and there actually is an heir to the Jones family's estate."

"But Albert can't have kids."

"Correct. Which means that the father—"

Molly gripped my shoulder. "Had to be someone else."

"Right. A few months later, news came out about Howard's divorce, attributed to an affair with Juliet. By then the rumors about Albert sleeping around with all the women in town had already spread. According to Clara, Piers had been doing his best going around town, trying to stop those rumors. But what if every detail we know about that story is wrong?"

She frowned. "Okay, now I'm lost."

"We already know that Albert can't have kids, so where did the rumor about him being the father come from?"

"Piers," she said, understanding starting to crack its way through. "Piers wasn't stopping rumors. He was spreading them. To distract everyone."

"Which, since Albert is incapable, makes the father?"

Molly's grip tightened on my shoulder. It started to hurt. "Howard."

"Which makes his affair with Juliet?"

"Just another part of the coverup."

"Exactly." I stood from the chair and walked to another corner of the library with Molly close behind me. "This is where the conjecture really starts, but my guess is Juliet agreed to be known as Howard's mistress under the condition that she was promised a majority stake in the company in the future."

"Which would make sense for her to be the killer, but she ended up being a victim. But wait—" Molly, distracted by her thoughts, bumped into me when I stopped in front of a huge shelf of Jonesboro High School yearbooks. She said, "I'm still lost here. If those stories about Albert were all a lie, why is he such a bad person?"

"My guess?" I said, scanning the yearbooks. "Self-fulfilling prophecy. His dad sacrificed his son on the altar of his own reputation. Over time, Albert figured he might as well just be a piece of shit if everyone thought he was anyway. That, coupled with his embarrassment at not being able to have kids of his own."

"That's sad. But I still don't get it. If there was no secret, why would Albert kill Jack, Juliet, and Piers?"

"That's just it," I said, grabbing a yearbook from the shelf. Jonesboro High School 1988. "I don't think Albert is the one behind the murders anymore."

"Then who is?"

I walked back to the front desk. "The one person involved in this whole thing that we haven't taken into account yet." I opened the yearbook and started looking through the senior class.

I flipped a few pages before Molly whispered, "Howard?"

I laughed. "No, no, nothing supernatural about this case. Howard died ten years ago and is still dead." There were a few women in Albert's senior class. Melinda Adams. Annabelle Keaton. Katelyn Somers. Patricia Watson. Jessica Wilson. Stacy Young. Angie Zobrowski.

"No," I said, "the person we haven't considered is the woman Howard actually *was* having an affair with." I opened the winery's security footage on the computer. "I'm guessing the Big Three paid her off to keep quiet. Maybe even had her leave town. She was a senior in high school, she may have gone to college or something. Whatever they did, they found a way to keep her quiet. The winery was just starting to get the momentum it needed, and this could have ruined it in this little town."

As I started clicking through the computer, Molly said, "You really think she came back after all these years? How would she have gotten into town without being recognized?"

"That's where things get interesting. We wouldn't know about any of this if someone hadn't shown up at the winery last week asking about 'the Jones family's long-lost heir.'" I paused the surveillance footage and pointed at the woman rushing out of Albert's office. Long red hair, white, low-cut V-neck tee shirt. "There's our culprit."

"But why? Why would she start asking around beforehand? Why wouldn't she just pick them off?"

"I'm guessing she always planned to pin the whole thing on Albert. Making him nervous about this gives him a motive." I continued clicking through the files on the computer; I had kind of started to pick up which cameras were which over the past several days. I followed the reporter's path out of the building, eventually finding her walking down the front steps of the winery. She dropped something on the steps in her rush, quickly turned to grab it, then continued back down. I rewound the video and paused it just as the item dropped on the stairs. It wasn't what I was hoping to find, but it was better than I could have asked for. A familiar bottle-shaped keychain stood out clearly on the white front steps of the winery.

"She came to settle the score," I said. "It's not like she could take the business for herself or anything. She came to disgrace Albert. Ruin the winery, and Jonesboro along with it."

We stared at our new suspect on the monitor.

"So," Molly said. "Who is it?"

"That's the hard part." I looked between the yearbook and the monitor. None of the women in Al's graduating class looked like the reporter, but it was impossible to tell in the footage. I went back to the main foyer's video and watched the woman walk around and talk to the winery's employees. There was something familiar about her movements that I couldn't quite put my finger on.

Who the hell is it?

I picked up the article the woman gave Albert. It was someone from his senior class, but who? Who showed up in Jonesboro and killed three people, all to ruin the winery and make the Jones family suffer? I looked the packet over intently when the staple holding it together caught my eye.

The staple was purple.

"Holy shit."

I looked at the monitor and watched as the reporter walked around the main foyer of the winery. As she strolled from one end to the other, I mentally replaced the background, transitioned it into the morgue of the coroner's office.

"It's Catherine Sinclair."

"Who?"

"Catherine Sinclair. Sheriff Wilson's assistant. She's been helping at the coroner's office while Dr. Lancaster's out of town for his anniversary, but she packed up to leave yesterday." I thought back to my last conversation with Catherine and realized what was bothering me the day before. She normally had a beauty mark on the right side of her upper lip, but it was on the left. A disguise.

"But that doesn't make sense," I said. "Catherine's younger than me. She can't be the woman from Al's graduating class."

"How old is she?" Molly asked.

"Maybe thirty at the oldest."

"Chris." Molly put a hand on my shoulder. "What if it wasn't the woman Howard slept with that killed everyone?" She was staring at the monitor. "What if it was Howard's long-lost heir?"

I leaned back in the chair and stared at the ceiling. "Shit. But there wasn't a Sinclair in Albert's graduating class, so that could be a fake name, too. And I don't know where she is now."

"It sounds like she might have gotten scared and bailed on her plan. Maybe you were getting too close."

I sat back up. "Maybe."

There was still something bothering me. Catherine being the killer answered a lot of questions. Working at the station, she would have had easy access to a police car, which would have gone completely unnoticed parked next to the welcome sign. She probably pulled Juliet over and made her park the Corvette in front of the sign at gunpoint. She could have gotten the code to shut off the mansion's alarm from Juliet before killing her since she used to live there, then used Juliet's personal keys to unlock the front door when she went to kill Piers and frame Albert for it. Acting as assistant coroner, there's no telling how much she told me was truth and how much she made up. The one thing I knew for sure was that Albert's gun was used for the murders. The gun was registered in his name, and if she wanted to get away with all of this, that one detail needed to be true. But that's the exact thing that bothered me.

How did she get Albert's gun? And how did Jack really play into all of this? What happened on June 5th, 1992? And ultimately, who the hell was she?

"The journal."

"What?" Molly asked.

I pulled out my phone and called Robby. It rang for a long time. I was surprised when it didn't go to voicemail.

"What do you want?" he asked.

"Where are you right now?"

"I'm at the shop. Why?"

"Do you have that journal from 1988 on you?"

"Yeah, why?"

"Albert isn't the one behind all this. I'll try to explain more later, but I need you to try and find a name for me. Somewhere in there, probably late June or early July, a woman interrupted a meeting saying that Howard got her pregnant and it caused a big scene. I need you to see if your uncle wrote anything about it."

"Okay, but why is that important?"

"That woman's the mother of our culprit. I need you to find her name. I'll head to the shop here in a minute to help you."

"Wait, you're still in town?"

"Yeah, long story. I'll see you in a minute, just start looking for me." I hung up and stood from the chair.

"So what's the plan?" Molly asked.

"I'm gonna make a quick phone call and then go help Robby find this woman's name, then I'll go from there." I called the sheriff. It rang once then went immediately to voicemail. "What the hell?" I tried calling again. Same thing. I called Ralston, and his phone rang a couple times before he answered. "Ralston, is Wilson there?"

"Is Wilson where?" he said. "I'm at home. Sheriff told me to take today off, too."

"Really?"

"Yeah, he did. Why? What's up?"

"Catherine resigned yesterday. Do you know if she's already gone?"

"Catherine resigned? Damn, I didn't even know that happened."

"Right, you were already gone for the day." I rubbed my eyes. "Keep your phone close by. Might need your help."

"You got it, Harris."

I hung up and kissed Molly on the cheek before running out of the library.

Something didn't feel right.

FORTY-FIVE

The front door of Jack's Bait & Tackle was open. The store was empty. Robby's bike was nowhere to be seen. I called Robby. It went to voicemail. I called again. That time he answered.

"What, Seej?" he shouted. His breathing was labored. "What is it?"

"Where are you?"

I heard his bike clatter to the ground. "I'm finishing this."

"Robby, what the hell are you talking about? What's going on?"

"Doesn't matter who the girl was, man." He was shuffling around, doing something on the other end of the line. "It doesn't fucking matter."

"What?" I stepped into the tackle shop. The journal was still on the counter. "What do you mean it doesn't matter? Who was it?"

"Doesn't matter 'cause she's dead, man." I heard glass shatter. "But I know who can give me answers about what the fuck is going on."

"What are you talking about?" I started reading over the journal.

A gun cocked on the other end of the line.

"Whoa, Robby, where are you? What are you doing?"

"Like I said, I'm finishing this."

The line went dead.

"Fuck." I frantically scanned the pages of the journal. As soon as I found the name, I knew exactly where he was. I sprinted out of the tackle shop.

"Jessica Wilson stormed into the conference room today..."

I jumped over Robby's bike and up the stairs to the front doors of the police station. I ducked through the broken glass of the front door, a rock nestled in the shards crunching under my feet. I made my way to the stairwell, sweeping each room with my Glock before stepping through. I quietly made my way through the precinct, the entire building uncomfortably silent.

The last time I'd been in a building this quiet was after Charlie's funeral. Everyone else had left the church building, leaving me alone with my brother's picture in the sanctuary. Church staff had left for the day, all except for the last custodian who was kind enough to leave me with my thoughts. I sat in the front pew, staring down the unblinking eyes of his military headshot. I sat for what seemed like hours before standing and leaving the church. A week later, I drove to Jonesboro.

I walked down the empty hallway, lit only by the emergency fluorescents. I could hear voices from the holding cell block. One was frantic. Blubbering. Albert. The other was calm. Soft. Cold. Wilson. Albert was pleading with Wilson, begging him to let him go. Wilson said little, the few words he used demanding: "Shut up. Get up there. Be a man." He killed Jack, Juliet, and Piers, then gave Ralston the day off so he could finish the job.

A third voice, with nervous anger, sprang to life as I approached the holding cells. Robby. He started shouting at the sheriff, "What the fuck are you doing?" Wilson responded, completely unshaken by his arrival, telling him to leave. I quickened my pace down the hallway and swept my Glock around the corner, pointing it into the cell.

Albert stood at the edge of the bunk bolted into the cell wall, his belt strapped around his neck, the other end looped around a pipe in the ceiling. A hand-scrawled note was pinned to his chest. Sheriff Wilson had his pistol pressed firmly into the square of Albert's back and stood grinning at Robby, who had his arms outstretched with a Beretta clumsily gripped in his hands. The same one Reggie tried to sell me just days earlier. As I stepped forward, Wilson shifted his gaze from Robby to me, his grin unwavering.

"Harris," he said. "Good to see you."

"Wish I could say the same." I kept my gun trained on him. "Robby, get out of here. Now."

"No goddamn way, CJ," he said, tightening his grip on his pistol. "This bastard killed Uncle Jack. No way in hell he's getting out of here without paying for it."

"Don't have time for this shit, Romero, get the hell out—"

"No!" Robby shouted. Tears ran down his cheeks. "I'm seeing this through even if it kills me."

There was no reasoning with him. I turned my attention to Albert, who stared at me, sweating, whimpering, his eyes watering. The man who I'd always seen stand so proud, who'd rumbled his cars along Main Street to draw everyone's gaze to himself multiple times a week, had been reduced to a blubbering mass. In that moment, I could see that Albert Jones, CEO of Jonesboro Winery and Vineyards, was still just a boy.

I adjusted the grip on my gun. "Where's your niece, Sheriff?"

"Ah," he said. "Figured it all out, did you?"

"For the most part."

Albert whimpered. Wilson punched him in the hip with his empty hand and said, "You wanna explain it all to poor Albert here before he takes the plunge?"

I closed my eyes and took a deep breath. I'd learned so much about Jonesboro and its past in the past week. Hell, in the last forty-eight hours. I took a brief second to get my ducks in a row, then released my breath. "Okay."

I took a step further into the holding cell. "In 1988, Al got a girl in his graduating class pregnant. Jessica Wilson, if my research is correct." Albert cocked his head to the side. I said, "Except Al wasn't the one sleeping with her. No, Howard Jones was the father."

Wilson nodded.

"Jessica interrupted a meeting at the winery. The business was still in its early days, but Howard, Jack, and Juliet couldn't risk the winery going down in flames because of a scandal. So they came up with an idea to keep her quiet. They paid her off somehow and made her leave Jonesboro. Howard's wife caught wind of it and filed for divorce, but before that became public, Howard sent Piers about spreading the rumors that Albert had been sleeping with all the women in town to throw everyone off the scent and make it seem that his son was responsible for everything. Better him than the CEO of the company."

Wilson nodded again. Albert turned his gaze to the floor.

I pressed forward. "Jessica had a baby girl. After four years as a single mom somewhere in the world by herself, she came back to Jonesboro for your graduation, Mike. While she was here, she wanted something. Maybe she wanted her daughter written into the will, maybe she wanted more money. The winery had started picking up steam. If she was smart, she threatened to reveal her secret to the press if her demands weren't met. So Jack, Howard, and Juliet put another plan together. Maybe they already had one cooked up should she ever decide to come back. Whatever it was, it worked."

"The hell you talking about, man?" Robby said, the Beretta shaking in his hands. "Uncle Jack would never have done anything like that."

"Settle down, Robby," I said.

Albert whined uncontrollably. Wilson jammed the pistol harder into his back.

"So Jessica left again," I said. "Alone. And this time, without anything to show for it. The Jones family's success had come at a small cost to them. But at a huge cost to the Wilson family. Then, five years ago..." I breathed in and readjusted the grip on my Glock. "Jessica died. You were there at her deathbed. And maybe that's the first time you met your niece, whatever her name is, who was studying forensics. And I'm guessing that's when the truth finally came out, both to you and your niece. She was Howard's daughter, Al's sister, and deserved at least a portion of the company."

Wilson said nothing.

"You came back to Jonesboro. You went back to your job in the town built by the men who ruined your sister's life. You lost your passion for police work, and as you sat in the darkness of the sheriff's office watching porn, you started to develop a plan."

A grin cracked through Wilson's intensity.

"You called Liquor Enforcement two years ago, didn't you?"

Wilson nodded.

"You brought your niece out here so the two of you could carry out the murders of the people who ruined Jessica's life."

He nodded again.

"You went to the dock that morning and went out on the lake with Jack. You murdered him in his own rowboat while the gun club that you started months ago was in session. When I realized Jack was murdered in his boat, I told you I was going to check it out the next morning. You tossed Juliet's keys into the boat, which is why Robby and I didn't notice them the night before. You pulled Juliet over outside of town, made her park in front of the welcome sign, then shot her point blank. But not before getting the information you needed to break into the Jones family mansion and kill Piers two nights ago. And Piers may not have even been necessary for your plan, but he recognized your niece when he and Al came into the precinct the other day. She was the reporter who visited the winery last week, putting Al on edge.

"Your plan was always to pin the entire thing on Albert, then bring him here, then have him apparently commit suicide in his own cell over the guilt of his actions. You got ahold of his gun at one of your gun club meetings so you could use it to commit your murders, then switched it back when you broke into the mansion the other night with Juliet's personal keys that you 'accidentally' kept here at the precinct. Hell, selling all the station's Glocks was probably your idea, too. And all of this would go over without a hitch because you're the sheriff. Everyone would believe everything you said."

Albert continued to whimper. Wilson's grin had turned into a full smile.

"There are still a few gaps in there," I said, "but it all still connects. Now I just have a couple final questions for you. First, what did Jack Romero have to do with any of this?" Robby glanced my direction as I leveled my gun at Wilson's head. "Care to enlighten me?"

FORTY-SIX

The sheriff didn't blink, but took a deep breath, flaring his nostrils before saying, "Jessica came home for my graduation. She seemed exhausted when she came back. She had been raising a daughter on her own for four years, after all. Left Regina, my niece, back home with a friend so she could come to town. The day after she got back, Jack asked me to go fishing with him. I told him my sister was in town, but he insisted. Said he didn't have anyone to go with, but really wanted the company, so I agreed. Jack and I went out on the lake that day. We talked about life, I told him I wanted to be a police officer someday. He said I should pursue it. That I'd be good at it. That I could be the sheriff if I really wanted to. We didn't catch a thing. I thought nothing of it."

Albert tried to step back from the edge of the bunk. Wilson gripped his arm and yanked him back up. "What I didn't know was that on the shore of the lake, not even a hundred yards away, Piers was taking a walk with Jessica. Howard couldn't do it himself, couldn't risk being seen with her in case people started putting two and two together. They stopped on the shore and looked at the single boat out on the lake. He told her that if I happened to die, fall into the water with something weighing me down, that it could be months, maybe even years, before anyone found my body at the bottom of the lake. That it would be a shame if it happened that day, with her watching, but it would be even worse if Jack decided he needed a fishing companion some other day to cope with the stress of Howard's scandal getting out."

June 5ᵗʰ, 1992 – Went fishing today. Piers took care of everything.

"It's not true," Robby whispered, the Beretta lowering toward the floor. "It can't be true."

I fought to keep my hand steady. Wilson smiled and said, "So you know what I did that morning, Chris? Do you?"

"You took him fishing."

"You're damn right I took him fishing. He was thrilled to have a companion that morning. I didn't have a rod on me, but I offered to row. He smiled and got himself situated and started yammering on like he always did. We got out to the middle of the lake, and he threw his line over the side before I pulled the gun on him. Had a nice little chat, we did. If I remember right..." His smile widened. "We waved to each other that morning, didn't we?"

We did. I waved at Jack and his fishing buddy on my run that morning like I did any other day. One of them waved back at me. I was right there.

"Regina met me at the dock with my car," Wilson continued. "No one was there to see me load him up and drive off. Thanks, by the way. I need to get that oil leak fixed."

I heard Robby's grip tighten on his gun.

Wilson's smile was joyless, dead, empty. "How many people do you think Jack took out on that lake over the years, Chris? Hm? How many people's *kids* did he take out there with him? And how many times do you think Piers, or Howard, or Juliet, for that matter, was taking someone else for a walk on the shore?"

"You're lying!" Robby shouted, lifting the Beretta once more. "Uncle Jack would never—"

"Robby, put the goddamn gun down!" I shouted. "Put the gun down and get the hell out of here!"

"What're you gonna do, Seej? Kill me like you killed your own brother? Just do your job, whatever that's supposed to mean?"

I swallowed and steadied my hands. "I wasn't trying to kill him, Robby. I was trying to keep him from making a huge mistake. One that could ruin his entire life." I cast him a glance, but his eyes were focused on Wilson. "Look, kid, whatever you're thinking about doing right now, it's not worth it. It won't make you feel any better after all's said and done."

Robby sniffed and said, "We'll see." The Berretta didn't stray from Wilson's head, but his finger slipped subtly off the trigger.

I took that as a sign he was listening and turned back to the Sheriff. "One last question."

Wilson nodded.

"Why me? Why did you rope me into all of this?"

"You were the only hitch in my plan, Harris," he said. "This entire operation was supposed to go down a while ago. Regina wasn't even meant to be a part of it unless she wanted to come out of the woodwork and claim her inheritance. I didn't really care either way what she wanted to do at that point. But then you had to start giving me your tips, solving our cases, flaunting your experience. All the other idiots in this town would have eaten up whatever I told them. But you—the young, hotshot, 'real' cop from the big city—no, you wouldn't have bought a word. I had to do something about you. Once I found out where you came from, it didn't take long to research your background. Found out about Charlie. Damn shame, that one."

I shifted my weight and took a step forward. Wilson jammed the pistol harder into Albert's back. I stopped moving. Albert sobbed.

"You could have ruined everything," Wilson said. "I knew as soon as people started dying, you would start looking into it yourself. Especially since you were such good friends with Jack. I had to make some changes to my plan. I had Regina come out here to help me. Paid for Dr. Lancaster's anniversary trip on the station's tab and had her set up as the assistant coroner. I knew you would believe whatever she said, even if I needed her to lie about what actually happened."

He smiled. "I had to break you. I had to beat you to the punch and get you involved myself before you decided to investigate on your own. So I threw the body in the ditch the next morning, knowing you'd probably be the first person to find it on your run. Ultimately, I needed to get you to leave town. Since I knew about everything with Charlie and how you jumped ship after all that went down, planning the rest was easy. I told you to keep everything a secret. Then I left that envelope on your truck. I convinced the mayor to host that press conference months ago. And Regina was planted in the crowd to help get everyone riled up. She's the one that spilled your little secret. It went over exactly as I planned it would. You're supposed to be hours away from here by now."

Wilson and I stood on opposite ends of the cell, eyes locked together. The only sound was Albert's occasional sob, accompanied by Robby's deep, steadying breaths.

"So," I said, "what happens now?"

"Now?" Wilson smiled. "Well, since you're here and not halfway to Los Angeles..." He moved his gun away from Albert and pointed it at me. "I'll kill you. I'll blow your goddamn brains out, drive you somewhere far out of town and leave you to rot. Or toss you in the middle of the lake with rocks tied to your ankles. I like that idea better."

"You don't think anyone will notice I'm gone?"

"You?" He laughed. "A bartender-turned-detective who, just a few days ago, said in front of everyone that he hated this town and was leaving as soon as he solved the case? No, I don't think anyone will notice you're gone. The kid's a different matter, but it should be simple enough."

I made eye contact with Albert. He looked like he was trying to communicate something to me, but I quickly shook my head. In the distance, I could hear the muffled bells of the church chime. Noon.

"So all of this," I said, "every part of this plan was just one grand scheme to destroy Jonesboro from the inside, starting at the top. To absolutely obliterate the town that Howard and Jack spent their lives turning into the success it became. It was never actually about the business."

There was a ferocity in his eyes, a relentless determination to see his plan through.

"No," I said. "You just wanted to bring the motherfucker down and watch it burn."

Wilson began to chuckle, a low, menacing laugh, driven to the point of lunacy by loss.

"But why resort to murder?" I asked, stepping forward. I had to keep him talking while I figured a safe way out of this. "And why get Regina involved in all of this? I'm sure there's something the two of you could have done within the law that—"

Wilson's laughter ended abruptly. He glared at me and screamed, "I am the goddamn law!"

Albert moved. His foot flew to the side as he tried to kick Wilson's hand, but he lost his footing and was suspended in the air by his neck, choking. Wilson turned and shouted at him, but then quickly turned his gun back toward me. Robby shouted.

I squeezed the trigger.

Two gunshots went off in the holding cell.

FORTY-SEVEN

I shut the front door to the Muenzingers' condo. "Well," I said, "guess that's it, huh?"

Abby and Lizzy laid on the couch where it sat on the sidewalk next to their Uhaul. "Yep, I guess so," Abby said. "Wish we were gonna be here to meet your mom. Sounds like a cool lady."

"I'll have you all come out and visit together sometime. Promise."

Abby grabbed one side of the couch and I grabbed the other. "Come on, Liz," she said. "Hop off."

Lizzy locked her phone and sighed. "You know, I was just starting to like this place." She sat on the curb, watching as we maneuvered the couch into the trailer.

I pulled the door shut behind me as I hopped out and hitched the trailer shut. "Do you have a place lined up in New York yet?"

Abby shook her head, the golden hoops in her ears swinging back and forth. "Not yet. I'm sure we'll find something out there, though. It's a big city. The dance studio said they'd help me find something in my budget."

"Well," I said, looking at both of them, "make sure you call me if you need anything."

"You got it, Sheriff Harris," Lizzy said with a mock salute.

I chuckled. "The title's only temporary. I'm just running the precinct until Westcliffe finds someone to take over permanently."

"And then what?" Abby asked.

"Not sure yet. We'll see what happens when Molly finishes her degree."

"You're welcome, by the way." Abby punched me in the shoulder. I winced in pain and rolled my arm back. "Shit," she said. "Sorry. How's that feeling?"

I pulled on my left shoulder with my right hand and stretched it. "It's all right. Could be a lot worse. Lucky for me Mike Wilson's a lousy shot."

"You're one to talk, considering he's still alive," Lizzy said.

"He fucking shot me, can you cut me some slack?"

We all laughed and Lizzy stood, dusting off the back of her pants. "Well, just don't be a total moron and get yourself shot again after we're gone."

"I won't. Promise." I held my arms out and the two of them came close for a hug. "I'm gonna miss you two."

"God, Chris," Lizzy said, sniffling. "Why can't you just shut the fuck up for once and let a moment happen?" They both took a step back from me and wiped a few stray tears from their eyes.

"What do you say, girls?" I said. "One last shift at O'Callaghan's?" They both nodded and Lizzy jogged to my truck. I started walking after her when Abby grabbed my arm.

"Hey," she said. "I hope you don't think I'm—"

"What? Running away?" She looked down at the ground. I pulled her close and gave her a hug. "Don't worry," I said. "I know. You're not running away from anything. You're chasing something great." She squeezed me tighter. I said, "But if I go even a month without hearing from you, I swear to God I'm flying to New York to hunt you down. Deal?"

She pulled away from me and smiled. "Deal."

<hr>

At 7:00, the bell above the bar door jingled. Everyone turned to greet Robby Romero as he stepped in, right on cue. He nodded at everybody with a huge grin on his face. He sat down at the bar next to Jack's stool and knocked on the bartop. "Mind grabbing me a beer?"

I threw my dishrag over my shoulder. "Mind showing me an ID?"

He reached into his back pocket, pulled his driver's license out of his wallet, and handed it to me. I looked it over, held it up to the light, smacked it on the bartop a couple times with a loud *thwack*, then looked it over again. He still had a huge grin on his face.

I smiled. "Happy birthday, Robby."

Abby popped out of the back room holding a cake with twenty-one lit candles as everyone in the bar sang. He blew out the candles as Mick, the Dinsmores, Amanda, and all the other regulars clapped him on the shoulders and congratulated him. He thanked each person in turn while Abby handed out slices of cake.

As the crowd dispersed and returned to their usual spots, I leaned across the bar in front of him and asked, "What'll it be?"

He scanned the taps along the back of the bar and looked at all the liquor bottles sitting on the shelves on the wall. Then he looked at his uncle's barstool, permanently bolted to the floor just in case he ever sauntered back in, and said, "How about a Jack and Coke?"

I smiled, put a couple cubes of ice in a glass, poured a double shot of Jack Daniels over them, and filled the glass with Coca-Cola. I set it on a coaster in front of him.

"What?" he asked. "No lime?" Abby tossed a lime from behind me, which he caught and squeezed into the glass. He took a sip of his drink.

"What do you think?" I asked.

He grinned. "Just what I needed."

I fist bumped him. "How's running the tackle shop going?"

He took another sip and said, "It's been good, man. I don't have Uncle Jack's business sense or anything, so it's been hard, but it's been good all the same. Aunt Clara's been helping me out quite a bit and Albert's taught me some of the business-end shit that Uncle Jack taught him. Al and I are skipping our weekly meeting this week with the relaunch and everything, but we'll be back at it next week if everything goes okay." He grinned. "If you'd told me a few months ago that Albert Jones and I could almost be friends, I woulda said you were crazy. He's like a different person the last couple months. Uncle Jack's tackle shop, I think it's been good for all of us."

"Good. I'm glad," I said. "You've really come a long way, Rob."

He laughed. "Come on, Seej. It's Robby." He looked at the clock. "Hey, don't you need to get going?"

I checked the time. "Shit, you're right." I tossed my dishrag in the sink and circled the bar. "Hey Abby," I shouted, "lock up for me, will you? I've got a date." Everyone in the bar turned and shouted, "Ooooooh!" I flipped everyone off before shutting the door behind me.

———

"What's this surprise?" I asked.

Molly walked a few steps ahead of me with her hands deep in the pockets of her trench coat. "You'll just have to wait and see," she called over her shoulder.

I was full after our dinner and just wanted to sit on the couch and watch a movie or something, but she took off like a madwoman toward the board-walk the second we left Vineyard Grill. The lack of creativity in Jonesboro was astounding. Had the perfect opportunity to rename Howard's Grill something clever and they went with "Vineyard." Again. Christ.

The sun had set, and Jonesboro was beginning to quiet down for the night, the only sounds coming from the back patio of the restaurant. She walked along the boardwalk to the big sliding door of the pedal boat shack.

"What?" I said. "Are we breaking into the pedal boat shack again?"

"Unlike you," she said, "I decided to ask Clay for the key."

"I don't know, I feel like breaking in added to the fun of it all."

She slid the door open and the two of us sat in one of the blue plastic pedal boats. We floated into the middle of the lake, laughing and reminisc-ing as we pedaled. Eventually we settled into a slow, delicate rocking motion in the water. We laid back and looked up at the stars.

"Beautiful night," I said.

"Mmhm," Molly said, and laid her head against my shoulder. "Are you ready for tomorrow?"

"The Relaunch?" I felt her nod on my shoulder. "I'm ready for it to be over. Hiring all these new guys at the station to prepare for it has been a pain in the ass. We'll see what happens. Could end up that no one cares after all's said and done. It's been two years, after all." I shrugged. "But on the other hand, this town could start getting crazy again. They have the full fireworks display planned and everything, just like they used to."

"I'd love to see this town in full swing."

"It's really something. Families boating on the lake and fishing, kids swimming in the summer heat. Can't go anywhere without laughter following you. It's...amazing."

"You're amazing." She kissed me and laid her head back on my shoulder. The boat rocked us gently, the sound from Howard's patio carrying over the water. "This lake may never be this quiet again, huh?" she said.

"Possibly not," I said. "Guess we'll know after tomorrow."

"If that's the case," she said. She stood and pulled at the waistbelt of her trench coat, her chin lifted to the sky in a sort of defiance. "Sheriff Harris, I have a crime to report."

I grinned. "And what crime would that be, Ms. Bauer?"

"Someone," she said, pulling at the shoulders of her coat, "is skinny-dipping in the lake." She dropped the trench coat to her feet and jumped out of the pedal boat into the lake, leaving her high heels behind. I laughed as she kicked up water furiously, swimming away as fast as she could.

A few seconds later I dove in after her, leaving my clothes behind in the boat.

Acknowledgements

First and foremost, I need to thank my wife who has encouraged me through every part of this insanity known as self-publishing. We've been married for five years now, and I've been working on this novel even longer than that. She's supported me every step of the way, and I'll never be able to fully express my gratitude. Love you, baby. I also need to thank my family, especially my mom, for always telling me that I can do this, even when the process became frustrating or imposter syndrome set in. I wouldn't have finished this without all of you. I'd like to thank Kayla for editing and encouraging me in this process. I'd like to thank my college Creative Writing professor, who for the life of me I can't remember the name of, and I'll be kicking myself the rest of my life for forgetting. The idea for this novel started in your class, and you have no idea how thankful I am (just like I have no idea what your name is anymore). I'd like to thank my buddy Isaac Holtorf for designing such a kickass cover for me, and for dealing with my nitpicks throughout the design process. This book is better for it, and I appreciate you so much. And finally, oddly enough, I'd like to thank Nintendo, the late Cing, Inc., and Rika Suzuki for Hotel Dusk: Room 215 on the Nintendo DS. So much of Kyle Hyde and Louis DeNonno are infused into CJ and Robby, and I have you to thank for it.

About The Author

Conner Lee lives in Colorado with his wife and kids. Ever the daydreamer, he spends his waking hours mentally writing stories while working various jobs, typing out as many ideas as he can on his lunch breaks. On the rare occasion he has free time, you can find him spending time with his kids, enjoying narrative-focused video games, or playing Dungeons & Dragons.

To read more of Conner's writing and see what he's working on, you can follow him @connerleewriter on Instagram.